'You will do whatever I want, girl. Be whatever I want,' Quentin snapped, and caught her to him. The table between them was knocked sideways. The food and glasses and bottles crashed and thudded to the bare wooden floor.

Sapphira gave an angry cry. 'Are you so discontented with the world that you must take out your hate on everyone you meet?'

'Damn you, wench. I did not come here to listen to an attack on my character,' Quentin growled, reaching down to haul her roughly to her feet. His fingers, light as the touch of a feather, slid over her skin and she shivered at the touch of them, steeling herself for what was to come. He was so strong. How could she fight him?

As he drew her against him, his lips seeking the bruised area of her shoulder, she groped behind her desperately, seeking the bottle. Her hand touched it and she grasped it tightly. As Quentin's lips moved to the smooth hollow between her breasts, she brought it down over his head with all the force she could muster, and then, wide-eyed at what she had done, watched him slide into a motionless heap at her feet . . .

D0784928

Valentina Luellen has been a successful and popular author for some years, and until quite recently she lived in the English countryside with her husband and their son Jamie. However, her husband became seriously ill and she packed everything—including the car, two dogs and five cats—and went to live on a small farm in the Algarve, Portugal. There her husband's health improved, and she now divides her time between the kitchen and the study of her newly-renovated farmhouse.

BLACK RAVENSWOOD is Valentina Luellen's sixteenth Masquerade Historical Romance; others include PRINCE OF DECEPTION, THE SILVER SALAMANDER, WILD WIND IN THE HEATHER, ELUSIVE FLAME OF LOVE and MISTRESS OF TANGLEWOOD.

BLACK RAVENSWOOD

VALENTINA LUELLEN

MILLS & BOON LIMITED
15–16 BROOK'S MEWS
LONDON W1A 1DR

All the characters in this book have no existence outside the imagination of the Author, and have no relation whatsoever to anyone bearing the same name or names. They are not even distantly inspired by any individual known or unknown to the Author, and all the incidents are pure invention.

The text of this publication or any part thereof may not be reproduced or transmitted in any form or by any means, electronic or mechanical, including photo-copying, recording, storage in an information retrieval system, or otherwise, without the written permission of the publisher.

This book is sold subject to the condition that it shall not, by way of trade or otherwise, be lent, resold, hired out or otherwise circulated without the prior consent of the publisher in any form of binding or cover other than that in which it is published and without a similar condition including this condition being imposed on the subsequent purchaser.

*First published in Great Britain 1985
by Mills & Boon Limited*

© Valentina Luellen 1985

*Australian copyright 1985
Philippine copyright 1985*

ISBN 0 263 75100 7

Set in 10 on 10½ pt Linotron Times
04–0685–67,500

*Photoset by Rowland Phototypesetting Ltd
Bury St Edmunds, Suffolk
Made and printed in Great Britain by
Cox & Wyman Ltd, Reading, Berks*

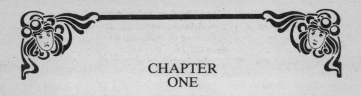

CHAPTER
ONE

'SAPPHIRA! DAMMIT! Where are you, girl?'

The loud angry bellow of Silas Bestwick, owner of the Black Horse tavern in Wapping, clearly reached the ears of the young girl in the kitchen, even though he was on the floor above. She had just seated herself at the long, well-scrubbed pine table to enjoy a bowl of meat stew and a thick wedge of bread, fresh out of the oven set in the wall opposite her. Her cheeks paled at a tone she knew well, a tone warning her that Silas, who was not only her employer, but her uncle too, was in a foul mood again.

It was not an unusual occurrence after a night of heavy drinking, and one she had become accustomed to over the past months since he had taken her into service. He would descend on all who worked for him, railing at them, threatening, cursing, until they scattered in all directions to find work out of his sight, and out of reach of the huge hairy fists which he was inclined to use with great gusto at such times. Only then would he go upstairs and sleep off the effects, often not appearing again until late the same evening, but in time to begin drinking with his customers.

'Let him wait. You've eaten nothing all day.' Molly turned from the enormous cauldron of stew she was stirring over the open fire, and stared at her adopted daughter. 'Sit down and finish your food.'

In a month Sapphira would be eighteen, and already her mother's blood was beginning to make itself apparent, she thought, as she watched Sapphira tentatively seat herself again and begin to eat the stew before her.

The proud way she always held her head, the grace
with which she moved, the gentleness of her voice and
manner. The mark of breeding. Of a lady. She was
reed-slender, with a waist so small that it could be
encircled by a man's two hands. Molly's lips tightened at
the thought of some common drunkard or womanising
Cavalier, like those who frequented the waterside
tavern, laying their filthy hands on her precious baby.
She had not protected her as long as this, only for a
nobody to have her. She was destined for better things.

Her hair was secured in a thick plait now, but when
loose it reached her waist in a torrent of burnished
copper. Her eyes were the rich blue of sapphires—
which had given her her name, Molly suspected—but
without the lustre of those precious stones, for they had
no reason to sparkle.

She was used as a work-horse from morning to night,
and paid a mere pittance for the long and arduous hours
of toil, the lewd comments and invitations which came
her way from customers, the bruised bottom constantly
pinched or slapped by some man who thought she was
there to do more than serve ale. There was barely
anything left over to buy food, once the rent for their
lodgings had been paid. Lodgings! Two small rooms at
the top of the narrow three-storeyed building. One bed,
bare boards and rats crawling over them as they slept,
and for that Sapphira had to part with almost all of her
precious wages. This was why Molly insisted that the
girl ate at least one substantial meal each day in the
tavern. Silas never knew, for he would have deducted
the cost of it or added it to their rent.

It was hard to believe he was her dead husband's
brother. He was a spiteful man when sober, vicious
when drunk, and she hated him for the degradation he
had forced on her as well as on Lottie—her own
daughter, not yet fifteen—and Sapphira, who was
beginning to attract his lecherous gaze more and more
as she daily grew more lovely. She had often thought

that the girl was the only reason Silas had offered them shelter and work. There were times of late when she had caught him watching Sapphira, his beady little eyes following her every movement, and it both worried and frightened her. Soon she would have to send the girl away. It would break her heart, but it had to be done. Before misfortune had overcome them—the death of her beloved husband Sam and the loss of the lodging-house which had kept the family in comfortable circumstances for ten years—Molly had taken pity on a young scholar unable to pay his bill with her. In return for a room and food, she had set him to schooling Sapphira, to teach her her numbers and letters, to read and write her own name. She could do all these things now, as though born to them. It was a well-kept secret from Silas, lest he found some way of putting her knowledge to some use for himself, for she knew he could neither read nor write.

As her name was called again, Sapphira sighed and put aside the bowl. Molly marvelled at her self-control. Never did she show anger, spite or bitterness at the lowly position to which they had all been reduced. Never did she complain at the deplorable conditions in which they lived. When Molly was low in spirits, Sapphira comforted her with talk of the bright future which surely lay ahead. When Lottie was ill with the coughing sickness which overtook her every winter, it was Sapphira who sat up at night nursing her, who worked longer hours for an extra coin begrudgingly paid out by old skinflint Bestwick—and never a word of complaint. She was an angel.

'I must go up, or he will come down here, and then he might turn on you if he sees this food. Quickly, mother, tip it back. I've eaten some.' Sapphira climbed to her feet and brought the bowl back to the fire. It was hardly touched, but Molly made no comment. She would hide away some bread and cheese to take upstairs for later.

'You look tired, child,' she said, touching the girl's pale cheeks. 'I heard you tossing and turning last night. Perhaps you are sickening for a cold.'

'Silas would never allow it,' Sapphira replied, forcing a smile to her lips. It would not do to let her stepmother know how ill she felt. She had to go upstairs and do an evening's work, or there would be no money for food or lodgings. It would give her uncle great pleasure to toss them out into the street, she suspected. 'Don't worry about me.'

'If only my Sam was alive,' Molly began, but Sapphira silenced her with a frown.

'We won't be here for ever, I promise. Perhaps I can find other work—better work—for us all, or for me alone. I can cook and sew, and my learning must count for something. One day we shall have so much money we won't know how to spend it.'

'You listened to what I said, then? You are going to try and find your real mother? She was a lady, Sapphira. She will be rich. She will give you everything you want. It is your right.'

'No.' The girl's face became stubborn. The eyes, a hard, brilliant blue, devoid of all warmth. Molly had noticed that she was always this way when talk of her true mother came up for discussion. 'She abandoned me as a baby; why should she want me now? She owes me nothing, and I owe her no recognition. You are my mother and will always be so. Now I must go before the "old barrel"'—it was her nickname for Silas, always used whenever he was well out of earshot—'has a fit.'

Silas was waiting for her at the door which led to the tap-room, already well filled with customers. It was a large room overlooking the river and Wapping Steps. A fire flamed in the stone hearth to warm the men who came in from a bleak February night and another heavy snowstorm. Well-worn leather armchairs set on either side were occupied by a group of noisy men with long ringlets. The table between them was littered with glasses and earthenware jugs. Empty, most like, Sapphira thought in disgust. The King's men again, out and about for another rowdy night of carousing and causing trouble. Why did they have to choose the Black Horse for their entertainment? She felt in no condition to withstand their crude comments and bold stares, but one look into her uncle's face told her there was no escape from it.

'Where the devil have you been, girl? The Earl and his friends have been here this past half-hour. Where were you? With some lad?'

'No.' Sapphira tried to stare back at him as penetratingly as he stared at her, but was forced to lower her gaze. There was something very alarming in the way his eyes considered her—undressing her in the most indecent manner. As the men in the room beyond would do the moment they saw her. One day, she promised herself . . .

'Get to work, you lazy slut. What do I pay you for? You owe me another hour tonight.'

She knew it was useless to argue, having tried on several occasions before when he had unfairly forced her to work extra hours. On two of those he had only given her half her rightful wages. The third time he had struck her across the face, leaving a bruise on her cheek which had been visible for days afterwards.

'No nonsense tonight, either, my girl,' Silas warned, as she picked up her skirts to avoid him as she passed. It was her way of showing her dislike of him, and it never failed to irritate him. High and mighty minx! Without him, she would be in the gutter where she belonged. 'You be nice to the gentlemen, do you hear me, or I'll take a strap to you!'

Sapphira bristled at the order, but continued to ignore him. Be nice to them, indeed! She was no tavern wench who accommodated the customers for extra money, as several of the other waitresses did. There were rooms upstairs where they took their pleasures. Silas had hinted several times how much she could earn if she followed their example. He had suggested that he should select her clientèle—only the best, he assured her. Men with titles who would pay well, give her presents. She would be able to buy clothes, extra food for the family and medicine for Lottie. Give herself to a man for money! The idea shocked and revolted her and increased her desperation. Somehow she must get away from the tavern and from her uncle. She was afraid of him and what might become of her if she remained much longer.

Long legs in breeches barred her path. Without looking up at the face of the man lounging in the chair in front of her, she said politely, 'May I pass, sir?' and waited for him to move aside.

His shoes had dainty silver buckles, a new fashion introduced by the King himself. Her eyes wandered up over the ruffles edging satin breeches of dark emerald green, adorned with yards of ribbon trimming of the same colour, to the short doublet, open almost to the waist, and revealing a strong, muscular chest, dark with hair. Quickly she looked at the man's features, and found a pair of black eyes, so cold that they made her inwardly shiver, examining her also. They considered the plain brown dress she wore, the bare feet thrust into well-worn shoes, the trim ankles just visible beneath the patched cotton. A slight smile touched the lean mouth as they centred on bare, shapely shoulders and moved lower to rest almost insultingly on the firm swell of her breasts. Sapphira felt her cheeks burn as, without a word, the man swung his legs aside and she hurried past to the men around the fire, not daring to look at him again.

'At last! Ale, wench. Bring us ale! Jugs of it. And brandy!' one of the Cavaliers cried at the sight of her.

'Yes, sir. And food, too?'

'The sight of you has whetted my appetite for something other than food,' a second man laughed, and she was pulled roughly backwards as he caught hold of her skirt from behind.

Angrily she struck out at the hands outstretched to grab hold of her, and one of her clenched fists struck the man's grinning face. Reeling away from him, Sapphira lost her balance as she ducked to avoid being caught by his companion, and sprawled across the lap of the man who sat by the door. Amid roars of laughter from his friend and encouragement to continue further, he took her in his arms and soundly kissed her. Sapphira nearly fainted in horror. She was held in too tight a grip to free herself, and was forced to endure the torture of a hard mouth grinding cruelly into hers, the touch of a hand against her wildly beating heart. There was no pleasure for him in it, she realised, as she fought to contain her senses. He was kissing her as if he hated her—but he did not know her! She had never seen him before tonight. Who was he pretending he held as he explored the soft mouth trapped beneath his own? Who was he punishing with such savage kisses?

In silence, he set her on her feet again and thrust her in the direction of the door, amid disappointed groans and jeers. Sapphira stumbled outside and leaned against the wall, gulping in great mouthfuls of air. She had felt as if she was being suffocated.

Silas, who had seen the incident from across the other room, came hurrying up to her, wiping his hands on a grubby apron. Every day she knew that Molly provided him with a clean one, but he was such a filthy man with revolting habits that it was stained and creased within the hour.

'Don't stand there like a ninny. Get the ale and brandy. What did the Earl say to you, eh? Taken a fancy to you, has he?'

'The—the Earl?' Sapphira looked at him almost stupidly, and then it dawned on her that he was referring to the man who had kissed her.

'The Earl of Ravenswood. Fine-looking gentleman,

isn't he? Very rich, and with the ear of the King, I have heard. Don't displease him with your airs and graces. You'll not lose by it if you are pleasant to the likes of him.'

'Shall I not?' She looked at him challengingly. No woman was safe when the King's fine gentlemen roved the streets seeking entertainment. They swore, gambled, bullied and used the foulest of language. They sought their fun in the many coffee-houses which had sprung up in the City after the return of Charles from exile, or invaded the theatres and made mock of the plays and actors until it was impossible to continue with a performance. They broke windows and defaced signs, and insulted respectable women until only the very brave ventured out after dark. Often rival gangs of young gentlemen met and fought until soldiers were brought in to disperse them. And it was allowed, because they were sons of wealthy citizens or came from good families, and were said only to be indulging in a little light-hearted sport to pass away the time. 'You pay me to serve them with food and wine. I shall do no more and no less.'

From beneath dark brows, eyes which gleamed with a blue-black hue in the candlelight stared out of the hard aquiline face at the men at the table beside him. Save for one man, Blaise Courtney who sat at his right hand, the only man he had ever called a true friend, Quentin Tyrell, Seventh Earl of Ravenswood, knew that all the rest were afraid of his black moods and quick temper. 'Black Ravenswood' was what they called him behind his back—too cowardly to say it to his face, for they knew the consequences. Milksops all of them, he thought in disgust. Not a real man among them. Hangers-on at Court, overdressed, too rich and idle— and soft. They wore swords at their sides to show off their manliness, yet he knew that only Blaise could ever come near to equalling him in a fight, and not even he could best the man who had taught him to use both sword and dagger.

They were comrades-in-arms who had come together under strange circumstances as enemies and yet had become staunch friends. Many times had they brawled together to alleviate the boredom which was part of their everyday existence and unburdened the agony of memories together on a long night over endless jugs of ale and brandy.

'What are we doing here?' he demanded ungraciously as he reached for the tankard at his elbow. He had a hard head where drink was concerned, and the past hour of rapidly consuming both ale and brandy would normally have done nothing to him, but he had begun to drink the previous evening, angry and bitter, and had continued throughout the day, so that by this late hour he was in a dangerous mood. One Blaise had recognised immediately, and, also understanding the cause, had wisely held his tongue and taken it upon himself to try and draw his friend out of his gloom.

'You are in a foul humour, Quentin, so I'm trying to provide you with some fun. I thought the sight of people you dislike making fools of themselves would amuse you,' Blaise returned, casing an amused glance at their companions who, more than a little drunk, were engaged in wagering large sums of money on who would bed a certain married lady that evening. 'It usually does.'

He was six years younger than Quentin, with dark brown hair, and eyes that looked brown until a closer inspection revealed bright specks of blue. His young face registered concern as his gaze returned to Quentin's morose features. God knows how the evening would end with him in one of these moods!

'You are too young to be so cynical,' Quentin chided.

'Some of yours must have rubbed off on me. If this doesn't please you, let's find some women.'

'Women!' Quentin's eyes narrowed to angry slits.

'Deuce take it, boy, who do you think has put me in this frame of mind?'

'Corinna,' Blaise said, and suddenly understood. Damn that woman. She ruined every life she touched. How many had there been before him? Now she was hell-bent on depriving her own brother of everything he held dear—and yet still Blaise loved her. It was beyond his comprehension why he should. It was just something he could not control, which would not die and give him peace. He would always love her, and Quentin knew it. She was the only thing which could cause friction between them—she had done in the past and would continue to do so as long as she drew breath.

'Yes, damn her!' his friend ejaculated violently, and gulped down his ale. Immediately the waitress was at the table to refill his glass. Pretty little thing, Blaise thought, considering the slender figure, too thin for his taste, beneath the worn dress. She looked cold and tired. Quentin looked up at her and immediately colour flooded her cheeks and she turned away from them. 'Have you been arguing over the will again?'

'Yes.' Quentin glowered at him. The drink was beginning to affect him more than he liked to admit, and he was having to fight to keep control of his faculties. 'When did I tell you about that?'

'Months ago. You were very drunk at the time—and angry.'

'I seem to have been that way for a long while, and the closer it gets to my accursed birthday, the worse I am. I shall lose everything, Blaise! It will all go to her to squander away. I've got to prevent it. But how?'

'You know there's only one way to stop her. It was what your father wanted, after all,' Blaise told her quietly.

'Marry? Me?' Quentin looked at him as though he had taken leave of his senses. 'I shall never do that.' Not again, he added silently to himself.

'You must, if you are to save your inheritance. Think

of it as a business venture. You don't have to love the woman, or bed her. Only wed her.'

'Love! I shall never love one of that treacherous sex. I've seen the other side of the coin, remember, in France and Holland, and now here at Court. They sell their bodies for baubles. There's not one honest woman left in this country, if there ever was one.'

'Then pick the first one who takes your fancy, and marry her. Pay her off afterwards. The will says only that you have to be married on your thirty-second birthday . . .'

'There's more I didn't tell you, drunk or not,' Quentin interrupted. 'I have to remain married for a year after that . . .'

'Then set her up in some town house with adequate funds, and forget she exists. Unless, of course, you find her accommodating.'

'I have a mistress who is that.'

'You are fortunate.' Blaise's tone was dry. Quentin scowled at him, as Corinna rose between them once again. His gaze centred once again on Sapphira. He had found himself watching her many times throughout the evening. She was most careful to avoid him when she came near the table, he noticed, and his lip curled in sardonic amusement. She had a way about her which was beginning to annoy him in his present condition. A tavern wench acting the lady. Painful memories came flooding back, and he finished his drink without tasting it.

'More brandy, girl,' he thundered, and she spun around instantly to attend to him. For a moment her gaze met his, and he was struck by the startling blueness of her large eyes. Like Blaise, he thought her too thin and far too pale, and ordinarily he would not have given her a second glance, but too much liquor had roused the vicious streak in him that only Blaise—and his mother, now dead—had ever been able to temper. Before her death he had rarely raised his voice to a living soul, had been fair in all his acts and always restrained the devil he knew dwelled deep inside him. But five years' absence from his beloved home, fighting in France, living from hand to mouth in Holland afterwards at the King's side, watching the way men grovelled before Charles for favours, sold their honour and often that of their wives for a place at his side at the Court in Breda, soon changed him. Watching young women flutter their eyelashes adoringly at the man who would soon return to England as its king, hoping to find a way into his bed, sickened him. There was no honesty and damn little decency left in the land he had returned to.

'I shall have to fetch a fresh bottle, sir.'

Again that refusal to look at him which stirred the malice in him. It was a ploy, a game her kind played to attract interest. He would never be caught that way again! A show of fear, of coyness. A tavern wench— coy? As Sapphira disappeared from the room, Quentin said with a slow, ugly smile,

'Make the arrangements, Blaise. You are right, we need a little diversion from this crowd of popinjays. Tell the landlord I require the blue-eyed wench upstairs. I suppose you already have one picked out for yourself?'

Blaise gave him a crooked grin; pleased at his capitulation, yet at the same time disturbed by it. Quentin was ripe for a quarrel or a fight, it mattered not who with. He did not envy the waitress who had served them, although he knew she would be well paid for her services, however inadequate to the needs of his friend. And again, despite his love, he cursed the woman who had brought so much disruption into their lives. While Quentin began to drink from the fresh bottle of brandy which arrived, he went in search of the landlord.

'Sapphira?' Silas's eyes almost started out of his head at the suggestion. He knew she would never consider it. Unless . . . 'Why, of course, my lord, both wenches will be at your disposal within half an hour. I must make the rooms ready. The Earl is taken with my young niece, then?'

'Niece?' Blaise could scarcely contain his disgust. 'She is a relative of yours?'

'My dead brother's child, my lord. A good girl. Untouched by any man. I may have a little difficulty persuading her to agree to . . .'

'Untouched, in this place? Get her upstairs, man, or I shall not answer for the consequences. My friend requires her to bring him food and wine, and to partake of it with him. See she understands that, and gives no trouble, or I shall deal with you. If there is anything left of you to deal with when the Earl has finished with you,' Blaise added warningly, and Silas's ruddy face went an unhealthy shade of grey. He knew only too well the havoc these young men could wreak at will—and without recompense to their unfortunate victims.

'She is at his command, I assure you. The girl is a trifle high-spirited, that's all. She has notions above her station, if you understand me.'

'See that she has none of them when she goes upstairs,' Blaise replied, and went back to rejoin his companions.

'The Earl and his friend are entertaining upstairs, my girl.' Her uncle ordered, 'Take him some cold ham and chicken, a bottle of my best claret and a bottle of brandy.'

Silas had found Sapphira washing a mound of glasses that she had been too busy to attend to before. She was relieved to be out of the tap-room and the gaze of the man he referred to as the Earl. When she left, he had been engaged in a game of arm-wrestling and had beaten all his opponents. He despised them, she thought, as she slipped unseen out of the room. There was something very frightening about the man. Not only the way he had stared continuously at her, but the light in which he regarded men who were supposed to be his friends.

To only one of them had he been civil all evening. Cavaliers! They disgusted her.

'Upstairs?' she echoed. There were other waitresses to serve the men and women who took rooms upstairs for the evening. She had never been called upon to do so before, and her eyes searched her uncle's face suspiciously. 'Is there no one else? I have so much to do here.'

'Leave it—I shall find someone else. Don't dawdle, girl; the room must be made ready before the Earl arrives. He is to entertain a young woman.'

'Oh,' was all Sapphira said as she wiped her hands dry and began to prepare the tray of food and drink. Those few words said so much.

Silas smiled to himself as he left her. If she was attractive to a man like the Earl of Ravenswood, then there would be others. All would be willing to buy her favours, and, after tonight, she would be his to command.

Rosie, a young Irish girl who had been working for Silas for several years and who had befriended Sapphira when she first arrived, eyed with a smile the tray she was preparing.

'Joining us tonight, then, are you?' There was no malice in the suggestion, only amusement, but it made Sapphira pale with apprehension.

'I am not,' she declared vehemently. 'I am merely taking this to the Earl. He is to entertain upstairs tonight.'

'Oh, my poor unsuspecting little chicken,' Rosie declared in her strong brogue. 'Has the lecherous old Bestwick not made it plain that you are to be the one entertained? The Earl wants you! I have his friend. He's harmless enough, and pays well for my company. But you! Silas will fill his pockets with gold tonight if the Earl is pleased with you. He's been hoping for something like this for months, but was afraid Molly would scratch his eyes out if she learned of it.'

'Me?' Sapphira stared at her, the horrible realisation of her words gradually beginning to have an effect. 'Me? He expects me to . . . Oh, no! He could not! Would not! Rosie, he knows I will never . . .'

'Out, Rosie! I'll deal with you later.' Silas's angry tones behind them froze both girls into silence. Rosie snatched up her tray and fled from the kitchen as if a thousand devils were after her. She knew only too well the effects of Silas's temper, and she was not about to provoke it further. The sympathy in her eyes as she passed Sapphira filled the girl with a deep feeling of helplessness—of betrayal.

'You take the tray up yourself,' she declared, backing away from it. 'I shall not go up to him. I will not become one of your—your strumpets.'

'You will do exactly as you are told, my girl, or tomorrow you and your mother and that sickly little sister will find yourselves out on the street, without a halfpenny, without a roof over your heads. How long do you think she will last in weather like this, eh?' Silas came close to where she stood, thrusting his beery features close to hers. She cried out as he caught one slim wrist in his hand and exerted such pressure on it that she cried out in agony. His free hand fastened on her shoulder, and the thick fingers bit deep into her soft skin until the pain made her feel faint. 'You will go upstairs and you will do whatever is asked of you. Do I make myself clear?'

'No, I won't!' Sapphira cried. To degrade herself thus! She could not. There had to be some other way.

The pain grew. Silas's face blurred before her tortured gaze, and she slumped back, near fainting, against the wall.

'I shall not mark you, my dear Sapphira. But, believe me, I can hurt you just the same. Fetch the tray, now, like a good girl, and take it upstairs. See that the room is warm and comfortable, and wait for the Earl. You will not lose by it. No more shall I. Tomorrow, we shall talk. Perhaps you will have come round to my way of thinking by then. Between the two of us we could make a great deal of money.'

Sapphira stumbled away from him, rubbing her bruised wrist where the marks of his fingers plainly showed. They were on her shoulder, too, and she quickly adjusted the neckline of her dress to cover them. She was trapped! What could she do? Perhaps the Earl was a reasonable man, who would listen to her, but as she mounted the narrow stairs to the upstairs rooms she remembered the look in those dark eyes as he considered her, and knew that drink had made him beyond reasoning.

Silas's rooms were not known for their comfort. There was a bed, with clean sheets and covers, a table and a couple of chairs. The fire in the small hearth needed rekindling when she entered, and it took her a full ten minutes to produce any show of life from the dull embers. At last flames appeared, and she sat back on her heels, wiping a hand across her forehead. How hot she felt; yet she was cold, too. The thin dress she wore, with nothing but a cotton undershift underneath, did nothing to keep out the winter draughts which howled throughout the bleak tavern. There was a thin film of perspiration across her forehead, yet she was shivering.

She must not have a cold, she thought apprehensively, or she could not work and earn money to help keep them. Heaven only knew it was little enough! Yet if she did not do as Silas demanded, tomorrow they would have no roof over their heads, no work, no money. He could not be so cruel! She knew he could, and the knowledge sent her sinking into the depths of despair. Without realising what she was doing, she turned down the bed, placed the tray and the bottles beside it on a table, and sat down to await the arrival of the man who had demanded her presence. She would appeal to him. It was her only chance.

When Quentin opened the door, so quietly that it did

not even rouse Sapphira from her thoughts as she stared into the flickering flames of the fire, his first impression was one of dejection and unhappiness. Of a little lost waif with nowhere to go and no one to turn to. Sapphira's shoulders drooped with tiredness. Her head was resting against the back of the worn chair in which she sat, and her hair was spread out about her shoulders like a thick cloud. How the fire deepened the redness of it, he thought, as he stepped inside and closed the door after him, just as quietly. For a long moment he considered the slender profile of her neck and throat, and suddenly found himself imagining her adorned with jewels, in a dress of watered silk and lace. He blinked to dispel the apparition of beauty and grace which presented itself. She was a common serving-girl, prepared to give herself to him or to anyone who paid her. No different from the whores he associated with at Court.

'I am sorry to have kept you waiting.' She spun round at the sound of his voice; what little colour there was in her cheeks drained from them immediately. As he advanced towards her, he dismissed the thought that the fear in her eyes was genuine. He took in at a single glance the adequate supply of food and drink. For two —not one. She had come prepared to stay, despite those blue eyes.

He splashed claret into two glasses, and held one out to her. She made no move to take it, and his face darkened in annoyance.

'Enough of this charade, girl. We both know why you are here. Drink up and let us enjoy ourselves,' he said in a curt tone.

'Enjoy ourselves, sir?' Sapphira rose to her feet, still refusing to accept the glass pushed her way. 'Is that why you are here? I thought you were angry with the world, and wished to lose yourself in drink and the other indulgences that men of your station seem to take pleasure in, these days.'

Quentin gaped at her. An educated girl in a tavern! What game was being played here? He was doubly angry that she had so correctly assessed his state of mind. He drank his claret and refilled the glass, and again held out the second one to Sapphira.

'Drink, girl,' he commanded. Usually men jumped to do his bidding, but she did not move.

'I do not drink, sir. Nor shall I . . . entertain you as my uncle wishes me to do. There are others more— worthy—of your attentions than I, and more competent to carry out your wishes,' came the scornful answer to his order.

'You will do whatever I want, girl. Be whatever I want,' Quentin snapped, and caught her to him. The table between them was knocked sideways. The food and glasses and bottles crashed and thudded to the bare wooden floor.

Sapphira gave an angry cry. Far from being afraid of this man, she now found herself annoyed by his supposition that he could take her at his pleasure, and that she would have no say in the matter. She was not an object to be bought or bartered at will. She struck away the hands meant to restrain her, and Quentin was so surprised at her action that he released her. She bent to straighten the table, and replaced on it the bottle of brandy, which luckily had not broken. The opened bottle of claret was seeping through the boards at her feet. The glasses smashed into a thousand pieces.

'Are you so discontented with the world that you must take out your hate on everyone you meet?' she cried, her eyes flashing as she stared up at him.

'Damn you, wench. I did not come here to listen to an attack on my character,' Quentin growled, reaching down to haul her roughly to her feet.

As he did so, the neckline of her dress slipped away from the milk-white shoulders, and he found himself staring at the red marks that Silas's cruel grip had left on her soft skin. She saw the dark eyes narrow in puzzlement, and for a moment he hesitated in what, she suspected, was the launching of a determined attack on her helpless person. His fingers, as light as the touch of a feather, slid over the bruises and she shivered at the touch of them, steeling herself for what was to come. He was so strong. How could she fight and win against him? He had already shown he thought her show of modesty to be nothing more than a ploy to entrap him, hoping for more money, perhaps.

'Was your last customer difficult?'

The cynical comment broke the last remaining thread of her self-control. As he drew her against him, his lips seeking the bruised areas on her shoulder, a hand cupping one of her small breasts, she groped behind her desperately, seeking the table. Her hand touched the bottle there, and grasped it tightly. As Quentin's lips moved down to the smooth hollow between her breasts, she brought it down over his head with all the force she could muster, and then, wide-eyed at what she had done, watched him slide into a motionless heap at her feet.

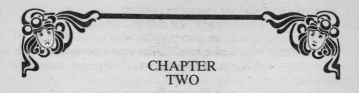

CHAPTER
TWO

How LONG Sapphira stared down at the unconscious form of Quentin Tyrell, she did not know. The claret from the bottle she had broken over his head was soaking into the rich green of his doublet and waistcoat, darkening it to an ominous red. Fragments of glass littered the floor about him. Was that blood beneath his head or merely more wine, she wondered in sudden alarm, and bent to touch the thick black hair, her fingers searching for an open wound. He moaned, and she sprang back from him as if touched by a red-hot poker.

What was she to do? She could not leave him lying there. And yet, why not? It was more than he deserved. Why should she care what happened to him?

Silas! Momentary panic seized her. She could not tell him the truth, or she and her mother and Lottie would find themselves without lodgings and work by morning. She would say that the Earl was so drunk that he stumbled and fell, knocking himself out. As she opened the door, praying he would not recover his senses until his friends had taken him well away from the tavern, Silas almost fell into the room. The realisation that he had been either listening at the keyhole, or attempting to see what was going on inside the room, made her disgust of him intensify.

'He—he fell,' she began to stammer nervously, as her uncle swore at the sight which met his eyes. 'He is —so drunk . . .'

Her heart was in her mouth when he knelt beside the man. To her horror, she saw Silas begin to search him. A leather money-pouch came into view, and was immediately stowed away beneath the grimy apron.

'What are you doing?' she asked, horrified.

'If he's as drunk as you say, he won't miss this, will he? Or have you lied to me?' Silas's eyes were suddenly filled with suspicion. 'His hair and clothes are covered in wine!'

'He knocked over the bottle when he fell—and the glasses.' Sapphira went to begin gathering up the shattered fragments of glass. Silas grabbed her by the arm, pulling her to her feet, and shook her violently.

'You little liar. You've struck him! Don't you realise what you have done?' He was beside himself with rage. 'You useless baggage!'

'He insulted me,' she cried in defence of her actions. She would never forget the smile on Quentin's face as he held her, or the cruel taunt, 'Was your last customer difficult?', as he saw the bruises on her shoulders.

'Insulted you!' Silas sneered. He could have struck her for her insolence. 'You need teaching a lesson, my girl, and when I've got myself out of this mess, I'm going to give you one. We've got to get him out of here. Go downstairs and fetch Mick and two of his lads. They can carry him to some quiet alley, and when he comes to he will think he was set upon by footpads. With any luck he won't come back here again. For all our sakes, let's hope he doesn't remember you. If he does, and he comes back here still wanting satisfaction from you, by God, he'll get it!'

Sapphira fled to go in search of the men her uncle wanted. They were in one of the smaller rooms, where the air was thick with smoke and stank of sweat and spilt ale. They were sailors from one of the ships moored by the Steps who threw out the unruly elements in return for free drinks for the duration of their stay. She did not return to the room. She wanted neither to see the Earl taken away nor to face her uncle again, and slipped up a back staircase to her own room and closed the door firmly behind her. It could not be locked, for there was no key—Silas had removed that the first day they arrived, together with what meagre pennies had been among their belongings. The small window was barred, and could not be opened to allow even a little fresh air into the stifling atmosphere which usually prevailed, and she hoped her mother and Lottie would soon come to keep her company. As she sat on the bare, dusty boards she was shivering, and knew it was not from the cold. She was terrified of the reprisals Silas intended for her disobedience and the aggravation she had caused him.

Crawling across the floor, she pushed away her mattress and prised up the loose floorboard beneath. She thrust her hand into the hole and held her breath as she groped, then sighed with relief as her fingers touched what she had concealed there. With trembling hands she took it out, and gazed in awe at the pendant shining up at her. Two magnificent sapphires formed the centres of a large letter 'S'. The craftsmanship of the silver filigree work which made up the letter was flawless.

This jewel had been round her neck when she had been abandoned outside the Convent of the Sisters of Mercy. Despite all the hardships that had befallen them, Molly had never sold it, nor would allow her to do so. One day, she declared firmly, this pendant would lead Sapphira to her true mother and her rightful inheritance! Until now she had kept it hidden, and bided by her mother's ruling, but no longer. The money she would get from selling it would give them a new start far away from the Black Horse. Another boarding-house, perhaps, where they could all live and work together in comfort, without fear.

She was afraid of Silas, of what he intended her to become. Tomorrow she would slip out of the house and find a moneylender to buy it from her, and she would not mention it to Molly until the money was in her hands and nothing could be done about it.

Footsteps on the stairs brought her sitting bolt

upright, her eyes widening in fear. Heavy steps. Those of a man. Silas's fat body pushed its way through the narrow doorway. In his hand he held a thick leather strap. She had once seen him beat one of the kitchen lads with it for not washing out the tankards to his satisfaction.

'Don't you dare touch me,' she cried, trying to sound unafraid as he advanced towards her, but her voice shook and she saw his eyes gleam. 'If you beat me, I won't be able to work.'

The strap descended over her bare shoulders, and she cried out in pain and tried to protect herself with her hands, but it came down again and again without mercy on every part of her body. She got to her knees, trying to rise, but Silas kicked her down again and she sprawled at his feet, helpless, whimpering in fear and agony as he continued with his lesson.

An hour later, Molly and Lottie, climbing the stairs to their bed, found the door of the room open, and Sapphira prostrate on the moonlit floor like one dead. The sapphire pendant was nowhere to be seen.

'Oh, my poor baby. What has that brute done to you?' It was her mother's voice, but a long way away. Sapphira tried to open her eyes, but the lids felt so heavy, and she could not move. Why could she not move? With a great effort she flexed one arm, and immediately cried out in pain as a thousand red-hot needles pierced her skin. At least, that is what it felt like. 'Lie still, dear. You must lie still. As God is my witness, I swear that one day I will kill that man for what he has done to you!'

At last, Sapphira opened her eyes on to Molly's tear-streaked face. Close by sat Lottie, her hands clasped together in her lap, her face whiter than snow. It was several minutes before she was able to focus her gaze properly. It was light outside! She felt disoriented —confused—and so very stiff and tired. Silas! Molly's hands rested gently on her shoulders as terror registered in her expression, but for all her gentleness, Sapphira winced visibly.

'I ache all over,' she whispered.

'That inhuman monster beat you. I thought you were dead . . . you were so still and cold. Don't talk, but sleep, and I shall bring you some hot broth later on.'

Tentatively Sapphira raised trembling fingers to her mouth. It felt swollen. No wonder it was so difficult to speak. Her cheeks were tender, too. She must have fallen face downwards when she lost consciousness, and bruised them.

'Bring me the mirror, Lottie?' Molly shook her head vigorously, but Sapphira insisted, and inspected her reflection in silence.

There was a vivid bruise on her forehead, another on her cheek, and the corner of her mouth was cut. She did not remember that happening. Pulling away the single drab blanket which covered her, she found that her arms and shoulders were a mass of dark blue and purple bruises which stood out with startling clarity against the whiteness of her skin. She knew that, beneath her shift, her breasts and thighs and legs were marked. Silas had taken great satisfaction in the beating, the vindictive streak in him aroused still further by her refusal to beg for mercy.

'He says that, when you are better, he is going to give you to the first man willing to pay a golden guinea to spend the night with you,' her younger sister said in a low tone, and instantly earned herself a sharp rebuke from her mother.

'He'll not lay another finger on you,' Molly assured her, 'nor turn you into one of those women. As soon as you are well, we are leaving here. You said that there must be work somewhere else for us. We'll find it.'

'Oh, mother!' Sapphira laid her head against Molly's thin bosom and wept. Brave words, but that was all they were. If they left the tavern they might wander the

streets for days, finding neither work nor shelter, and
they had no money to invest in better accommodation
—Silas had seen to that. He kept them so poor that
they were reliant on him for everything. Lottie would
never survive the cold, Sapphira thought, as the girl
began to cough painfully into a patched handkerchief.
Even though every fibre of her being cried out against
it, she knew she must give in and do what Silas asked
of her. The only alternative was to run away herself,
telling no one, not even her mother, where she was
going and try to earn some money honestly; but dare
she risk what he would do to the two dear ones she left
behind? He would work them unmercifully, perhaps
beat them too for allowing her to go—or turn them out
to fend for themselves and she would return to find
them gone.

She could not think now. She wanted only to sleep.
Her eyelids drooped wearily, and Molly laid her back
on the mattress and covered her again with the blanket.
Loud voices on the stairs outside roused Sapphira to
painful reality again. As she struggled up onto one
elbow, expecting the door to fly open and Silas to
appear, gloating over his victory, Quentin Tyrell
stormed into the room and she fell back with a gasp.
Which of them was the worst, she did not know, for
she feared them both for different reasons. Molly
crouched low over her as he advanced across the room,
his face as black as storm-clouds.

'I thought you would still be here. The landlord said
that you had run away with my purse, but I think you
are too useful to him to be allowed to leave. Where is
it, girl? My money-pouch. Return it to me this instant,
before I whip you within an inch of your life!' he
demanded in clipped tones.

Sapphira's eyes were glued to the riding-whip
clutched in one hand. He meant it!

'I haven't got it.' Her voice was hardly audible. She
saw his gaze focus on her bruised cheek and split lip,

and a frown creased the handsome features. He looked as he had done the previous evening, when he had seen the marks on her. Had she not known differently, she would have thought he was concerned for her. 'My uncle took your purse.'

'It's the truth,' Molly started up protectively, positioning herself between Quentin and her daughter. Like a she-cat protecting its young, he thought, before reaching out and sweeping her aside.

'He said you would say that. Where have you hidden it? Close by, I'll warrant.' He bent and pulled away the blanket and froze at what he saw. For a moment he said nothing, then tersely snapped, 'He has already taken you to task for your thieving ways, I see. Give me my purse, and we shall say no more about it.'

'I do not have it. I swear it.' Bright tears welled into Sapphira's eyes. She raised a hand to dash them away, and his mouth tightened at the scratches and welts along her bare arm. She had been viciously beaten. Even he in all his anger would never have used the whip he held on her. The threat of it was usually enough to cower a disobedient servant, let alone a slip of a girl. 'He—I was beaten because I would not—could not . . .'

'She is not a wanton,' Molly interrupted, glaring at Quentin with hatred in her eyes. How she loathed the rich! They looked down their noses at poor folk like her, never realising that she had once been a woman of substance. Their ladies moved their silken skirts aside to avoid her in the street, or their men pushed her into the gutter with a comment that she belonged there. 'Although he would turn her into one. You men are all alike. You steal innocence from a young girl and then toss her money as if that could compensate for the loss of that which she treasures most. How many of your precious fancy ladies at Court are as virtuous as my Sapphira, grand lord?'

'Hold your tongue, woman! Do not make my quarrel with you also,' came the low warning. 'Does she speak true? The landlord forced you to that room?' The question was addressed to Sapphira, who nodded. She no longer cared whether he believed her or not. A great drowsiness was creeping over her, and she felt very cold. Quentin went down on one knee beside her, and his fingers drew away the bodice of her shift. Molly cursed him, but he ignored her, and then she saw that he was not caressing Sapphira but examining in great detail the abrasions on her body.

'She is in need of a doctor. Fetch one,' he ordered, straightening.

'He will not allow it, and if he did, we have no money to pay,' Molly said fiercely.

'But of course she shall have a doctor,' Silas declared from the doorway. He had been eavesdropping outside for several minutes, awaiting an opportune moment to show himself. He had been right. The Earl was taken with Sapphira. Instead of a whipping, he was thinking of giving her help. She shall have her physician, he thought; when she is well, I shall put her to good use. He had been in fear of his life when the Earl appeared, seeking his lost purse, expecting a dozen revenge-seeking Cavaliers to descend on the tavern in his wake, but the man was alone. Too angry to be placated, Silas had made Sapphira the scapegoat, and sent the Earl upstairs. 'Go and fetch one, Molly. In a few days she will be as good as new, my lord,' he whined, drawing closer to the mattress where the girl lay. Quentin did not miss the way she shrank back at his approach, her large blue eyes growing terrified. 'Shall we say a week?'

Quentin turned on him slowly, his eyes angry slits which Silas, so absorbed in his new notions, failed to notice.

'A week?' he echoed. 'For what?'

'Why, to make her available to your good self and your friends. The girl is a little slow, my lord, if you understand me. I shall instruct her as to your requirements . . .'

The flat of Quentin's hand, delivered with great force, sent him staggering back against the wall. The Earl unfastened his cloak, and then, lifting Sapphira from her bed, he wrapped it round her so that only her ashen features showed against the dark blue velvet.

'There will be no need to bring a doctor,' he said to Molly, still hovering in the doorway. 'I am taking her with me. She will be well cared for.'

'No!'

Molly ignored Sapphira's distressed cry. She did not like Quentin Tyrell or his kind, but he was rich, and he moved in Court circles. He would give Sapphira everything she could ever dream of wanting—clothes, jewels, a place in the world. Albeit an unrecognised place, for as his mistress she would never have his name and the position that went with it; but what did that matter if she had clothes on her back and a roof over her head and a man to protect her against the world?

'Take her, sir. But, I beg you, be kind to her. She is all I've said, and more. But for her, that wretched man would have cast us out into the streets long ago. He kept her to use her as he does other poor girls working here.'

'No!' Sapphira said again, and fresh tears cascaded down over her cheeks. The salt from them touched the cut at her mouth and stung sharply, evoking more. Some of them dropped on to the hand Quentin was resting lightly on her shoulder, and a strange expression settled over his features as he stared down at her. He had seen many women cry in his time, but none had touched him so deeply as the sight of this dejected child, weeping silently beside him. He had returned in order to vent the full fury of his wrath upon her for her part in what had happened last night.

He had recovered to find himself in some stinking alley, lying beneath foul-smelling rubbish that someone had recently tossed out of a window. A cat was sniffing at his feet when he opened his eyes, and he heard the scurry of rats in the shadows. For a moment he thought the ache in his head had been caused by too much drink, but then as he staggered to his feet and tried to get his bearings, memory returned, and, with it, the realisation that his full purse was missing. Stolen! He had been in no condition to return to the tavern that night to settle his score with the rascally landlord and his thieving wenches, but at first light he had been up and preparing to leave his house in the Manor of Hyde. As he rode through the deserted streets, with the damp London mists still clinging to every rooftop, past the beggars and drunks still sleeping in the doorways and alleyways, he cursed himself for allowing his guard to drop. Not for many years had he been caught out so successfully, and all because he had allowed a moment of sentiment —even pity—to cloud his wits and mar his judgments. The sight of the bruises on Sapphira's shoulders, the apprehension in those blue eyes, had momentarily halted him in his chosen path. And, for his pains, he had a racking headache and was missing a purse full of guineas.

The anger in him which had demanded some kind of satisfaction—revenge for the humiliating experience, the attack of his person, which he suspected had been deliberately planned, using the girl as a ploy—disappeared as he slowly traced the path of a tear down over Sapphira's cheek. Damn it! What was the matter with him? He would let her have the purse of gold, and leave. She could find a safe haven away from the tavern and start afresh.

'Here, my lord. Your money.' Silas thrust the money-pouch towards him. 'I kept it for you. Took it off her and kept it for you. It's all there, I've not touched it.'

Quentin took it without a word. *Give it to her and go,* his instincts cried. *She was nothing more than a tavern wench, doubtless not as innocent as he had been told. How could she be, in such a den of iniquity? And* yet there was something about her which stirred him, roused in him a feeling he had sought to repress over the years. He thought he had done with pity the day his father died, and he had learned how his own sister had schemed and lied behind his back to deprive him of his heritage. And would succeed within a month, if he did not find himself a wife . . . No, it was too incredulous to consider. This girl, this unknown, pathetic little creature, his wife! Yet he would never marry for love. Not again! He had considered making propositions to two of the women he knew at Court, but had dismissed the idea as useless. They were greedy creatures, both of them, who would never have been satisfied with his name and a sizeable settlement in return for their services. But this girl, who had nothing—no prospects—would jump at such an offer.

'Here, woman. Take this and put it to good use,' Quentin said, and tossed the pouch to Molly. She dropped it in her amazement, then scooped it up from the floor and hugged it against her, blessing him in a husky tone. Silas could only stare at him in a shocked silence. Give the money to her! She would not have it for long. 'If you touch her, I shall come back and flay you, my friend.' Quentin was looking at him with narrowed gaze.

'The girl,' Silas gasped, seeing his newly-made profits slipping away from him. 'I have kept her, clothed and fed her since her father died. Am I to get nothing for all that? You cannot take her from me . . .'

'You've used her and these others for cheap labour, to my way of thinking,' came the terse reply. 'If they wish to leave, and I advise them to do so, you will not stop them. If I hear of one sharp word to them, one incident meant to cause them grief or pain, I shall come back. And if you make that necessary . . .' His fingers reached for the dagger at his waist meaningfully.

Silas saw the cold features and took to his heels, almost tumbling down the stairs in his haste to hide himself. Lottie began to cry loudly as Quentin gathered Sapphira up into his arms. Molly drew her close and soothed her, strangely calm in herself, even though she knew she might never again see the girl she had cared for since she was a baby. The pouch of gold was heavy in her hands. She loosened the leather thonging, unable to resist a look at the abundance of coins which would make a new life for her and Lottie.

'Wait!' Quentin came to an abrupt halt at the door, as she called out. The pouch did not contain only coins. She withdrew the pendant, held it out to him. 'Take this. It belongs to her.'

He looked at the intricately-laced silverwork and the sapphires in the palm of his hand, and raised suspicious eyes to her face. 'Where did she come by such a thing? These stones are real.'

'It belonged to her true mother,' Molly told him, a resigned look in her eyes. She had always dreamed that, one day, Sapphira would find her true parents and become part of the world which had been denied her from birth. This man could make it happen for her. 'My husband and I adopted her from the Sisters of Mercy when she was but six months old. That was round her neck. I kept it for her so that, some day, she would be able to find out who she really is.'

'A love-child,' Quentin said softly, almost to himself. Now, more than ever, he was convinced that this girl was the answer to all his problems. Sapphira struggled weakly in his arms, desperate appeal in her eyes as she stared up at him, at Molly, at Lottie. He could not take her away from her family. Life with him as his mistress, for she was sure that was what he intended for her, would be little better than if she stayed at the tavern and did Silas's bidding. A man she did not love would own her. Her feeble strength ebbed, her resistance ceased. 'She shall want for nothing. She is to be my wife,' Quentin said.

At his words, Sapphira gave a low moan of disbelief

and despair, and her head fell back against his shoulder, her loose hair shadowing a face bereft of all colour. She was his, he thought, and for some reason the knowledge was exhilarating.

'You will do no such thing,' Mrs Grayson declared, when Sapphira voiced her intention of getting out of bed. 'I have instructions from the Earl himself to see that you stay abed for a whole week until those dreadful marks disappear. You cannot show yourself looking like that! What will people think?'

Sapphira gave in, allowing the pillows to be placed more comfortably behind her back, and settled down to another day of doing nothing at all. It was her fourth. She had been feverish for the first two, she was told by Mrs Grayson, the Earl's housekeeper, who was in sole charge of the new arrival. There was a young maid who came and went from the bedroom, bringing food and a change of nightclothes, but it was the housekeeper who came several times into Sapphira's presence to inquire if she needed anything or wished to make a complaint about her conditions. Sapphira could not believe it! Complain—her?

She had never seen the like of the bedroom where she lay. As the tall, stout figure of Mrs Grayson in her black dress and crisp white apron left the room, Sapphira's gaze travelled slowly, still a trifle incredulously, around her. It was a pleasant—no, beautiful— room. The furniture was in the style lately introduced by the brilliant young King of France. She had seen pictures in a book her teacher had once lent her, or she would have been unable to identify it. The wardrobe and the dressing-table beneath the window, where heavy burgundy curtains were tightly drawn to keep out the cold night air, were inlaid with exquisite marquetry. On the floor was a mat the colour of warm sunlight. The four-poster where she lay could accommodate six people, let alone one rather small girl, she thought, stretching languidly. The terrible pain in her back and the aches in her arms and legs had all but disappeared, hastened by some preparation administered during her fever by the Earl's own doctor, who had arrived to attend her within an hour of her own admittance to the house. She remembered very little of what had taken place after Quentin Tyrell carried her from the tavern: a faint memory of a coach and the sound of horses' hooves clattering noisily over cobbled stones, of gentle hands undressing her, and a blissfully soft mattress receiving her abused body. But, after that, nothing until she awoke to find herself in this strange room, where she was treated as an honoured guest.

She felt a strange thrill run through her as she traced the pattern of rosebuds on the silken coverlet beneath her fingertips. The sheets and pillowcases were silk, too, as was the nightgown she wore. She blushed as she looked down at the flimsy material, which left bare her arms and shoulders, frilled with an abundance of pure white lace. A velvet robe trimmed with fur lay at the bottom of the bed. She had been told she could ask for anything she wanted, but when she expressed only her desire to leave the Earl's house as soon as possible, she received no answer, although she remembered that the housekeeper gave her a scrutinising look.

The true reason she had been brought to the house and was being given such royal treatment, Sapphira thought she appreciated. It was all part of Quentin Tyrell's scheme to get from her what she had refused to part with at the tavern. He had tried force, and it had failed; so now he, with great cunning, was trying to bribe her. She would never become his mistress, she told herself fiercely. Never! As soon as she was strong enough she would run away and find Molly and Lottie again. The money he had given them would take them far away to a new life, and he would never find her. Until then she would play at his own game, pretending a continued lack of strength while daily she grew stronger, to keep him at arm's length. He had not come near her so far, although she had been told that he inquired after her health daily. So solicitous! The hypo-crite—did he really expect her to believe that he was concerned over a poor tavern wench he had tried unsuc-cessfully to seduce? Most likely he had made a bet with his gaming friends. Yes, that was it! He had wagered a certain sum of money on her capitulating to his terms within a given time. There were not many girls without money and resources of their own who would turn down the chance to be his mistress for even one short evening, Sapphira thought, as she listened to a clock somewhere in the house, chiming eight times. He would be sure he could bribe her with money and clothes, perhaps even jewels. How wrong he was! It seemed that he needed to be proved wrong about her character for a second time.

By the end of the week her strength had all but returned, and with it a growing determination to flee the house before another day passed. She had had no word from Molly and did not know where she might be; she was sure only that, once she had sufficient funds to move on, she would have quit the tavern and Silas's detestable company as quickly as possible. Why had she not tried to contact Sapphira? Or had she tried, and the message had been deliberately kept from its desti-nation?

Early in the evening, when the maid had been in to light the candles and rekindle the fire which kept the room as warm as toast, Sapphira made up her mind to leave now, before she began to grow too accustomed to the touch of silk against her skin. Slipping out of bed, she went across to the wardrobe and flung open the door. It was full of clothes, and she gasped in amaze-ment, knowing full well they had not been there before she fell asleep that afternoon.

There were gowns of every material imaginable, trimmed with sable fur and ermine, adorned with pearls or other jewels. Laces and satins, velvets and brocades. Bright bold colours and subdued colours. There were fur cloaks and dainty little shoes. She could not resist the temptation to try on one pair, of red leather, and her cheeks began to burn as she found they fitted easily. Spinning round, she ran to the carved chest in one corner and threw back the lid. It was full of undergarments and night attire. Were these meant to tempt her further? How dare he! The arrogance of the man in taking her for granted!

She contained her anger, selected a dress of blue velvet and went to consider her reflection in the ornate gilt mirror against the wall. Since she had no other clothes to wear, she would take this one, and a warm cloak. He would not even miss it.

'Do they meet with your approval?' Quentin asked from the doorway behind her. She had been so absorbed in her thoughts that she had not heard him enter. The amused smile on his face made her immediately return the dress to its place in the wardrobe. Cheeks flaming, she stepped back towards the bed, aware she was wearing only a thin, almost transparent, nightgown, which revealed far more to his gaze than she would have liked. His hard, bright eyes glittered as they surveyed her.

'Why should they?'

A shadow of annoyance crossed his face at her hostile tone, but he decided to ignore it. She was naturally still frightened, and believing that the worst was about to befall her. He had deliberately delayed coming to see her, hoping she would be in a receptive and agreeable mood when he did. Time was growing short. A decision had to be made soon and action taken before his birthday.

'They belong to you.' He closed the door behind him and advanced into the room. Sapphira leapt back into bed and sat hugging the clothes high around her shoulders. 'I have not come to assail your virtue presuming, of course, you are as innocent as that woman at the tavern insisted. I choose to believe otherwise, but as I shall not be bothering to discover whether or not it is the truth, it is of little importance to me.'

'You—will not . . .' Sapphira swallowed hard, unable to believe her ears. He was playing some game with her. 'Why—why, then, am I here?'

'Would you prefer to be back at the Black Horse with your devoted uncle?' Quentin asked sardonically, and she shook her head. In the candlelight, strands of her loose hair were turned to fire. Her real mother had been a red-head, he thought, and wondered if she were numbered among his many acquaintances at Court. 'What are you called, girl?'

'Sapphira. If I am not . . . I mean, if you do not want me, why am I here? Why have you been so kind to me, after I . . .'

'Gave me an unpleasant headache? I, too, think I have taken leave of my senses, but you are the answer to a problem which has been plaguing my life for a long while. Do you like your surroundings, Sapphira?' No common name; and, now that he saw her with eyes not glazed with drink, his mind clear and sharp, he could see the fine bone structure, the grace with which she held herself. With the right clothes and jewels to adorn that lovely neck, those slender milk-white shoulders, she could pass anywhere for a lady. Not that he would be seen much in her company.

'They are very—fine.' She chose her words with care, suspicious of the question, and he nodded understandingly.

'Would you like to continue living here?'

'As your kept woman! Never!' Sapphira threw back her head, and her eyes blazed like brilliant sapphires out of the paleness of her face. His words had drained all colour from it again. She had been right about him, after all. 'Have you tired of your fine ladies of rank that you want one such as I to warm your bed, my lord? I have little of my own to give any man, but what I have shall be given freely or not at all. If you touch me—I shall kill you!'

'Damn you, girl, I'm offering you a life of luxury,' Quentin snapped. Wheeling about, he tugged at the bell-rope to summon a servant, then, opening all the wardrobe doors, he stared at the contents for a full minute before selecting a black velvet gown lavishly trimmed with sable. Sapphira's eyes widened as he tossed it across the bed. 'You will get up and allow yourself to be dressed, and then you will come downstairs and have supper with me. We shall talk then. If I remain here a moment longer, your arrogance will anger me greatly. Give Mrs Grayson no trouble,' he warned, as the woman entered. 'Dress her, and bring her to me within the hour. Do not make it necessary for me to come back here again.'

'I will not do his bidding,' Sapphira gasped, as the door slammed noisily behind him.

'I think you should.' The housekeeper moved round the room, taking out petticoats and a linen shift, stockings and shoes. 'The Earl is not a patient man. He always gets his own way in the end; so why not be sensible now, young lady, and save us all the sharp end of his tongue.'

In silence, Sapphira gave herself into the woman's hands. She sat in a miserable silence as her hair was brushed until it shone in the flickering candlelight. 'Up, I think,' Mrs Grayson murmured, as she twisted it into a mass of tiny curls which fell in profusion over one shoulder. A simple bandeau of ribbon encircled her head. When it came to her face being powdered, her lips rouged and a black patch being fixed to one cheek, Sapphira rebelled and threatened to retire to her bed again unless her face was left untouched. She did not want to look like one of those women at Court who puffed their hair out in outrageous styles, and thought it chic to parade with stars of circles on their cheeks or foreheads. What a ridiculous fashion that was!

'There, now, what do you think? I find the transformation quite startling. Look in the mirror, girl. Is it not
an improvement?'

Was that her? Sapphira blinked several times at the
reflection that stared back at her. That girl had style
and elegance, where she had none. She was beautiful,
graceful in her movements. How the black dress clung
to her slim figure, accentuating curves her old cotton
dress had hidden. She looked—a lady! Why was he
doing this to her? Why had he given her such lovely
things to wear, made her aware of what could be hers
for the asking? It was too cruel. He was clever and subtle
in his approach, making each refusal more difficult to
utter. One day, when she had money of her own and a
position, she would remember how he had humiliated
her and mocked her pride.

Quentin looked down the length of the dining-table at
the uncommunicative figure seated at the far end. Her
manner continued to annoy him and rouse the devil he
knew he must contain if he was to succeed in his plan.
She had waited a full hour—deliberately, he suspected
—before joining him. She had accepted the chair pulled
out for her by a liveried page with a slight inclination
of her head, and a smile which had utterly captivated
the impressionable young lad who had scarcely been
able to take his eyes from her since. Yet she had not
looked in his own direction or acknowledged him in any
way.

Quentin had to admit, although he would never have
condescended to tell her so, that she looked beautiful.
The transformation from tavern wench to a creature of
elegance had amazed him when she first entered the
room, and once again he was aware of how well she
carried herself. Her carriage and poise would fool many
of his friends, who usually looked no further than a
woman's face, if it was pretty. He noticed that hers had
been left untouched, and wondered whose idea that had

been. Her own? Had she no wish not only to act, but to look the grand lady?

There was no warmth in her expression when she did look at him, however, but he chose to make no comment and ordered the meal to be served. She barely touched the thick oxtail soup, heavily laced with red wine, and only picked at the succulent chicken basted in pungent oriental spices, a recipe he had brought back from abroad. Neither did she attempt to try the full-bodied claret at her fingertips, or the port which was poured out for her when she refused even to touch the orange pudding.

By this time Quentin's temper was at a dangerous level. She was determined to vex him. Damn the girl! What was the matter with her? He doubted if she had ever sat down to such a meal in all her life. She was a typical woman, feigning reticence until the price was right. She and Corinna would make a fine pair!

'I have a proposition for you, Sapphira.' He sat back in his chair after a servant had refilled his glass with port, and then withdrawn. She stiffened visibly. 'Let us call it a business arrangement, which will be mutually beneficial.'

'I will not become your mistress,' Sapphira declared defiantly. 'I cannot be bought, my lord, poor as I am. You have been wasting your time and your gifts. When I leave in the morning, I shall take nothing of yours with me. Contrary to what you suppose, I am neither a thief nor a liar.'

'You shall become whatever I wish you to become,' Quentin snapped, his eyes narrowing to angry slits. 'In this house, I am master. *Your* master, if I so choose. Let us make your position quite clear, you little fool. You will do exactly what I ask of you, or I shall have you arrested the moment you leave here and charge you with stealing my purse of gold. Which you gave to your mother, and will be found in her possession,' he added meaningly.

'You would not—could not—be so cruel . . .'
Sapphira saw by the set of his jaw that he meant every
word. Who would believe her word against that of a
titled gentleman? She would be thrown into prison;
perhaps Molly and Lottie, too, as accomplices. He was
an inhuman monster!

'I see we understand each other at last. However,
you may not wish to drive me to those extremes when
you have heard what I have to say. I am prepared to
provide for every need you have for clothes, jewels or
money. You shall have a house of your own, if you
wish, where you can entertain your own circle of friends.
I should like you to cultivate new ones; but I shall assist
you in that matter—that will come later.'

'Later?' Sapphira echoed. Why did she suddenly feel
like a tiny bird trapped in a small barred cage?

'In return for these things,' Quentin continued, 'and
believe this, girl—for once the deed is done, I want
nothing from you—you will be free to do as you please
and go where you wish. So long as you do nothing to
sully my name, we shall live two different lives. I want
you to marry me.'

'Your humour is in bad taste, sir,' she gasped. She
remembered now: he had told Molly she was to be his
wife, but she had thought it a lie to placate her mother
lest she caused a fuss as he left the tavern. He had been
in earnest! 'Is this some new bet you have arranged with
your friends?'

'My reasons do not concern you. However, I shall
tell you this. It is necessary for me to be married on my
thirty-second birthday, which falls next month, and I
must remain thus for one year afterwards. That is all I
ask of you, girl. One year of your life. Twelve months,
during which you will be paid a small fortune if you
are anything like other women I have known. Think
of your family—of that pathetic little creature I saw
with you in that room. Think of what you could give
them.'

'Are you such a terrible catch that you have to resort to seeking a bride from riverside taverns?' Sapphira's tone was scornful. He could not be serious. It was a dream, and she would awaken soon in the tavern, with Silas bellowing for her to get to the tap-room. None of this could possibly be real.

'With careful coaching, you might pass for a reasonable facsimile of a lady,' Quentin drawled, ignoring the comment. He had come too far to turn back now; he would not be dissuaded. 'I am buying your time, wench.' He used the term deliberately to remind her of who she was and the precarious position she would find herself in if she continued with her fancy airs. Slowly his eyes considered her, from the top of her shining hair to the décolletage of the black gown. 'I have a mistress, whom I find quite satisfactory. You have nothing at all to interest me. You have an adequate wardrobe to be going on with at the moment, but you will need more outdoor clothes for the country. I shall arrange for a dressmaker to call on you tomorrow afternoon.'

Sapphira pushed back her chair and rose to her feet like someone in a dream. He sat watching her in silence, a smile tugging at the corners of the lean mouth. He looked so satisfied and confident, she thought apprehensively. 'I would like to go to my room.'

'Of course! You have a busy time ahead of you. Tomorrow I shall begin the necessary arrangements. It will be a quiet affair. The less you are seen in public for a while the better—until you have acquired a little finesse, I mean.'

Damn her! If only she had been more receptive, he would have treated her with more courtesy and kindness. He could afford to be lenient, after all. He had won. Corinna had failed after so many years of scheming.

'Here.' From beneath the napkin at his side that bore his crest, as did all the linen in the house, he withdrew a slim box and pushed it down the table towards her.

'That's what you are waiting for, isn't it? A first instalment.'

What the box contained, Sapphira did not know. She did not even move to take it as his insult sank deep into her. Did he think money could buy everything? Without a word she turned and swept out of the room. Not until she was in bed, enjoying the cup of hot chocolate the maid had brought her, did she realise that she had given him no answer. But then she knew he had not expected one. With the threat of prison hanging over her head and that of the two people dearest to her in all the world, she would do what he asked.

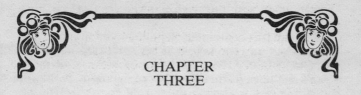

CHAPTER
THREE

QUENTIN CAME unannounced into Sapphira's bedroom the following morning as she sat in bed, a breakfast tray in front of her. Dismissing the maid, he walked over to her side and tossed something down on the coverlet. Sapphira stiffened as she found herself looking at a bracelet. Were those huge green stones real emeralds?

'You forgot that last night,' Quentin said in a guarded tone. He had come expecting trouble, but to his surprise she said nothing. So she had accepted the opportunity after all, he thought, and wondered why he should feel such annoyance when it was what he wanted. 'We are leaving at mid-day for the country, so I have not made arrangements for the dressmaker. That can wait until we return.'

'Where are we going?' Sapphira's appetite vanished, and she pushed the tray aside. She had slept very little, plagued by dreams in which first Silas was pursuing her with his strap and then Quentin Tyrell. Each man sought to use her for his own ends. Not for one moment did she believe the latter would ignore her once they were married. He would be the laughing-stock of his friends if it was discovered he had not bedded with his own wife. She had watched the sky lighten outside the windows, and resigned herself to the fact that she had no choice but to marry him. At least, as he said, there would be compensation. Money to keep her mother and Lottie, perhaps to provide them with a small house of her own. She knew that Molly had been dreaming of her own home again for many years. For their sakes she would accept the strange trick fate had played on her.

'I must see my mother and sister, and tell them I am well.'

'When we return.' His tone prohibited argument. 'I am taking you to Ravenswood, my estate in Devon. We shall be married there, and by the time we come back, I hope you will have begun to act—as well as look—like a lady.'

'I am sure I shall give good value for money,' she retorted, and saw his lips tighten at her frosty tone. Did he expect her to fall into his arms and thank him for her good fortune? Had it been offered without the threat of prison, which made a refusal impossible, she might have felt gratitude, not this resentment which rose up inside her every time they came together. 'Are you not afraid that your friends from the Black Horse will recognise me, my lord?'

'That is bound to happen, of course, but it is quite the fashion nowadays to lower one's standards. Even the King seeks diversions in the theatre, and he is by no means alone.' He shrugged his broad shoulders.

'But not many men marry their little amusements, do they, sir?' Sapphira asked, toying with the bracelet. She would sell it the moment she returned to London and give the money to her mother. What did she want with such things? 'But, then, you do not have a choice, do you?'

'You would be wise not to remind me of that again,' Quentin warned with a frown. 'I suggest you finish your breakfast, as we have a long journey ahead of us.'

The sound of a woman's voice raised in anger came to them clearly from the corridor outside. Sapphira heard Quentin utter a low oath, and saw him wheel towards the door as it was flung open. An attractive young woman in her early twenties stood on the threshold, staring at them both with cold, hazel eyes. She wore a riding-habit in a dark blue material, and a wide-brimmed hat with an ostrich feather was perched on top of her blonde hair. The riding-whip she carried was slapped noisily against her deep skirt as she declared loudly,

'Entertaining again, Quentin? She's a new one, isn't she? A little young, even for you.'

Sapphira gasped, and drew the bedcovers around her bare arms. The woman laughed at her scarlet cheeks. Quentin interrupted her harshly.

'Get out, Corinna. We shall talk, if we must, downstairs.'

'I'm not ashamed for your strumpet to hear what I say. As we both rely on you for your favours, we are little different, although I am more particular whom I sleep with. I need money. It's the only reason I ever come here.'

Who was she, Sapphira wondered, feeling embarrassed and tongue-tied at the woman's cutting words and baleful looks. Surely this was not his mistress?

'You have had your allowance for this month.'

'I need more. Damn you, Quentin, you'll give her a handful of guineas without a second thought, yet you make your own sister crawl to you for less.'

'Get downstairs. I'll join you in a minute,' Quentin thundered, stepping towards her with fists clenching, and she took a step backwards, paling slightly at his tone.

She sent one more scathing look in Sapphira's direction, and said bitterly, 'Yes, brother dear. I shall await your gracious presence while you pay off your—companion. For the moment, I have no choice.'

Quentin slammed the door behind him, his face a white, angry mask. The comment Sapphira was about to make was never uttered. There was something very frightening about the change in him, and she wisely remained silent. He strode to the window and stared down into the street, his back towards her. When he turned, his expression was unreadable. Without one word of explanation, he left her.

Her curiosity aroused, Sapphira slipped out of bed

and ran to the door. As Quentin reached the bottom of the staircase and moved in the direction of the sitting-room, where his sister was pacing the floor impatiently, she tiptoed to the edge of the gilded banister rail to listen.

The voices, which began low and almost inaudible to her ears, rose sharply within a few minutes. She heard Corinna declare shrilly, 'I must have that amount. I need it desperately.' Quentin's curt answer, 'A hundred guineas, and not one more until next month.' 'Next month?' Corinna's tone changed suddenly and became almost mocking. 'In one month, my dear brother, I shall be mistress in this house, Mistress of Ravenswood too, or have you forgotten the clause in our father's will? You have no wife! You are going to lose everything, and on the day you do, you will leave this house and never set foot in it again. Or Ravenswood. I shall sell it, I think. I have no love for it, not like you.' 'You bitch,' Quentin snarled . . .

Sapphira did not remain to listen to any more. Shaken, she returned to her bed and rang for the maid to come and help her to dress. So Corinna was the reason Quentin needed to marry. Something in his father's will made it necessary for him to have a wife on his thirty-second birthday, or his estates and money went to his sister. What kind of a father set brother and sister against each other in this way? There was too much she did not know about the circumstances which had driven him to take so drastic an action as to marry a perfect stranger—a nobody such as her. She shuddered a little as she remembered the hatred in his sister's voice as she mocked him with the loss of his home. What terrible thing had happened to drive them so far apart? She knew he would never tell her, and she wondered if she had the courage to ask him herself.

Ravenswood, the country estate of Quentin Tyrell, was set in a wooded landscape, miles from the nearest village. The house was an enormous, half-timbered manor house built in the reign of Queen Elizabeth. As the carriage turned through a large pair of iron gates and rolled down a tree-lined drive towards it, she leaned forward with wide eyes and tried to count the numerous windows shining in the early morning sunshine, but gave up when she reached fifty. There were orchards on both sides of it, and gardens still covered with the snow that had fallen the night before. The weather had been so uncertain that Quentin had called another halt when they reached the coast road, and they had spent the night at a comfortable hostelry. The place was crowded with travellers like themselves mistrusting the bleak weather, but she had been found a room. Not until morning did she discover that Quentin had slept downstairs in a chair.

He had rarely bothered to make conversation with her during the long journey. Some of the time he slept, his dark head resting against the padded seat, untroubled by the slow, sometimes unsteady, progress of the carriage. She had found herself studying him as the days slipped by and she was left to huddle inside her fur-lined cloak in a miserable silence. His manner had been changed by his sister's visit, she thought as she considered the set features, which had not relaxed even in sleep. He had become curt and impatient with her. On one day he had all but reduced her to tears with his cutting remarks, and she came to the conclusion that nothing she ever did or said would please him. She was a means to an end, and nothing more.

'You have a beautiful home, my lord,' she said, trying hard not to show her excitement as he helped her to alight. She was to be mistress of this! 'How proud you must be!'

'You think it beautiful?' Quentin looked at her with suspicious eyes. 'Corinna calls it an ugly mausoleum. Unfriendly and cold. Like me!'

'But then she has always been able to call it home,

and has always been warm and comfortable in winter and slept in a feather bed, whereas I am only just beginning to know—and appreciate—these things. Please don't misunderstand me,' she hastened to add, as his mouth crooked into a mocking smile. 'Molly has always been a good mother to me, even though I was not her own child, and I shall always love her for it. But not even all the long hours she used to work before her husband died, and we were reduced to the circumstances in which you found us, brought in enough money for us to enjoy such comforts as you and your sister take for granted.'

'We shall see how much you like it after you have been here a week,' Quentin returned, mounting the wide curve of steps to the front door and tossing his hat and gloves to the hovering servant. He did not like being coupled with Corinna. He, too, knew what it was like to suffer hardships and privations. God knows, he had had enough of them in Holland and France. 'Bring mulled wine for us both to the Great Hall—we are frozen. Instruct all the household I wish to see them in an hour. I have something to tell them.'

Still hugging her cloak about her, Sapphira followed him into an enormous room which must have been over seventy feet in length and half as wide. All the panelling on the walls was in dark oak, as were the massive beams which supported the roof. Two large chandeliers hung low on chains over a heavy carved table and twelve chairs with thick red velvet padded backs. The table gleamed, with not a speck of dust on it anywhere, and she could smell the pewter tankards that must have been freshly cleaned that morning. How many hours had she spent polishing the self-same things in the Black Horse?

Her steps slowed as she surveyed her new domain. The rich Persian tapestries which covered a smaller table, and a sofa beneath the double-latticed windows, the heavy dresser, some eight or nine feet in length,

also covered with pewter and silver plate. Her domain!
She would appreciate it, even if Corinna did not. For
one year all this would be hers. She did not want to
think beyond that. A fire blazed in the cavern of a
fireplace, and both sides of the hearth were stacked high
with logs. She went towards the flames immediately,
stretching out her cold hands to the welcoming warmth.
A coat of arms dominated the wall above her, between
a pair of crossed swords, bearing the Latin inscription,
'*Contra Mundum*'.

'*Against the World*,' she translated quietly, and Quentin, who had bent beside her to throw another piece of
wood on the fire, straightened up with a soft exclamation
of amazement.

'How do you come to read Latin, wench?'

'I am not completely ignorant, as I have already told
you, sir.' Sapphira felt pleased that she had surprised
him with her knowledge. Perhaps it might help to stop
him treating her like a ninny. She was a person in her
own right, simple though she might be by his standards,
and she would not allow herself to be ground underheel
by his domineering way. 'Is it your family motto?'

'For the past three hundred years.'

'Then I think your ancestors must have been very
brave, if not lonely, men.'

'Why so?' Quentin demanded with a frown.

'No one man—or woman—can fight the whole world,
sir. Such an existence would be unbearable. It is
unthinkable not to have friends: someone to trust and
confide in.'

'Sometimes a solitary existence brings less pain,' came
the terse reply, and her eyes searched his face, which
was suddenly grim. It was the way he chose to live, she
realised. His companions at the tavern had not been
friends, but merely people he had been with. He had
sat on his chair in the tap-room watching them with
narrowed gaze, giving her the impression that he
despised every single one of them. Perhaps not all,

though. The man who had sat with him, she recalled that someone had addressed him as Blaise, had seemed to reach him every so often, yet even he did not receive all the Earl's undivided attention. A part of him always seemed detached, kept separate from whatever he was doing. She did not think one short year could be long enough to get to know him or what went on in his mind behind those satanic features. Had anyone ever really known him, she wondered?

'You are pale. Has the journey tired you?' It was the first sign of consideration he had shown her since leaving London.

'Yes,' she admitted. 'My whole body aches.'

In fact her body and shoulders, still somewhat tender from the beating Silas had given her, were quite painful. Most of the bruises had become ugly yellowing blotches, which was why she had chosen a travelling-gown which covered as much of her as possible. Not knowing what awaited her at Ravenswood, she had brought most of her new wardrobe. The novelty of being able to change into a different gown six times a day, if she so chose, would take some time to wear off.

'I sent word ahead of our arrival, so you will find your rooms prepared. Warm yourself with that wine, and then go and rest. Tomorrow morning we shall have a visit from the vicar. The wedding ceremony will take place in the chapel here. I thought it best to tell him that you are an orphan, so as not to shock him. Please remember that, when you are with him.'

'Of course, my lord. Have you any other instructions for me? Am I to remain in my rooms until we are married, or am I allowed to wander freely about the place?' Sapphira asked stiffly, resenting the unecessary comment. Did he believe she wanted her background to be made open knowledge, subjecting her to the whispered comments and stares of his servants? It would be humiliating enough when they returned to London, and she was forced to face his friends. He had made it clear that, for a short while at least, she would have to appear with him in public. An introduction at Court, however, would be out of the question. She was good enough to be used to save his estates and thwart his sister, good enough to flaunt before his friends who would no doubt regard her as a huge joke with her lack of manners and sparse conversation, but not good enough to appear at his side as his wife in Court circles. For one moment she thought of reminding him that part of her was of noble blood, but she had never used that knowledge before, and she would not now. Her real mother, whoever she was, would remain a stranger. She did not want to find someone who had so callously abandoned her as a baby.

Quentin scowled at the taunt, aware of the servant at the other side of the table. 'You will be shown to your rooms when you are ready,' he answered, containing himself. Leaving his mulled wine untouched, he strode from the room and she heard him shouting for a bath to be prepared, fresh clothes laid out and his horse saddled.

With a tired sigh, Sapphira sat down in a chair by the fire and put him out of her thoughts. As soon as she returned to London, she would go to look for Molly and Lottie. If they had left the tavern, which she prayed they had, with the purse of money still intact and hidden from Silas's thieving fingers, she would soon find them now that she had money to pay for information. Perhaps Rosie would know. The warmth was beginning to make her feel drowsy.

'I should like to go to my rooms now,' she said to the silent servant, and he came forward to relieve her of her empty glass.

'This way, please, my lady.'

She brightened a little as she followed him up the oak staircase to a long corridor which must have led to more than a dozen rooms. If only Mollie and Lottie could see her now, she thought, as she was admitted to a suite of rooms consisting of a huge sitting-room, a bedroom, and a small antechamber where a maid could sleep if required. Or Silas! It was time she stopped worrying about Quentin's hateful attitude. To him, she was a necessary evil whom he must endure for twelve whole months, and he had made it plain how much he detested it, but she must not allow it to ruin the wonderful new world opening up before her. For the first time in all her eighteen years, she had a future—a bright, unbelievably promising future. She must never look back again.

The friendly attitude of the vicar who came to Ravenswood in the morning immediately put Sapphira at her ease. He was, in fact, in charge of the parish of Market Cross, a mile on the far side of the village that bore the same name, and which, she was amazed to discover, was included in the Earl's land. She began to realise how rich and influential her future husband was as she listened to the two men discussing estate business, and the growing prosperity of the village since Quentin had given money for the rebuilding of the church, with enough over to start a school. His ideas were quite progressive, and he was well liked and respected by those who worked for him on the estate, for there was talk of a celebration for him and his bride, if he agreed. To her great surprise, he did.

'And how is the Lady Corinna?' the vicar asked his companion.

'Well, sir; but unfortunately she is confined to bed with a cold and will miss the ceremony. Doubtless she will make up for it when we return to London,' Quentin replied with a smile. He lied with such ease, Sapphira thought.

'How are things between you, my son? Improved, I pray.'

'Never better.' Only Sapphira noticed the tightening of the muscles in his face, as if even to discuss his sister was repugnant to him. Whatever had she done to deserve such treatment, apart from wanting, quite rightfully she had begun to think, to share in her brother's inheritance from their father? Why should she not have an equal share in what had been left? Sapphira, although their initial meeting had not been to her liking, had thought Corinna a strong character and very independent. Was Quentin one of those men who looked down on a woman for showing strength and determination to control her own life? Not all women wanted to be mindless extensions of their husbands or fathers, as was so often the case in a society where men were the dominant force.

'You are very quiet, my child?' The vicar was looking in her direction. She had not involved herself in any of the conversation, knowing that Quentin would not have approved—besides, what did she have to say of interest to this man of learning? She had been introduced simply as the Lady Sapphira, an orphan who had been brought up by a maiden aunt, recently demised, in London, where they had met only a month before. How neatly he ensured there were no loose ends, no possibility of her fictitious maiden aunt appearing for the wedding.

'I fear she is a little overawed by the swiftness of my proposal,' Quentin chuckled softly, but the eyes intent on Sapphira were watchful, and warning in their intensity. 'But, since she has no one else in the world, I saw no reason to wait. Do you? Who better to take care of her in this time of grief than the man with whom she has chosen to spend the rest of her life? I did think, however, that a quiet ceremony here at Ravenswood was more suitable than a grand London affair. Our celebrations can come later, can they not, my dear?'

'Yes, indeed.' The endearment stung her, but she ignored it. He had missed his vocation, she thought—he should have been at Drury Lane.

'A sensible arrangement. Even as a young boy, you

were always most considerate, Quentin. I was afraid
that London and the decadence of the King's Court
might have changed you. I remember how your dear
mother used to sit here in this very room and reminisce
about your childhood. Those were happy days, when
you were all together,' the vicar sighed. 'A pity they
cannot return.'

'They are never lost to me, sir. I carry them in my
heart, along with her memory.'

For a moment Sapphira saw the mask drop, and the
pain mirrored in his dark eyes made her catch her
breath. 'Against the World'. Not only the family motto,
but his, and for a brief instant she saw how alone and
unhappy Quentin Tyrell was in his chosen existence.
Then the smile returned, the invitation for the vicar to
walk with him and admire the new stallion in his stables.
Left alone, unwanted and rather disturbed by what
she had seen, Sapphira returned to her room. That
afternoon she pleaded a headache and begged to be
allowed to dine upstairs. He sent a servant to her with
a tray of food, but no accompanying message. She had
not expected one.

Later, she slept fitfully in the four-poster bed with
its elaborate hangings, silken pillow-covers and
embroidered bedspread. The feather mattress, she estimated, was twelve inches thick, and so soft and comfortable that she had fallen asleep as soon as she relaxed
into it.

Pulling on a wrap, she slid her feet into warm slippers
and walked to open the curtains. The sky was dull
and overcast. Rain or snow, she wondered, and was
surprised to see a groom leading a horse towards the
front of the house. It was a magnificent beast with a
jet-black coat. Quentin came down the steps, huddled
inside thick outdoor clothing, and mounted with the
ease of an accomplished horseman. Would she have to
learn to ride? The thought terrified her. Where was he

off to at this early hour, and what was she supposed to do while he was absent?

She tugged at the bell-rope beside the bed, and minutes later a breathless maid came to see what she required, looking amazed to find her not only up, but wanting breakfast.

'I'm sorry, my lady . . . I mean . . . The master doesn't usually eat until nine. He likes to ride for two hours before breakfast each morning. There's nothing ready yet.'

'Then I shall wait until he returns,' Sapphira replied. The girl looked even more discomforted, prompting her to ask, 'Is anything wrong?'

'The Earl won't be back until this afternoon, my lady. He's ridden over to see Squire Havelock, and when those two get together, he is always away most of the day.'

'Then bring me something light to eat as soon as you can. Toast and jam, or a plain egg. Who is in charge of the house?'

'Wilcox, my lady. He's been here for years. He served the late Earl in his day.'

'Tell him I would like to speak to him after breakfast.' If Quentin was going to go off for most of the day, she would have to find her own interests. She would start with the house. As its future mistress, it was time she inspected it. He would not return and find her bored or miserable.

Wilcox was in his late sixties, grey-haired with slightly stooping shoulders. Despite his age, Sapphira noticed his sharp eyes, which would miss nothing that took place in the house. For a moment they took stock in silence, each weighing up the potential of the other's character.

'I am pleased to meet you, Wilcox. I am told there is nothing you do not know about this lovely old house, and so I am going to rely on you a great deal to help me in the months ahead. I am not a country person, you see; I was born in London. That has its advantages,

I assure you, but now I have come to this part of the country and seen how beautiful it is, even with all this snow about, I realise how much I have missed in the city.' The man said not a word, but remained with his gaze fixed doggedly on her determined young face. She sat down on a near-by chair, spreading her skirts about her, and laid her hands in her lap. Instantly his eyes reverted to her ringless fingers. Did he think it strange that she wore no betrothal ring? How she wished she knew what Quentin had told the servants about her. Had the story been the same as he had told the vicar?

'As mistress here, I fully understand the responsibilities which will befall me, but I shall need guidance, your expert guidance, when it comes to entertaining the Earl's friends. All this is very new to me, and I want to please him. I would not like him to think that, because I am young in years, I do not have a sensible head on my shoulders.'

'I am at your service, my lady.' Wilcox gave her a stiff bow, but she noticed a gleam come into his eyes. He had been waiting for the new broom to make a clean sweep, but she was too wise to start making changes before she was well established in his favour. 'Perhaps I might be so bold as to suggest that the servants be introduced first, and then an inspection of the house.'

'If you are not all too busy,' Sapphira said, hardly able to hide her satisfaction. If she could win this dour-faced old retainer over to her side, life at Ravenswood would be heaven for her. 'I realise that the preparations for our wedding are in hand, at very short notice. It must have placed a great burden on the staff.'

'For a short while only, my lady, as we have had to arrange for additional supplies of some requisites for the celebrations. With no guests, apart from the vicar and the Lady Margaret for the wedding breakfast, we have not been over-taxed, I assure you.'

He sounded as though he could have coped easily with a hundred guests, Sapphira thought, and remembered how flustered Silas became when the tavern was full and his customers grew ugly because there were not enough waitresses to serve them quickly.

'Who—who is the Lady Margaret? I don't seem to remember the Earl mentioning her.'

'A close friend of his, my lady, for many years now. Since he returned from France, in fact. She used to stay here often with the late Countess.'

His mistress! It had to be, and he had invited her here for the wedding! What a monstrous thing to do!

Wilcox excused himself, as a footman appeared, bowing, in the doorway. Sapphira caught sight of a carriage rolling to a halt outside the windows, and went to look out curiously. Quentin had ridden off on horseback, so it could not be he.

She watched a figure emerge, wrapped in a white fur wrap so voluminous that it covered her from head to toe. All Sapphira could see were cheeks tinged a bright pink from the cold, and a full, wide mouth.

'Lady Margaret Stafford,' Wilcox said behind her, as she stared at the woman ascending the stairs. 'Will you receive her in here by the fire, my lady?'

Receive her? Sapphira was aghast at the suggestion, and almost refused; then, aware that Wilcox was looking at her scrutinisingly, she nodded affirmation. He knew who she was, of course. He was waiting to see how the future mistress of Ravenswood received the Earl's mistress. A lady might have refused, Sapphira thought, as she returned to her chair by the fire and steeled herself for the ordeal, but she was curious to see what kind of woman had kept a man like Quentin Tyrell tied to her for so many years. She would be exceptionally beautiful, she decided, a woman of the world. She would know and wear the latest fashions, however outrageous, because she had confidence and poise. She would sparkle, radiant as a queen with the jewels that Quentin and probably other men had lavished on her over the years. What did Lady Margaret know about

Sapphira? Had Quentin told her how he had forced her into agreeing to marry him? Had they laughed about the little tavern nobody that he was going to try to turn into a lady? How she wished she had the courage to run away, back to London to find Molly and Lottie, and they would hide themselves so that he could never find them and send them to prison on a false charge of stealing. But common sense prevailed. He was giving her all she had ever wanted, and she, in her turn, could take care of her family. The importance of that far outweighed her dislike of Quentin or her growing humiliation at the position she found herself in. She would never have fine manners, even though she wore fine clothes. She had not been born to it.

'Thank heavens for a fire! I am so stiff that I can hardly move. Wilcox, a glass of the Earl's madeira if you please—a large one.'

From beneath the fur cocoon emerged a woman in her early thirties, Sapphira estimated, perhaps a little younger, with dark chestnut hair and blue-grey eyes that turned enquiringly in the direction of the seated figure. Attractive, but not the striking beauty she had expected.

'You must be Sapphira. Quentin has told me all about you. We must introduce ourselves properly later on, when I have thawed out,' she declared, smiling, and seated herself in a chair near-by, pulling back her skirt above her ankles and thrusting neatly booted feet out towards the hearth. 'My God, the journey! A nightmare. Why Quentin could not have married you in London is beyond my comprehension. Why has he dragged you down here, of all places, in such weather?'

'If, as you say, he has told you all about me,' Sapphira replied stiffly, not responding to the unexpected warmth that had taken her completely by surprise, 'then you know why. He wants me hidden away so that none of his friends can see him being wed to a girl who stands by his side before the clergyman because he has forced her into it. He is ashamed of me. I am to save his neck, and that's all. He scarcely has the time to be civil to me.'

The vehemence in the words had not been intended. She had meant to be calm and composed and at least hold her head up before this woman who had come to inspect her at Quentin's invitation.

'Have you seen all you wish to, my lady?' she asked, rising to her feet. 'If so, I shall leave you. I am sure you know your way about the place better than I, so I am not required to play hostess. Not that I even know how. You and Quentin will be able to laugh over the way he has outwitted his sister with this marriage. You will be the first of many . . .'

'My poor child, what has that man done to you to make you feel this way?' the woman declared, interrupting her. 'He gave me to understand you were quite happy with the arrangements, that you have a mother, and sister who is not in the best of health, and that his payment for your part in this affair will take them from a horrible tavern with money to start a new life. Is this not the truth?'

Bright tears welled into Sapphira's eyes at the kindness of her voice. She did not want false comfort! A servant arrived with a decanter of madeira and a glass. Lady Margaret waved him away, poured some out and offered it to Sapphira.

'Drink this. You are overwrought, my dear.'

'I do not drink.'

'Then you had better begin here and now, or you will never survive in our world. Do you not drink at all?'

'No. Molly, my mother, would not allow it. My father drank—he was a kind, gentle man, but people put upon him, and when things grew too much for him he would take to the bottle. He was drunk when he died —he fell downstairs and broke his neck,' Sapphira answered in a whisper. It was after his death that things had begun to go wrong for them. The lodging-house did not pay its way, and they were forced to sell. Then Lottie was always ill, and the doctor's bills took most of their money until Molly was forced to go to her brother-in-law seeking help. Help! One day God would punish Silas for the hell he had put them through. It came to her suddenly that, in her new position, she would be able to hasten that day if she chose.

'Very well, I shall not force you. It would appear that too much has been used upon you lately.' The glass was held to the full lips, and Sapphira watched her drink. She laughed in amusement at the surprise on her face. 'There, I begin to feel better already. We shall take the decanter upstairs with us and talk. No argument, young woman. If Quentin has mistreated or abused you in any way to get you to agree to this marriage, he will receive the sharp end of my tongue. I suppose you do know that we are—how shall I put it . . .'

'You are his mistress.'

Lady Margaret laughed again, not in the least offended by her bluntness. It was a friendly sound, and Sapphira, against her will, found herself beginning to like her.

'You will cause the fans to flutter if you speak out like that in London, but then I'd like to see a fresh breeze blow through the Court. You may be it. Yes, Quentin and I have had a very pleasant relationship for several years. Neither of us takes the other for granted. We are still free agents. Never take him for granted, my dear. He is a difficult man, for reasons I shall not go into now; I think you have enough on your mind without his problems, too. Come, bring the wine and let us see if we can make those lovely eyes shine, shall we?'

This was incredible, Sapphira thought, as they mounted the stairs together, Lady Margaret still complaining about the journey and her cold feet. She had been prepared to loathe this woman, and yet here she was feeling at ease with her in the space of a few

minutes. She did not know how it had come about or
whether it would last, but of one thing she was certain.
Lady Margaret was genuinely concerned about her. She
had found a friend!

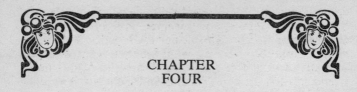

CHAPTER
FOUR

'So MOLLY is not your true mother?' Lady Margaret said, motioning Sapphira to help herself to some more of the toast, dripping with butter, on the table between them. For the past hour they had been closeted in the latter's bedroom, deep in conversation. Wilcox himself had brought hot chocolate, some broth for the visitor and toast spread with butter and honey. He had informed her that her rooms were prepared, but Lady Margaret had declined to go to them and he had left them alone, looking more than a little surprised. 'That will set the tongues wagging in the kitchen,' she had laughed. 'They expected us to claw each other's eyes out.'

'Why should they?' Sapphira had replied in puzzlement. 'I am only to be his wife. Everyone knows a mistress is more important than a wife. It is she who holds sway over the man.'

'How little you know of Quentin. No one, man or woman, holds sway over him. He is his own master.'

'And very lonely.'

'So you have realised that already. There is a chance for you yet.'

Now, an hour later the decanter of madeira half empty and a glow in Margaret's cheeks, not caused by the cold—she was no longer complaining about her feet, Sapphira realised—the bond of friendship had been firmly cemented. She had bluntly said, when they had first sat down, that she thought that Margaret was being nice to her only for Quentin's sake, and had been rebuked for her suspicion. Margaret was lounging on a couch, her head supported by several cushions. Sapphira sat opposite on a carved upright chair, and the wariness had gone from her expression. If anyone could help her to become what Quentin wanted, then Margaret could. But she was still too shy of this new friendship to ask any favours, and a favour it would indeed be. A large one. To teach her would be an enormous undertaking. She was completely unaware of the qualities she already possessed, which Molly had seen developing in her only a short while before she had left the Black Horse.

'Have you any idea who abandoned you?'

'None,' Sapphira said, shaking her head. 'All Molly could tell me was that I had been left outside the Convent of the Sisters of Mercy just outside Richmond, in London. I was well clothed, and there was a sapphire pendant round my neck, but no indication of my identity. A note pinned to a blanket simply said, "Please call her Sapphira and love her as I do." Love! How could I have been loved if I was abandoned?'

'Don't sound so bitter, my dear; there could be a hundred reasons why it happened.' Margaret surveyed the young face with new interest. There were many skeletons hidden in family closets at Court. What key would unlock the door to this mystery? She was curious about it. Of course Sapphira's true mother might have died at her birth and the baby had been abandoned by the father, or someone not wanting a scandal in the family. 'A sapphire pendant?' she said at last. 'Do you have it?'

'It was taken from me by my uncle. I expect he has sold it by now. It was the most beautiful thing I have ever seen.'

'Someone obviously cared for you to leave you with such a jewel—and to wish you to be named. An unwanted child would have been left with nothing. Why was the pendant not sold when you were in need of money? It sounds as though it were worth a great deal.'

'Molly would not let me part with it. She always said that one day I would want to find her—my real mother —and perhaps the jewel was how she could recognise me.'

'And accept back what she had perhaps been forced to give up eighteen years ago.'

'She will never do that—if she still lives,' Sapphira replied bitterly. 'Why did she not return to the Convent, and finding me gone, seek Molly out? Take me back, if I meant as much to her as you seem to believe? No, I was what Quentin called me—a love-child. Born the wrong side of the blanket and disposed of as quickly as possible. I do not want to know her.'

'So be it. We have more important things to think about at the moment. The wedding is tomorrow, is it not?'

'Yes. Wilcox seems to be taking care of all the arrangements. There are to be no guests, you see, apart from yourself and the vicar who is to perform the ceremony. My lord's secret will be safe. Is he taking me back to London with him, do you know, or am I to remain here—hidden?'

'Why on earth should you?' Margaret said, stretching lazily. 'He should have thought about any embarrassment before he got himself into this. But, knowing him as I do, I expect he will keep his side of the bargain.'

'Bargain!' Sapphira gave a shiver, despite the warmth of the fire. 'How cold you make it sound.'

'Isn't that exactly the way it is meant to be?' came the surprised reply, accompanied by a rising of well-plucked eyebrows. 'You went into this with your eyes wide open, just as Quentin did. In return for marrying him, he is providing for you; is he not? Clothes and jewels, a house? Money?'

'I tried to refuse him, and he threatened to have me put in prison for stealing his money-purse when he came to the tavern and tried to—seduce me . . .' she cried.

'I think you had better start from the very beginning

and tell me how you and Quentin became involved,' Margaret said, and Sapphira told her, blushing furiously as she recounted the incident which had taken place between them in the upstairs room. And then the colour fled from her face as her voice dropped to a whisper and she spoke of Silas and the beating she had received. Margaret listened in silence, and when Sapphira had finished, gave a heavy sigh and rose to her feet.

'I would never have dreamed him capable of such a scheme,' she declared, with a grimace of disgust. 'I thought I knew every one of his moods, but it seems he still has a dark side to his nature hidden even from me. No wonder the name "Black Ravenswood" still sticks to him at Court. Someone else has obviously been on the wrong end of this unsavoury side of him, too. Leave him to me. If he thinks he can leave you here while he goes back to London and celebrates Corinna's failure to break the will, he is very much mistaken! I like you, Sapphira, and I'm going to help you.'

'How would you go against him, and risk his anger, for me?' Sapphira was taken aback by the gesture. She had never before had anyone to fight her battles for her.

'I think I can handle him. Who knows, in time, you might learn yourself. You are very young and lovely and you have the advantage of innocence, God, how I wish I still had a little! Quentin has been deeply injured by people he dearly loved. Perhaps someone like you, untouched by the outside world, the greed and debauchery which dwell in it, the mistrust and betrayals, will be able to touch the heart he protects so well against attack, against more pain. I do hope so. I am really rather fond of the man, despite all his faults—heaven only knows, we all have them. I would like to see someone make him really happy. Well, I'm away to a warm bath and my bed. He's ridden over to Squire Havelock's, hasn't he? That means boring talk of horses and dogs over the Squire's best brandy. He keeps the best cellar in Devon

—apart from Ravenswood, of course.' Margaret smiled at Sapphira from the doorway. 'You should rest as much as possible. Tomorrow is going to be a rather tiring day for us all, with the ceremony and the villagers coming to pay their respects and bring gifts—and then the wedding breakfast. Don't look so worried! I shall hold your hand throughout the day, even if Quentin doesn't.'

There would be no chance of that, Margaret thought, as she walked quickly in the direction of her own rooms. Quentin had shown himself to be totally devoid of emotion where the poor girl was concerned, and she would have something to say about that. The tiredness she had felt earlier began to slip away. Ordering a bath to be made ready, she had writing-materials brought to her and began to make out several lists containing the names of guests suitable for Sapphira to invite to the town house upon her return. Then she turned her attention to the important task of writing out a detailed description of the clothes she would need. Every occasion had to be catered for. Quentin had taken himself a wife, for better or for worse. She was going to do her best to ensure that Sapphira received the better side of the marriage.

'Margaret! How nice to see you. I didn't expect you to arrive until this evening, or I would have stayed at home to receive you.' Quentin waited until they were alone in her rooms before crossing to where she stood by the dressing-table and taking her in his arms. 'I've missed you these past weeks.'

'You were such a bad-tempered brute that I thought it best to go away for a while.' She allowed him to crush her to him. As always, when they embraced, she was conscious of the influence he exercised over her. She had been determined to be angry with him for his treatment of Sapphira, and to show it the moment he arrived, but his lips on hers made her forget the other girl instantly. She wound her arms round his neck,

allowing him to lift her and carry her across to the bed.
'Quentin, my hair,' she protested. The maid had just
finished dressing it for her to go down to dinner.

'Damn your hair,' he growled, and she made no
further complaint. Later, as he lounged in a chair,
watching her try to rearrange the curls that had come
loose during their love-making, she looked at him
through the mirror and startled him with her quiet
comment.

'I think your treatment of that girl is beyond contempt.'

'I beg your pardon! So you've met her? Perhaps now
you understand how desperate I was—the depths I have
sunk to in order to best my own sister and her foul
schemes,' he replied, surprised rather than angered by
the remark. 'When you know the details, you will not
use that "holier-than-thou" attitude with me.'

'Sapphira and I talked at great length, soon after I
arrived.' Margaret swung round on the stool and stared
into the arrogant face. She, who had cause to hate men
for their cruelty, trusted this one above all, with his
strange moods and temper, because when he was kind
and gentle he was the most wonderful man on earth.
He gave little of himself to anyone, but then he took
nothing and expected nothing. How astute of Sapphira,
young in years, to have seen this. 'Corinna! Always
Corinna. She will win in the end if you continue in this
way, you know. You will destroy yourself, and so she
will win.'

'You are talking nonsense,' Quentin declared, springing to his feet with the litheness of a panther. 'The
journey has fatigued you, and my presence is obviously
not what you want at this time. I shall see you at dinner.'

'You are a fool!'

He spun round to face her, his eyes glinting angrily.
Drawing her wrap around her, Margaret crossed one
slender leg over the other and stared at him levelly.

'This girl—this Sapphira. She said you threatened her

with prison if she did not agree to marry you. I could hardly believe my ears.'

'My dear Margaret, the wench worked in a tavern. Her uncle was willing to sell her body for whatever he could get for it.'

'But she was not. She tells me she hit you with a wine-bottle.'

'A full one. Sacrilege!' There was no humour in the answer. 'For God's sake, woman. She now has more in her life than ever before, and I shall demand nothing from her after tomorrow, only that she conduct herself in a seemly manner.'

'Demand!' Margaret echoed, with a smile that heightened his annoyance. 'Yes, I forgot. You do not ask any more, do you, Quentin? You demand, as though we were chattels.'

Quentin's eyes darkened to black coals. He had never heard her talk this way before. 'What is it? What has happened to you since you arrived? Has that girl fed you more of her lies? She speaks of being the daughter of some titled lady . . . No, she does not; it was the woman who took her in who told me. And there is this.' From his waistcoat pocket he produced a pendant, which caught the sunlight slanting through the windows in front of him, and Margaret caught her breath at the sight of the two flawless gems. 'She stole it, of course —or one of her family did.'

'It was round her neck when the Sisters of Mercy found her.'

'And you believe that story?' he scoffed, returning it to his pocket.

'Why, then, if it were stolen, did no one sell it? Do you think they liked living in that hovel? Do you imagine she liked being beaten by that sadistic uncle? Quentin, why do you not accept that there is good blood in her? With the right—connections—shall we say, she might very well prove a suitable wife for you. After all, you have made it plain, not only to me but to any woman who comes within a mile of you, that you have no room in your life for love or sentiment. You, Quentin Tyrell, are above that. Yet a wife, an innocent like this girl, taken under the wing of someone who could train her to your liking? An heir, Quentin? Are you telling me you would not like a son? A daughter, even? Are you not concerned that any children you have will be bastards?'

'She has bewitched you,' he declared, totally unable to believe what he was hearing. Once he had had such a dream, but no more.

'A girl of eighteen? An innocent creature such as she —take me in?' Margaret's laughter echoed around the room. 'I have had two husbands. One I married for love, and he married me for my money and position. The second I married for security and discovered his distasteful preferences on our wedding night. Don't talk to me of innocence! Yet this child has it, and you have treated her so cruelly. Tomorrow she will be your wife.'

'In name only. That was our agreement.'

'And you intend to keep it?' Margaret was thinking of Sapphira's loveliness as she spoke. Could a man like Quentin really stay away from her? At her question he looked furious, and she realised that he had spoken the truth. He did not intend to make her his wife by bedding her.

'Yes. She shall have my name and the position which goes with that.'

'But you don't intend to present her at Court?'

'Have you taken leave of your senses?'

'You do her an injustice. Given the right schooling, our little Sapphira might astound you!'

'If you can convince me of that, then I shall have her presented,' Quentin sneered. 'If not, I shall find some suitable means whereby you can compensate me for this stupid conversation. She is an awkward, ill-mannered tavern wench, and no clothes or jewels will change that.

You disappoint me, Margaret. I did not ask you here to take her side. She has no need of your support. I have only to give her a trinket or a few guineas, and she will be well content. I am going to bathe and change. Perhaps at dinner this foolishness will have been forgotten. I would not like it to spoil the time we have here together.'

As the door closed behind him, Margaret's face set into a determined expression. Did he expect to spend all his time with her, while his bride remained alone and rejected before the whole household! Quentin Tyrell, you are going to receive a great surprise, she thought, as she rang for her maid to return.

'Look at her!' Quentin said in a low tone, and Margaret inclined her head in his direction with a questioning look. 'She is determined to anger me.'

Sapphira sat at the other end of the dining-table and, as before when she had dined with him, was eating very little. Her gown was of russet-coloured satin which somehow clashed with her hair and made her look pale and insignificant, he thought.

Enjoying the last of her peach sorbet, Margaret looked at him with consternation in her expression. 'Are you so blind?' she whispered, afraid that their words might reach Sapphira and make her more self-conscious than she already was. 'Do you not realise that she has never eaten at such a table as this? Not only the food, but everything else, overawes her! Quentin, how can you be so unfeeling?'

'For heaven's sake,' he declared in exasperation. 'How am I to know anything about her?'

'You are marrying her—to your own advantage. The least you can do is to see that your wife—your wife,' she repeated slowly, 'returns to London with confidence. Or does it suit you to humiliate her because she is a nobody? Your friends will destroy her. Is that what you want? Do you despise her so much? Must you be reminded that, without her, Corinna would take everything from you. You may not like this girl or have respect for her, but she is the instrument you have chosen in order to win your fight. She is in need of your protection, Quentin, and if she does not have it, you are not the man I have always thought you to be.'

'Why are you siding with her?' he asked in surprise.

'I like her,' Margaret replied truthfully. 'And I shall do everything in my power to see that she is accepted once we return to London. You do intend her to return with you?'

'Why should she? Here, she has more than she has ever had. Why should I drag her back to London?' Quentin replied sourly, trying to ignore Sapphira's lost expression as she stared at him down the table. 'I did not promise that she should stand by my side as my wife. She knows I want nothing from her. She will be well cared for here. On the odd occasion that I need her, I shall send for her.'

'How generous of you!'

He scowled into Margaret's mocking features. 'What did you expect?'

'Gratitude, at least. I know she is being well paid, but she is a person in her own right, Quentin, not a slave.'

'You have spoken to me once before like this. I do not like it,' he warned, and was surprised when she shrugged her shoulders.

'I am not going to allow you to degrade this girl any more than she has been already. She is of good stock, of that I am sure; given the opportunity, she will surprise even you. Give her to me for the rest of the week. By the time you are ready to return to London, she will be ready to be presented.'

'Never!' Quentin declared. 'Introduce her to the King? I would be the laughing-stock of London.'

'So. She is good enough to help you to beat Corinna, but not good enough to present before your friends as your wife.' Margaret pushed back her chair and rose to her feet. She could not remember when she had felt such anger. 'You do her an injustice, Quentin, and I shall not allow it.'

'You will not allow it?' he questioned, a smile tugging at the corners of his lean mouth.

'Exactly. Tomorrow is her wedding day. Has the child a gown to wear?'

'I do not know.'

'You have taken responsibility for her, so you should know,' came the sharp retort. 'Do you think you are the only one with pride? Never mind, I shall find something suitable for her. Afterwards, you will not neglect her, do you hear me?'

'Margaret, why are you behaving like this?' Quentin was completely mystified by the change in his mistress. 'The girl is well satisfied with what I have given her— and shall give her over the next year. She is a conniving, scheming little whore, despite that look of angel innocence which seems to have completely deceived you.'

'My dear man, I have been deceived by experts at the game! This child has no conception of the world, and I do not want you to be her teacher.'

Under his incredulous gaze she went to Sapphira, who rose, and they both turned in the direction of the door. He was being abandoned! By Sapphira, he did not mind, but by his accommodating mistress! Devil take them both!

'He thinks I am a ninny,' Sapphira said, near to tears as they mounted the stairs to her room. 'I am so ignorant! I never know what to do or say, and when I sit down at such a table . . .' The array of utensils had frightened her out of her wits that first time in London, which was why she had pleaded a headache and gone to bed. At Ravenswood she had been forced to sit with Quentin and Margaret, still ignorant of table etiquette, and that ignorance had made her inwardly fume, especially when Quentin had sent withering looks down the table at her, believing her to be deliberately obtuse!

'My dear, the man is a fool! Ignore him. Tomorrow you will be a bride, and at the moment that is all that matters. Afterwards, you and I shall spend time together. I sense in you a shrewd eye and a keen ear. Quentin will be amazed at the difference in you when you return to London.'

'I wish I had your confidence,' Sapphira whispered.

Margaret fixed her with a smile. 'You shall have confidence, and I am going to show you how to obtain it. Tomorrow, your wedding day, will be the beginning. Now, ring for your maid. You are going to have an early night. Where is your wedding gown?'

'I—I haven't got one.' Until that moment, Sapphira had given no thought to what she would be wearing. 'Will you choose something for me?'

'I shall indeed,' Margaret said grimly.

Downstairs, she found that Quentin had retired to the study with a decanter of port. He looked up as she came into the room and immediately rose to fill another glass.

'Tired of your new friend already, my dear?' he inquired sardonically. 'Come and sit down, and let us spend the rest of the evening without her between us.'

'She tells me she has no wedding gown.'

'It is only going to be a simple ceremony, Margaret. What does she want with some elaborate gown that she will never use again? The girl has a complete new wardrobe; surely she can find something suitable?' Quentin returned, his expression registering annoyance. 'Besides, there wasn't time.'

'A poor excuse, if I may say so.' Margaret made no attempt to touch her wine or to seat herself by him as he had indicated. 'From the beginning, you have shown very little foresight where Sapphira is concerned, but I suppose I should have expected this. Have you no idea what a girl's wedding day means to her? No, of course you would not! You are a heartless and callous man who, now he has got what he wants, cares nothing for the instrument he used to get it. I am deeply disappointed in you, Quentin. I do not know how I could have been so wrong all these years. I have always thought that, deep inside you, there was a spark of human kindness that would one day show itself.'

'I didn't ask you here to tell me my faults,' Quentin glowered at her. 'I am aware I am no saint, nor the Christian soul you would have me, but neither am I completely devoid of sentiment. For heaven's sake, go and find her something, if it troubles you so much. Trunks of clothes which belonged to my mother are in the attic, her wedding gown among them. If I remember rightly, there is also a veil which belonged to her grandmother. Take anything. But, I warn you, Margaret, if this lapse on my part produces more greed from her, more demands, I shall toss her back into the gutter where she belongs.'

'After the wedding, naturally,' Margaret murmured. She relented sufficiently to cross the room and kiss him. Quentin caught her to him possessively, his eyes glinting in the candlelight. 'You are going to compensate me for this little annoyance.'

'Not tonight. I shall be far too busy.' Disengaging herself with a soft laugh, she had left him before he could find a suitable answer.

The marriage between Sapphira and Quentin Tyrell took place in the small chapel which adjoined the house, with the vicar of Market Cross performing the ceremony and Lady Margaret as witness. The single room, with its oak-beamed roof, was crowded with people, however, and Sapphira's courage faltered as she stepped over the threshold and found herself under examination.

'Villagers,' Margaret whispered, urging her on to where Quentin and the vicar waited. 'They have come to wish you well. Smile—they will like that. Good girl. Now, let's see if Quentin can show you the same courtesy.'

Sapphira caught her breath as he turned to watch her approach. How handsome he looked in peacock-blue brocade and lace ruffles tumbling in profusion from his sleeves and collar. Rings flashed and sparkled on the hand he extended towards her, and she found herself accepting it as if in a dream and allowing herself to be drawn to his side. Did he consider her appearance satisfactory? Those dark eyes told her nothing, and she lowered her gaze in disappointment as the vicar began to speak the words which would bind her to this stranger.

His fingers were cool against hers, and she gained a strange comfort from their touch. He was so strong, so sure of himself and what he wanted from life. She should be more like him. She would be more like him. With his name and position, many doors would be opened to her, whether he liked it or not. She would take full advantage of everything new which came her way, and enjoy it for the short while it was available to her. She smiled as he slid a thick gold band on her finger. It was done. She belonged to him now. Sapphira, Countess of Ravenswood. A new pride swelled inside her. She had never thought it possible to feel this way. Her head tilted back slightly as Quentin bent to give her a light kiss on the cheek and found instead that his mouth brushed hers. He looked startled, and quickly drew back, and then Margaret was congratulating them. The vicar was adding an extra blessing that they would soon have the joy of many children. Quentin's fixed smile told her it was never to happen. Despite all her fears, she realised precisely then that he never intended to touch her, and wondered why it had suddenly begun to matter to her. She had everything she wanted. She would be content with things as they were.

'Congratulations, Margaret.' Quentin turned to the

elegantly groomed woman at his side as Sapphira was surrounded by well-wishing villagers. He stepped back from the throng, his gaze studying his bride for a long moment. 'You must have stayed up half the night to achieve such a transformation.'

'Not at all. I found a girl this morning who is good at sewing, and she needed only two hours to alter the gown. She does you credit, Quentin; at least acknowledge that. Not one person here guesses that anything out of the ordinary has taken place. Surely that pleases you?'

Quentin's interest was still focused on Sapphira. He had been unable to believe his eyes when he first turned and saw her. She wore a gown of creamy lace with full sleeves, slashed with gleaming satin of the same colour, as was the underskirt which fell in graceful folds between the divided skirt. From her shoulder hung a long mantle which spread out behind her and was held by a small child from the village. Her hair was caught up in a profusion of curls on each side of her pale cheeks. A headdress of lace, into which were sewn hundreds of tiny diamonds, covered her bare shoulders. There were jewels in her ears and at her throat. Margaret's, he realised, recognising the items he had himself given her, and cursed himself for not realising that Sapphira had no jewellery of her own. She was not even wearing the bracelet he had given her the night before they left London, and wondered why. How different this ceremony was from the other in France!

On all sides, he was being congratulated. Not one of them guessed that the girl he had married was no better than the commonest field-hand. She was saying very little, he noticed, and the apparent shyness of manner only served to endear her more to the people who had come to see their lord married.

Sapphira looked up expectantly as he came to her side and took her arm to lead her back to the Great Hall for the wedding breakfast.

'Do I meet with your approval, my lord?' she asked softly, and a smile touched his lips as he heard the tinge of mockery in her voice. She knew she did. The proof was all around her.

'I have no complaints, but do not let the adoration of simple people go to your head. After all, you should know how to deal with your own kind,' came the cruel retort. He had no intention of satisfying her vanity. There would be others to do that when she was in London. Before long—a month, two at the most—everything he suspected about her character would have been proved. Why the thought of other men dancing attendance on her should irritate him he did not know, but it did. He was done with weakness! She would not bewitch him!

In the Great Hall, the fire blazed in the hearth. Tables had been laid out for the bride and groom and the guests, and there was another beneath the window, piled high with gifts for the newly-weds. Such an assortment of presents, Sapphira saw, as Quentin led her to the top table and seated her on one side of him with Margaret on the other, and the vicar beside her. A new arrival, totally unexpected she thought by the look on her husband's face, was the Squire Havelock. A widower in his late fifties, with no children, he made no bones about the fact that he had come to inspect the bride. To her embarrassment, he insisted on kissing her, and she was powerless to prevent herself being seized in a bear-like hug which almost squeezed the breath from her body. Then, sitting opposite her, he spent the whole of the afternoon and evening drinking heavily, congratulating Quentin on his good fortune, and applauding too loudly the jugglers from a near-by fair who had been induced to perform for the occasion.

Never before, in all her life, had Sapphira seen such an array of food. There were pheasant and rabbits cooked over a spit in the hearth. Veal and mutton, and more chickens than could have been eaten in a week, she surmised. Did the rich live like this every day? She would never accustom herself to such extravagance or such waste, she thought, watching the Squire toss a leg of chicken to one of the dogs. That piece of food would have been a meal for three at the Black Horse, and been enjoyed! The cook himself brought in the enormous wedding cake and placed it in the centre of the table, eagerly awaiting her comments.

She ate under Quentin's watchful eye, and had been persuaded to drink a little, but he could fault her on nothing. Margaret had been right—she learned quickly. She had lost much of her awkwardness, too; as the festivities wore on, she actually appeared to be enjoying herself. He became aware how her blue eyes shone as the jugglers performed and a clown tumbled and rolled around on the floor in front of them. Like a small child, he thought, not a grown woman at all. She clapped her hands with glee at the brown bear which did tricks, her cheeks flushed with wine. It was the first time since they had come together that he had seen colour in her cheeks. It became her.

Dammit! What was happening to him? How could he feel so well-disposed towards her, knowing her background, knowing she had tried to steal his purse? He had only her word that she had not. The beating could have been a punishment for that, when her uncle discovered what she had done. No girl could retain her innocence in such a place. Patience, he told himself. He never accepted anything or anyone at face value, and he was not going to start with her. One mistake was enough.

'You have less than a week to complete the transformation,' he said, turning to Margaret. 'I think you are wasting your time. Let the girl stay here and play out the charade of being mistress. Look at her!' he exclaimed, as Sapphira signalled to a servant to come forward and refill their empty glasses, and then ordered jugs of Malmsey and plates of food to be distributed among the players. 'Already she considers herself the grand lady!'

'Even you must agree that she does it well.' Margaret continued, 'Unless you agree that she returns to London with you and assumes her rightful place . . . her rightful place,' she repeated stubbornly, as he stared at her angrily, 'I shall invite her to stay with me and you can go to the devil!'

'Despite your present low opinion of me, I have not made my decision for purely selfish reasons. It would be safer for her here, where the servants can protect her. Safer for her—and for me. She would not be embarrassed when the truth comes out, as it surely must, nor would she embarrass me! Of the two of us, I think I am sufficiently thick-skinned to withstand the gossip, or I would not have entered into this marriage in the first place. And then there is Corinna. Have you considered Corinna, my dear?' The look on Margaret's face told him she had not. 'That bitch will torture her! Doubtful as I am as to the innocence of my bride, I know she is no match for my foul-mouthed, wicked-hearted sister.'

'There we are in full agreement. You must, of course, side with Sapphira in all matters. Make it quite clear to everyone, whatever they think of her, that she is your wife and bears your name, and therefore to insult her is to blacken the name of Ravenswood. You owe her that, Quentin.'

He gave a heavy sigh, glancing sideways as he did so at his bride. He had not expected such an apparition of loveliness—so desirable. Neither had he been prepared for the way she so easily disturbed his thoughts, arousing memories he had thrust into the deep recesses of his mind to escape from the pain they brought him.

'Have it your own way, but do not misconstrue this as weakness. My opinion of her has not changed. You will see what I mean, once we are in London.'

'Will you bet on that?' Margaret asked, her eyes

shining with a wicked light. They were both notorious for their gambling habits; but whereas she wagered and more often lost, he nearly always won, much to her exasperation. This bet he would lose! She was sure of it. 'Will you wager that magnificent black stallion you have just acquired?'

'What? Do you know how much that animal cost me? Ask anything but that.'

'The stallion, Quentin. I shall settle for nothing less. Sapphira is worth every guinea you paid for him, and more, as I intend to prove to you.'

'If you continue to make her such a tempting morsel, perhaps you are intending to place her in my bed.'

'Perhaps . . . You could do worse. She is young. She will be able to give you what every man desires—sons. You are no different in that respect from any man I have ever known. I cannot give you a child, you know that, and if it had been possible, you would never have loved it as you would your true heir. In your own way, darling Quentin, you are so old-fashioned—perhaps that is why I love you so. You are still untouched by what has happened around you. So is Sapphira. Consider it.'

'And if you lose your wager?' he countered, not wishing to consider the outrageous suggestion.

'You may do as you please with her, and I shall not lift a finger to stop you.'

She was too sure of herself. Quentin did not like the confidence which shone from her face, but he found himself agreeing nevertheless.

For the remainder of that week he saw little of Sapphira, who spent most of her time in Margaret's company. They all dined together, but otherwise went their separate ways during the day. If it was common knowledge that he did not visit his wife when they retired, had not done so even on their wedding night, the gossip did not reach his ears, and he was grateful for it.

Daily, Sapphira found the role thrust upon her easier to accept. She had lost her awe of Wilcox and now regarded him as a friend, and the other servants were polite and respectful to her in her new position. With him at her side, she conducted her inspection of the house as though it were the most natural thing in the world for her to do.

She had furniture changed round, moved from one room to another, discussed a different décor for the rooms in which she was installed and, despite her misgivings, allowed herself to be persuaded by Margaret to take riding lessons. Her first encounter with a horse was the disaster she had fully expected—and feared. She felt awkward in the riding-habit her friend provided, with its voluminous trailing skirts, and in dismounting she slipped and fell into inches of mud.

The laughter on Quentin's face as she hurried upstairs to her rooms in a miserable silence, far from deterring her from a second attempt, strengthened her intentions to do everything a lady should be able to do—with grace and elegance, with competence without recourse to her own stupidity when she failed.

The following morning she astounded Quentin by going out again on the same mount. By the time they were due to leave for London, she had begun to enjoy her daily excursions and, begrudgingly, he was beginning to admire her for her determined efforts.

She was relieved that Margaret accompanied them in the same carriage back to London, and stayed overnight at Quentin's residence before returning to her own house in the City. Suddenly, arriving back at the house to which Quentin had first brought her as a tired, dejected, half-starved individual suddenly drained her of all the confidence and courage she had gained at Ravenswood. This was different. Here, people—his acquaintances—know her, and here, the gossip, the whispers behind fluttering fans and white gloves would begin. She did not know if she had the stamina to withstand it. At Ravenswood it had all seemed so simple, but here . . .

CHAPTER
FIVE

As THE days passed, Sapphira became increasingly aware of the fact that no one came to the house in the Manor of Hyde to pay respects to the newly-married couple. Not even Quentin's sister, Corinna. Margaret had warned her how it would be, but she had half hoped that someone would befriend her. She felt lonely and unwanted in her solitary existence. Her daily routine never changed, and for someone accustomed to hard work eighteen hours a day, she began to find herself growing bored.

Breakfast in bed was followed by fittings for the clothes Margaret insisted she must have (she was beginning to wonder when and where she would ever wear them), then came the household business, which Quentin had told her was now her concern. She was pleased at first that he had involved her, but then gradually discovered that, with the capable servants headed by Mrs Grayson, the house all but ran itself. The housekeeper was kindness itself and went out of her way to make her feel at home, but by no stretch of her imagination could Sapphira consider an alteration she wanted in the daily menus to be of great importance.

Her mornings and evenings were spent reading or sewing, and if her husband was at home, they dined together. More often than not, in those first two weeks, she ate alone.

Her despondency had been heightened by a visit to the Black Horse to find Molly and Lottie. She was thankful that Silas was out at the time. Rosie, her eyes wide with envy at the sight of the elegant creature wrapped in sable, told her that they had left the day after Sapphira herself, after a violent argument. Sapphira had spent an hour after that wandering round the waterfront seeking information, and had left word that a large reward would be forthcoming for anyone who brought her news of the two women.

Where had they gone, and why had she not been sent word of their present address? It was as though they had deliberately chosen to vanish from her life—her new life. Did they think, because she now had money and position, she would abandon them? How she yearned for the comfort of Molly's arms and Lottie's talk of the day she would meet the handsome man she would marry. It was her fault that the girl had these ideas, Sapphira knew, for she had filled her head with fairy stories and fantasies to pass away a cold night. When she found them, she would make both their dreams come true, and she would ensure they were never parted again.

'My sister will be dining with us,' Quentin informed her in one of the rare occasions that he was still in the house when she came downstairs. He was dressed to go riding. With Margaret, no doubt, she thought, and bit back the urge to ask him to ride with her. 'Mrs Grayson has been told there will be extra guests. Three, in fact. I took the liberty of inviting Margaret and Blaise Courtney. You will no doubt remember him from the tavern where we met.'

'Was that necessary, my lord?' It was very easy to be stiffly formal with him, to keep a wedge between them so that their relationship did not wander from the path on which it had begun. 'Do you find my conversation so limited that you have to invite your mistress, and others, to amuse your sister? Perhaps, if I were allowed to meet more people, it might develop to your satisfaction.'

Quentin's face registered immediate anger at her

insolence. Her tongue grew sharper every time they spoke together.

'Margaret and Blaise will be here for your benefit, not hers,' he snapped. 'Why my sister has this sudden desire to see you, when last week she spoke to me of wanting to claw your eyes out—and mine along with them, I might add—is beyond me. I suspect her every move, her every word. The presence of the others might just prevent the evening from being a total calamity.'

'You have left the arrangements to Mrs Grayson, so how can it be that?' she returned with equal sharpness. 'Oh, I may be consulted on the menu—after it has been prepared, of course—but otherwise I shall have nothing to do with the evening's entertainment.'

'If Corinna has her way, you may very well be providing it.' Quentin glared at her. No woman had ever succeeded in rousing him to anger so quickly. 'If you are so eager to meet people—my so-called friends, the society I have deprived you of with good reason, these past weeks—invite them here. Invite whom you like, it's of no consequence to me. You will regret it, believe me. They will humiliate you.'

'A tavern wench is accustomed to dealing with the most difficult of customers,' Sapphira said, her small chin jutting stubbornly. Did he think she was afraid to accept his challenge? Of course he did. If she failed, he could banish her to Ravenswood on the pretence it was for her own good. 'Clothes and jewels no more make a lady than a title does a gentleman.'

The taunt stung him, and she saw a slow flush steal over his cheeks. His mouth tightened, and she knew she had gone too far.

'Our guests will be here about noon. Please be ready to receive them. If you find yourself unable to do so, remain in your room and I shall find some excuse for your absence.'

'And have you brand me a coward, as well as—as a

trollop?' Sapphira cried. 'Never! Until mid-day, my lord.'

Picking up her skirts, she brushed past him and went back to her rooms. The house reverberated with the slamming of the front door behind Quentin's departing figure. Let him sulk, she thought, suddenly brightening. She was going to accept his challenge—and more!

'Sapphira, how remiss you must think it of me not to have come before this, but this appalling weather plays havoc with my chest. I have been confined to bed for over a week.'

Corinna smiled at the girl seated at the head of the table. In her place! Despite the plea of a cold to explain her absence, her gown was daringly low, exposing more of her full breasts than Sapphira thought modest in any woman, and had certainly not been chosen for the warmth it could provide. Beside her sat Blaise Courtney, with Margaret opposite them.

She had known, for a full minute after Quentin had introduced them, that he did not believe her to be the girl he had seen in the Black Horse. She wore her long hair loose, surmounted with a tiny headband of pearls. The dress of plain burgundy wool trimmed with lace was, she considered, complementary to her burnished tresses and her colouring. She had spent an hour choosing it, knowing well that Corinna would inspect her appearance in great detail—which she had, and had turned away, a trifle disappointed, Sapphira surmised, because she could find no fault. Her only jewellery was the emerald bracelet Quentin had given her. He had provided her with many others, but she chose to wear nothing else except the wedding band on her finger.

How she wished she had the sapphire pendant that Silas had stolen from her. At least that was her own personal property, not something given as payment for services rendered. She suspected that Quentin was waiting for her to begin making demands on him. His

attitude was making it very hard not to do so, out of
spite!

'I hope you are fully recovered now,' Sapphira said
in honeyed tones. 'You must not be a stranger here,
Corinna. As Quentin's sister, you will always be welcome. And you too, Blaise.'

'You have left out Margaret,' Corinna purred. 'But
then she has always treated this house as her own. My
brother has never been known for his tactfulness. Wife
and mistress beneath the same roof! I am astounded
you are not at each other's throats.'

'Why should they be?' It was Quentin who replied,
eyes glinting dangerously at her comment. Sapphira
had grown a little pale, but she remained composed,
although lost for an answer. 'I assure you I am man
enough to accommodate two women in my life.'

Blaise made a spluttering noise over his soup as he
exploded into laughter, caught Quentin's gaze on him,
and wiped the smile from his face. Margaret bestowed
a smile on her lover, indicating that he had her full
approval for his timely intervention.

'Has anything interesting been happening while I
was away?' Quentin asked Blaise. He had deliberately
remained out of the way of friends and acquaintances
and the questions that he knew would come his way
when he returned to Court, spending most of his time
at Margaret's house in Richmond.

Of late she had been urging him to produce Sapphira
and finish with the gossip, and reluctantly he had come
to the conclusion that he must do so. He had set events
in motion, so he must now see them through—and
watch the transformation of his bride from the demure
creature who had stood at his side in the chapel at
Ravenswood into the grasping, ambitious monster lurk-
ing beneath that mask. The monster she had held in
abeyance until it was the right time for her to begin
asserting her rights as his wife. The price he would have
to pay for thwarting Corinna was to be a high one,

he thought grimly, as Blaise leaned forward and said something to his wife and she burst into laughter. Already she found the attentions of another man pleasing. The sound was an infectious one, and utterly genuine, not a ploy to attract attention to herself.

'Nothing you would find interesting,' Blaise returned in all innocence, for he was unaware of his friend's many visits to the house in Richmond and thought him to be enamoured with Sapphira, spending all his time with her. 'Thomas Greenwood fought a duel with young Masterson a few weeks ago and took three fingers off his left hand. The fool asked for it. Made some remark about Thomas's wife, and you know how insanely jealous he is about her. And too blind to see that he's being cuckolded by every man who knows her. There were enquiries about you, of course. Several charming ladies have missed your company, not to mention half the taverns and ale-houses in London. The King took me aside two days ago and hinted that he would like to see you again soon. Something about no one else playing him at backgammon like you do.'

'I shall pay my respects tomorrow,' Quentin nodded at him.

'With Sapphira?' Corinna inquired sweetly. 'The whole Court is intrigued by this sudden romance, Quentin—you can't appear alone. Lady Castlemaine is almost dying with curiosity to see the woman who has stolen your misogynous heart. Even I don't know how you first met her, and I certainly don't believe the rumours that you found her in some tavern in Wapping. Why, look at her, anyone can see she has good blood in her.'

Margaret threw Sapphira a half-smile, meant to comfort her. She had not expected Corinna to broach openly the subject as early as this; she was usually more subtle.

'The rumour happens to be true, Corinna.' Sapphira spoke before Quentin could counter the remark with one of his own, equally biting, and he sat back in his chair, not knowing what to expect. 'I am of good blood, although I never knew my real mother. Only that she was a lady; and my husband did find me in a tavern, the Black Horse in Wapping, where I worked as a waitress. I do not mind who knows my background—I have nothing to be ashamed of. Poverty is not a mortal sin, and from what I have heard of the Court, the high moral standards my adopted mother taught me to maintain will prove rather old-fashioned, but perhaps they may return when promiscuity is not the order of the day.'

'No wonder Quentin has hidden you away for the past few weeks,' Corinna declared, looking offended by the coldness of her tone. 'My dear girl, you do not go around boasting of such things. Have you no consideration for your husband's name and position? You are right, Quentin. She must not be allowed to mix with our friends yet, not until she learns to conduct herself with more decorum. She would make you the laughing-stock of London.'

And I hope I shall be at your side to watch it happen, she thought with malicious glee. Quentin had married this girl to keep his home and lands, the inheritance she considered rightly hers, and she was overjoyed that it brought him no satisfaction. By morning she would have told the story to enough people to have it circulated throughout the Court by nightfall. If he dared to show himself with her, she would be shunned. She would see to that!

'My husband does not agree with you, fortunately.' Sapphira was suddenly aware that if she did not come out of this conversation in full control of the situation, she might as well return to Ravenswood and hide herself away, for she would never have the courage to face the gossip. She hesitated only for a moment before committing herself to a drastic course of action. Margaret was watching her expectantly, yet with a shadow of doubt in her eyes. Did she, too, expect capitulation? As Quentin did? It was written on his face for her to see. 'Only this morning he kindly gave me permission to invite whomsoever I pleased to be entertained here. Of course, with my limited knowledge of his friends, and yours too, Corinna, I shall have to call on you both for the names. Margaret has already kindly given me some advice.'

'I am sure I can think of some more,' Margaret said quickly, and Sapphira smiled at her gratefully. There was no backing down now.

'I admit I have no experience when it comes to such things, but I shall manage.'

'On what scale are you planning to entertain?' Corinna asked, thunderstruck by the suggestion that she should help the very girl she had come hoping to humiliate and degrade. Yet, if she failed now, and she knew she had—miserably—what a perfect opportunity was presenting itself. 'Quentin has many friends. We both do. And, of course, if the King could be persuaded to attend . . .'

'Oh, would that be possible?' Sapphira looked at Quentin in sudden excitement. What a triumph that would be for her! The King beneath her roof! No one would dare to shun her then.

'I shall speak to Lady Castlemaine. She will know how best to approach him.' Corinna spoke quickly before her brother could reply. She had no intention of allowing him to spoil this second opportunity. 'You are a sensible young woman after all, Sapphira. Prove yourself here in your own home, and the invitations will come flooding in. Send word to me when the preparations begin, and you shall have all the help you need. I think perhaps I have been unfair and too hasty in my judgment of you. You know why, of course. Your marriage to Quentin has deprived me of a great deal of money promised to me in my father's will, but it is not your fault, and I should not hold you to blame. A ball . . .' She lifted her glass of wine, and held it out towards Sapphira with a smile which masked the hatred she felt for this usurper and for the man who had placed her in such a position of importance—above his own sister. She was still reduced to living on the income he allowed her, while Sapphira had everything. Her money, her house! They would regret taking these things from her, both of them! 'To the success of your undertaking, my dear.'

Quentin was the last one to raise his glass. He did so, wondering how many men he would be forced to challenge before that evening was over.

Later, as he escorted Margaret to her coach, she voiced her satisfaction at the suggestion and her pleasure that he had not opposed it.

'It is time she faced people. She is far stronger than you think. Corinna is about to discover hidden strength in that child.'

'I have no illusions as to what she will find,' Quentin replied, raising her fingers to his lips in a gesture of farewell. 'I begin to think they are well matched. The evening will be a disaster.'

'You malign the girl,' Margaret said crossly, pulling her hand away. 'Could you not bend just a little, my unyielding oak, and help her? It may very well turn out to your advantage.'

'She shall have all the help she needs. Whatever monies are required, I shall supply. Shall I tell you what will happen? She will take every guinea I give her and spend it recklessly, and little of it will be for her guests. All the planning and hard work will fall on you and Mrs Grayson. When this is over, and I have to count the cost of an evening of extravagance solely for her to show herself off to people who will attend only in order to inspect her like an animal at a zoo, I will remind you of our wager.'

'I am having a new riding outfit made,' Margaret informed him, confident of her success.

He would never understand how such an intelligent woman could be deceived by Sapphira's false air of childlike innocence. Was he the only one to realise her true character, the scheming treacherous character all women possessed? Not for one moment did he ever believe that his judgment could be at fault!

Sapphira was seated at the table beneath the window in her sitting-room when Quentin visited her one morning. Her maid instantly withdrew, and she turned to look at him curiously. He had had little to say to her since Corinna's visit, and she had been far too busy with her great new adventure to notice his usual absences. Before her were suggested menus, and lists of names, entertainers and musicians who might prove suitable for such a grand affair. She had never experienced such excitement.

'May I ask why you have refused Margaret's help in arranging this ball?' he demanded stiffly, and she knew battle was about to commence. She had been preparing for it ever since she had decided to do everything herself. Both Margaret and Corinna had supplied her with lists of names, as had Quentin, though this had been the shortest. It told her that he was not really interested in what was to take place. That had heightened her determination to show him she was neither the simpleton nor the adventurous, heartless creature he took her for. His continued condemnation of her character both angered and wounded her. Once and for all she felt she had to prove herself to him. When she had, she would be quite prepared to return to Ravenswood, if he still wanted her to, so long as she had found Molly and Lottie and could take them with her.

'Do you consider me capable of dealing with this alone, sir?'

'You? Heavens above! It is not going to be the same as serving men with jugs of ale, you stupid girl!'

Sapphira bristled at his scornful tone. She turned her back on him and continued to write. Quentin scowled at her. Did she want to make a fool of herself? Of him? She was a figure in elegant *déshabille*, with her long hair falling in profusion upon milk-white shoulders. The loose satin robe she wore was simple and uncluttered by fripperies. Again she wore no jewellery. She needed none to enhance her natural beauty, he realised. The pendant that Molly had given him burned a hole in his waistcoat pocket. He carried it with him continuously and had made discreet enquiries, seeking to find the rightful owner. No one recognised the design, and he had begun to wonder, very much against his will, if it had not been a special gift made for a woman—the woman who, for reasons of her own, had abandoned her baby, leaving it with perhaps the one thing she treasured most. Sentimental rubbish, he thought, moving into Sapphira's line of vision.

'You have not answered my question.'

'I thought I had.' She had no intention of allowing herself to be intimidated. 'I have three lists, from which I shall draw up a final list of the guests to be invited. I have half a dozen menus from which I shall choose several. I thought a cold buffet, as it makes it so much easier for people to mingle and meet each other, do you not think so?'

'You seem very sure of yourself,' Quentin remarked drily.

If only you knew, Sapphira thought. The very thought of facing his friends made her quiver in her shoes. Was he so blind, so oblivious to her as a woman, that he could not sense her apprehension?

'Would you have me otherwise, sir? Your friends will be expecting, nay, hoping for, a gauche, illiterate female who will provide them with an evening of lavish entertainment, hoping to buy your friendship. If it can be called that. I intend to prove to them, and to you, that I am neither to be laughed at nor displayed as an object of derision because of my lowly background. I am a person in my own right, demanding fair recognition for what I am.'

'You little idiot! If it is so important to you to be

accepted, why have you refused Margaret's help?' he asked in exasperation. Without it, the evening would be the fiasco he feared.

'I would have preferred that of my husband, but that is impossible.' She looked at him levelly, and succeeded, much to his astonishment, at making him feel as though he were somehow in the wrong. Had he not been supplying money without question for the past week? 'I shall manage alone.'

'And if you do not?' he asked grimly. 'If you fail in this, as you surely must, inexperienced as you are about such matters, and you make us both the laughing-stock of London, give me one reason why I should not banish you to Ravenswood.'

'Which is what would please you the most.' Sapphira gave a sad smile, which made him frown. Suddenly he found himself wanting to offer help, but did not know how. And, if he did, it would be a weakening of his resolve not to become involved with her. He looked at her sharply as she added, 'But if I do succeed in pleasing you . . .'

'The accomplishment will be amply rewarded. What would you have? A carriage and fine horses? Jewels?'

'Will you promise me to use every means at your disposal to find Molly and Lottie? I am so worried about them. They left the tavern the day after I did, and have not been heard of since,' Sapphira pleaded. 'I left word that there would be a reward for news, but no one has come forward . . .'

'That is all?' Quentin was openly astounded by the reply. He had been imagining the most expensive of requests. It was a trick! Yet he could not see what she would gain from it. His sympathy, perhaps? But why?

'What more should I ask from you? I have everything I want. A roof over my head, clothes, food. More than I have had in years. I am not discontented. Nor am I what you think, to demand of you what I do not need.'

'Are you happy?' Quentin asked, and wondered why

such a question had entered his head. What did he care?

'What is happiness? My idea of it would not be yours.'

'Would this go part of the way to achieving it?' Sapphira's eyes widened as he produced her pendant and held it out to her. She had thought never to see it again.

'But Silas—my uncle—took it from me . . .'

'It was in the money-purse I gave to Molly. She thought you should have it.' He watched her open a drawer and place it inside, closing it again with no trace of the satisfaction he had expected registering on her face. 'Have you no interest whatever in who you are? I find that strange. Would that knowledge not bring you happiness?' What a complex little creature she was!

'I think . . . only pain. For me or for the woman who abandoned me. Perhaps both,' came the quiet answer. 'No, sir, I have no desire to know who I am.'

After he had gone, Sapphira found that she could no longer concentrate on her important lists. With a sigh, she pushed the papers to one side, rang for a glass of hot milk to be brought to her, and took the pendant from the drawer.

The cold stones, as they lay in the palm of her hand, seemed somehow to mock her lack of interest. She ran her fingertips over the filigree silverwork, once again marvelling at its intricacy of design. What had the letter 'S' originally stood for? Her mother's name? Sarah? Susanne? Who had given it to her? Her lover, Sapphira's father? Why had it been left with her when she was abandoned? Was it, as Molly thought, given to her infant child by a mother distracted at the desertion forced on her by stern parents, or at a lover who did not want a daughter? Or was it, as Sapphira chose to believe, meant to be an enducement for someone to take the child and care for it, thus relieving both callous, unfeeling parents of the problem?

She went to the mirror and held the pendant to her throat. It matched her eyes. Despite the way she had come to own it, she was very fond of it. She had not yet decided on material for her ball gown, much to the distraction of her dressmaker, but now the decision was made for her. A blue to match the sapphires. Quentin would find no fault with her arrangements or her appearance. Would his attitude change towards her if she was really of good blood, she wondered. Why should she care? When the ball was over, a triumphant success, and she had been accepted by people who had come to gawk at her, and he had found Molly and Lottie, then—then she did not care if he never spoke to her again!

Liar, she thought silently, turning from the mirror. She had been telling herself for days that all this was for herself, to prove herself, but she knew it was not true. It was for him! Just once, she wanted those dark eyes to look at her without contempt or indifference. A little warmth, a kind word, would mean so much. She knew that love between them was impossible, but friendship . . .

Hurriedly she tugged at the bell-rope to summon her maid to come and help her to dress. There could never be anything between them, not even that. His mistrust of women separated them like a high wall. Even to hint that she might consider a change in their relationship could have disastrous results, she thought, remembering with reddening cheeks the way he had seized hold of her at the tavern and kissed her. It was better to leave things as they were.

The house of the Earl of Ravenswood was in a frenzy of activity. Even Quentin, himself an early riser, breakfasted in his room to the sound of the continuous tramp of feet past his door, the noisy arrival of heavily laden carts and delivery wagons in the street outside. From the window, he watched crates being unloaded, of fruit, meat, fish and wines. Sapphira was leaving a great deal until the last moment, or was she so overcome by the vastness of what she had undertaken that she could not manage any longer? Hurriedly he dressed and went in search of her. If he brought in Margaret now, the day might still be saved. Damnation, here he was worrying about her again. As if she needed his concern! Yet there were times when he had to admit, albeit with great reluctance, that she did remind him of a lost waif greatly in need of someone to befriend her. Lucy had looked like that the first time he saw her. Young, innocent, desirable . . . as Sapphira was to him now.

'I think the mistress is in the kitchen,' a passing servant told him. The downstairs floors screamed of chaos. The enormous music-room, which also housed his superb collection of books, was being cleared of furniture. It was here, Sapphira had stated, that she intended to lay out the buffet. The communicating doors to the dining-room had been thrown open to make it one very large salon. How many guests were they expecting? When she had showed him her final list, he had advised her to cut it by half!

To his left there was the sitting-room, where maids were busy polishing and cleaning and arranging masses of fresh flowers, brought from the market at the crack of dawn. The air was filled with the smell of narcissus, reminding him of Ravenswood when his mother had been alive. She had adored flowers, and the rooms had always been filled with them whenever possible. Abruptly he turned in the direction of the kitchen, pushing the painful memory to the back of his mind.

'What on earth!' On the threshold he came to a halt, his eyes wide with amazement, which in turn disappeared to admit blazing anger at what he saw. 'Have you taken leave of your senses, wench?'

It was the term he always used when he wanted to insult Sapphira and really hurt her, and again he succeeded. She was standing at the kitchen table, surrounded by bowls and pots, and gawking servant-girls. Her arms were covered up to the elbows in flour! An apron covered her morning gown, and her hair was hidden beneath a tight cap. For a moment she regarded her husband in silence before resuming what she was doing.

'More flour, Betty. No, that's enough! Mix it for me, as I showed you.' She returned her attention to Quentin's furious features. 'Have you come to help or to criticise, my lord?' she asked quietly.

'Is—is this how you consider a lady should conduct herself?' he thundered, and a page turned away at the door, not daring to squeeze past him.

'A lady should know how to act in an emergency. That is all I am doing. The cook slipped half an hour ago and sprained her wrist. Luckily, nearly everything was done last night. I mixed the meat myself so that is all ready to go into this pastry. Do you like venison pie, sir?'

'How many guests did you invite to this—this occasion?' Quentin changed the subject, realising that he was getting nowhere. His wife, covered in flour, and herself preparing food! It was unheard-of. All the servants present saw the warning in his eyes as he looked at them, and understood the consequences if they spoke of this incident.

'You saw the list yourself. Two hundred, was it not? About thirty are unable to attend.'

'You ignored what I said?'

'How could I delete names, when I knew not whom to exclude?' Sapphira answered, brushing a hand across a warm cheek. It left a smudge of flour, which made her mouth tighten still more.

'You had only to ask.'

'I have seen so little of you lately, sir, that I thought you had no interest in the matter. If I am mistaken, then surely you could have offered,' she countered, her young face growing stubborn at his reproachful expression, and behind her a girl giggled at the exchange.

'I shall see you this evening. More suitably attired to receive our guests then you are at the moment,' Quentin said, before turning on his heel.

Within the hour he had left the house. She did not know where he had gone or when he would return. Surely he was not so angry with her as deliberately to leave her to greet their guests alone? He had looked furious, and perhaps she should not have spoken to him thus before the servants, but then he should not have ridiculed her with so many ears present. Long before he quitted the house, the whole place was buzzing with what had taken place. Hard as she tried to maintain her composure, Sapphira retired to her room not long afterwards and burst into tears. She had failed miserably —she knew it now. It was too much for one person alone to tackle. Her pride had pushed her into making the gesture, and her pride had refused to allow her to accept help once she had so confidently proclaimed herself capable of accomplishing everything single-handed. What a fool she was!

'My lady, will you see Wilcox?' A maid disturbed her melancholy daydreaming some while later, and she looked at her, not comprehending at first what the words meant.

Wilcox! He was like a miracle from heaven. If anyone could save her face, it would be he!

'Yes. Yes! Send him up at once.' She jumped from the chair and quickly tidied her hair. When the man was admitted, she could hardly conceal her delight. 'Wilcox, what are you doing here? Has the Earl sent for you?' It was just conceivable, she had begun to think, that Quentin had demanded his presence to help with the occasion, but he shook his head,

'Not exactly, my lady. Before he left Ravenswood, the master instructed me to collect together certain items which he thought might be useful here. Pictures, some wall tapestries and other things that barely see the light of day in the country. I have two large crates of

Venetian glass—upon which my life rested, he said, should even one piece of it be broken when it arrived.'

'Glasses,' Sapphira breathed. 'Wilcox, you could not have come at a better time. Tonight there is to be a ball. Nearly two hundred guests.'

'Mrs Grayson has acquainted me with the details.' Wilcox's impassive face gave nothing away.

'It's going to be a complete failure,' Sapphira said. 'And it's all my fault. I wanted to do something all by myself . . . Now cook has a sprained wrist, and I was making pastry when the Earl . . . Oh, it doesn't matter. He's quite right about me, I shall never become a lady. Perhaps the kitchen is where I belong.'

'Are you by any chance having some trouble with the servants? Mrs Grayson feels that they do not always show the respect they should.'

'Is it any wonder? Why should they take orders from someone who is no better than they are! Do you know where the Earl first met me, Wilcox? In a tavern! I was serving ale. Knowing this, can you respect me?'

'You are the Countess of Ravenswood, my lady, and my duty is to serve you to the best of my ability,' the man returned, quite impassive at the revelation. If he had known before, she knew he would never tell her. 'If I might suggest that you show me what arrangements have been made regarding food and wines, and if you have a copy of the guest-list too.'

Sapphira brought them from the desk and handed them over in silence. He perused them for several minutes while she waited in an agony of suspense.

'Far from being a failure, I think this is quite a remarkable achievement. Bearing in mind, my lady, that you have not done this kind of thing before. Why even the Countess of Clarendon, who entertains frequently and has everything down to a fine art—or so she tells her friends—cannot manage without an additional thirty servants in the house and the kitchen staff working full time every day. You have done all this yourself? Who selected the meats? The wines? The flowers?'

'I did,' Sapphira confessed. 'Don't say it is going to be all right just to please me. The downstairs rooms are in utter disorder, and I cannot face having to go and watch the preparations. I know I should, but . . .'

'You must show yourself again,' Wilcox told her firmly. 'If you are to have any authority at all in this house, you must go downstairs, give your instructions, and look as if you will take a stick to anyone who idles away so much as one precious minute.'

'You are right, of course. Will you stay, Wilcox? Will you take over the supervision of the final arrangements?'

'I was about to suggest that, with your ladyship's permission. You have to prepare yourself for this evening. Shall we take a look round? Tell me how you want things to be, and I will ensure that your wishes are carried out. But you must be seen to be in charge, if you understand me.'

Not a single servant passed one comment or smiled to another as Sapphira, accompanied by the rigid-faced Wilcox, toured the rooms. She gave her instructions in a clear, firm voice, sent a maid scuttling back to change half a dozen chipped glasses, together with a sharp reprimand for the others present to be more alert, and retired to her room, feeling light-headed with elation. Worn out from her activities over the past days—she had secretly left the house on three consecutive mornings to be at the market early— she fell asleep quickly and did not wake for several hours. She did so with the awareness that the hour of her triumph or failure was growing horribly close.

She was too apprehensive to have any appetite when Mrs Grayson appeared with a tray.

'Lightly scrambled eggs, a little toast. Steak and fresh vegetables. I have Wilcox's orders to stand over you while you eat it, my lady,' she said, setting it down beside the bed and ignoring Sapphira's grimace. 'How can you expect to stay on your feet tonight if you have no food in your stomach?'

She was right. Sapphira knew only too well the effects of having little or no food. She ate slowly but steadily while the housekeeper began taking out the clothes she had selected for the evening.

'Dare I ask how it looks downstairs?' she said tentatively.

'The flowers are being arranged in the hall, and the last of the chairs in the music-room. Then there is only the inevitable clearing away to do. The food is ready to be laid out and the wines are being chilled. Wilcox himself has seen to the unpacking of the Venetian glass.'

'I gather that the Earl was rather specific about his fate, should there be any breakages,' Sapphira said, and for the first time that day she found it possible to smile. What would be Quentin's reaction when he returned and found the house ready and waiting for his guests?

Sapphira's dress, which had arrived from the dressmaker only the previous day, was carefully arranged over the couch. She gazed at it, still unable to believe that she could own such a marvel. The overskirt and bodice were of lace, the underskirt and the tiny bows, of satin. Both materials were exactly the colour of the sapphire pendant she intended to wear. She had taken great interest, while making her purchases, in the clothes and hairstyles worn by other women, and had discussed them at great length with her dressmaker. The gown had been designed to enhance her slender shoulders and tiny waist, and because of the modest size of young breasts she had decided to do away with the usual fichu which covered many a low-cut neckline. Hers was daring, but not immodest, and would show off the jewel at her throat to perfection, she decided. Her shoes were of blue velvet, dyed to match the gown, as was her feather-tipped fan.

For a long time she contemplated the jewellery Quentin had given her since their marriage. He had not been ungenerous in his gifts, but he never made them personally, always leaving them to be delivered with her breakfast or dinner when she ate alone. There were rings of every description, bracelets of diamonds and rubies, necklaces of gold set with emeralds, diamonds or ropes of pearls, perfectly matched.

As Wilcox had reminded her, she was Sapphira, Countess of Ravenswood. She must not only act like a lady, but look like one. She selected a diamond bracelet, and matching sapphire earrings to go with the pendant, and a small diamond pin in her hair.

At five o'clock Wilcox presented himself to tell her that everything was ready for a last-minute inspection. Hesitantly she made her way downstairs. In the kitchen, the tables and cupboards bulged with food. She smiled to herself as she saw the tray of venison pies. She had done everything but place them in the oven, and she was proud of the fact. There were pigeons, whole joints of beef and mutton, the latter stuffed with garlic. Chickens and roasted suckling pig. A shoulder of venison rested appetisingly beside the meat pies, which would be eaten with sugared mustard.

Casks of ale and cider waited to be carried into the other room. Hundreds of bottles of wine from France, rare clarets and cognacs, stood lined up beside them. A suitable number of bottles had already been uncorked and either decanted or left to chill, Wilcox pointed out as she stared at the array in amazement.

For dessert, if it should be required, there were roasted pears, pasties, jellies and assorted mounds of cheeses

The music-room glowed with candlelight from the chandelier suspended in the middle of the room. The Venetian glass sparkled and shone, the pewter and silverware gleamed. The air was heavy with the perfume of flowers. For a long moment she stood drinking in the elegance of it all, the luxury and extravagance, that she herself had brought into being.

'Would my lady care to sample a little of the champagne we shall be serving?' Mrs Grayson came to her side with one of the Venetian glasses filled with a sparkling liquid which was as colourful as the flowers on the table before them. Sapphira had never seen or tasted anything like it before. It slid down her throat like nectar and, before she realised it, she had finished the whole glass. The amusement on the housekeeper's face told her that it should be drunk with more respect another time.

'Thank you,' Sapphira said quietly, and a trifle awkwardly. 'I don't know what I would have done without you.'

'I know I speak for Wilcox, too, when I say it is a pleasure to serve you, my lady,' Mrs Grayson replied, retrieving the Venetian glass. 'We both hope that this evening will be all you want it to be.'

If only that were possible, Sapphira thought, as she turned towards the door. Five-thirty, and Quentin had not returned. Very well, she could manage without him, she told herself, and went back to her room to take a bath in hot scented water and prepare herself for the arduous hours ahead.

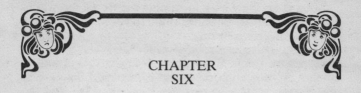

CHAPTER
SIX

'HAS THE master returned yet?' Sapphira asked, looking at the clock for the tenth time in as many minutes. A quarter to seven, and he had not come to her. She was dressed and ready to go down. Would it be alone?

'Yes, my lady. His man went to him not long ago.' The reply brought a sigh of relief from Sapphira's lips, and immediately she brightened. Turning slowly before the mirror, she inspected her reflection for a last time. 'How do I look?'

Mrs Grayson, who had insisted on dressing Sapphira herself and attending in fact to all her toilette, stepped back and nodded in approval. If anyone passed disapproving comment tonight, it would be out of sheer jealousy. She doubted if even the most notable beauties at the King's Court could match the girl who stood before her.

'Beware that you do not catch the King's eye, my lady. He is known to have a fancy for beautiful women! Here is your fan. Now, hold your head high and look straight at everyone you meet. You have nothing to be ashamed of, and a great deal to be proud of, this evening. The Earl asked that you wait for him in his sitting-room, so that you can go down together. No one has arrived yet except for young Blaise Courtney, and he was sampling the claret when I left him.'

Sapphira's eyes were decidedly misty as she glided, rather than walked, along the corridor and was admitted to the apartment of her husband. Blaise, lounging in a chair—a decanter of claret which he had brought with him, on a table, together with two glasses—gazed open-mouthed at the figure who entered, swallowed hard, and then rose with a warm smile to take her hand in his and raise it to his lips.

'I thought angels resided only in heaven. My lady, you look glorious. You will be the envy of every woman who sees you, and every man will be wishing he were in Quentin's place. I must have been mad not to have snatched you up myself while I had the chance.'

'You have a smooth tongue, sir,' Sapphira replied, but she was not annoyed by his words. 'And you have a short memory.'

'Nay. I remember how it came about. I must confess to instigating the whole plot. Quentin needed a wife, and I suggested he marry the first girl who took his fancy. He has the devil's own luck!'

So that was what made Quentin so determined to marry her. Blaise had put the idea into his head.

'And who selected me? You?' she asked, with eyebrows rising quizzingly.

'No, I did.' Quentin came out of the dressing-room behind her. Slowly she turned to face him and waited for his reaction. He was angry to discover her discussing with Blaise how they had met, for it was not a moment of which he found himself particularly proud any more, but the reproach which rose in his throat was never uttered as his eyes became transfixed on this apparition of unexpected loveliness. Her appearance was scrutinised in great detail, but he could find no fault with her gown, her hair worn a new way—an abundance of shining curls each side of her unpowdered face—nothing! It astonished him. Even the jewellery she wore had been chosen with taste and forethought. As his animosity drained away, a feeling of pleasure came over him. Never had he imagined escorting such a delightful-looking creature downstairs.

As he gazed at her, he saw her mouth begin to tremble slightly with apprehension. She was everything he could ever want in a wife, he thought. Young, lovely, capable of giving him the heir he secretly longed for; but if he touched her and found her no innocent, the illusion would be destroyed, as it had been with so many other women he had known. It was better that she should know nothing of his dreams, his hopes. Better that their relationship remain as it was. Safe, uncomplicated, the vision before him intact.

'Turn round,' he ordered, breaking free from the intensity of his thoughts. She obeyed, aware of Blaise's eyes riveted on her every movement. Nor was Quentin ignorant of his friend's interest, but it gave him no cause for concern. For years Blaise had loved no other woman but his sister Corinna, and although his affairs were numerous, they were meaningless. He would never love anyone but her, despite the way she kept him at arm's length, dangling like a puppet. He loved her despite her rejections, the unfulfilling of her promises. His interest in Sapphira meant nothing. If she was safe in the company of any man, it was Blaise. 'You have achieved perfection, madam. I congratulate you. But before you allow this one success to go to your head, remember that we have guests awaiting us below. Not all of them will be as free with their compliments.'

Quentin did not know how his praise swelled Sapphira's heart with pride. What did she care for the gossip-mongers? She had pleased him. She was already more than half-way to victory!

At the head of the stairs, Quentin paused to survey the scene below. Perhaps two dozen people had now arrived, and Sapphira realised that she should have been present to receive them. Curious glances began to be cast up towards them. Quentin felt the ringed hand laid lightly on his arm begin to tremble, as she suddenly had misgivings.

'I—I cannot,' she breathed. Now that the moment of truth had come, she knew how lacking she was in the social graces. Margaret had taught her much, even the latest dances, and she knew she was more beautiful than most of the women below, but she was no more than a common little tavern wench, and they all knew it!

Quentin's hand closed over hers and held it fast. In a low, fierce whisper he said, 'You have come too far to turn back now. This is what you wanted, isn't it?'

Mutely she nodded and allowed him to lead her down the sweeping staircase. Heads turned, fans fluttered discreetly to hide a whispered comment, as Quentin, resplendent in burgundy silk, with a matching embroidered waistcoat from France of the same colour, white breeches, and dark red leather shoes, descended beside the slender figure in blue. He was fully aware that they made an elegant pair, aware, too, of the ripple of surprise which ran through the onlookers as they began to wonder whether the rumour had been true after all.

This quietly-spoken young woman, who moved among them with ease and charm—a trifle tongue-tied at times, but that made her all the more appealing— was no commoner. Her poise and bearing made her stand out even among the distinguished gathering which followed her every move most keenly. Sapphira's head began to reel at the names she heard. She was introduced to Marchionesses, Countesses and Duchesses, had her hand kissed time and time again by bold-eyed Dukes and Lords, even a foreign Prince! Her husband's circle of friends was astonishing. For an hour he remained patiently by her side, but she became aware of his increasingly impatient manner. The music-room was crammed to capacity. People flowed over into the hall and the dining-room, drinking, talking, inspecting passers-by with the same scrutiny that she had been subjected to. From the conversations she overheard as she mingled, desperately trying to keep track of names and faces, it seemed that the favourite topic of the men was the women present, and who had been unfaithful to whose husband that week. And the women, after they had dissected every other attractive female in the room, turned their attentions to talk of lovers and affairs. Accustomed to lewd comments and tavern gossip, Sapphira was nevertheless shocked by the intimate details, described in great detail. Was this how Quentin expected her to act? It would explain his manner towards her. When no husband could trust his wife and no wife her husband, how could any marriage, any worth-while relationship, survive?

'Margaret has just arrived. Come and greet her; then I will leave you,' Quentin murmured, relief in his tone. He had long ago grown bored with such functions, and they gave him no pleasure. Most of the people bored him, too. The limited conversations irritated him, and the continual betting which always accompanied such a gathering left him cold with disgust. He had already overheard a dozen assignations being made.

He glanced down at the girl at his side as they threaded their way to where Margaret stood just inside the door. So poised and cool. Part of him was proud of her achievement, but part of him also despised the ease with which she seemed to adjust so readily. There was no sign of nervousness now that she was the centre of attention. How many men would try and seduce her before the night was out, he wondered, brows furrowing?

'Sapphira, my dear, what a triumph!' Margaret declared, and his frown grew as she smiled only briefly at him and proceeded to take Sapphira in her arms. 'Confidence, did I not tell you? And you have it. Let me look at you. Does she not look a picture, Quentin?'

'I have told her so.'

'I should hope so, And the arrangements? What fault have you found with them?' Margaret asked lightly. 'Everything looks as if it is superbly set out. All that food. One of my maids saw you at Covent Garden yesterday, Did you make the purchases yourself? I can hardly believe it!'

Sapphira nodded, aware of Quentin's dark gaze on

her. 'I've been there many times. I used to do the buying
for Silas, so I knew where to go for a bargain.' She
wondered why Margaret smiled. 'I—I was afraid I
would run out of money, as I had no idea how much
things would cost, you see. We didn't entertain like this
at the Black Horse! But in fact I have some left over.'

Margaret laughed aloud at the growing puzzlement
in Quentin's eyes. This was not what he had expected
at all.

'What a resourceful little thing you are.' Margaret
took a glass of wine from the tray held by a hovering
servant. Sapphira and Quentin followed suit. She had
already had at least three glasses, which had resulted in
her completely losing all self-consciousness. The warm
glow stealing through her was very pleasant. She knew
people were looking in their direction, no doubt specu-
lating on the friendship between Quentin's wife and his
mistress. It would keep them occupied if they had no
one else to tear apart, she thought without malice. It
did not disconcert her—she had accepted it from the
beginning, and was glad of it. 'I think we should drink
a toast. To Sapphira! May heaven continue to smile on
you.'

'I think Sapphira is capable of making heaven work
for her on her own terms,' Quentin remarked a trifle
ironically, and saw a shadow cross her face. 'I concede
defeat, Margaret. You have won your bet.'

'Bet?' Sapphira echoed, softly. What did he mean?
Margaret looked slightly out of countenance.

'We had a wager. She thought you would succeed
tonight. I did not,' he replied slowly, and her cheeks
blanched. Without a word she turned and walked away
from them. 'Damn!' he ejaculated under his breath, and
Margaret's eyes burned with anger.

'I could think of a stronger word than that. Whatever
possessed you to tell her? If anyone was going to humiliate her tonight, why did it have to be her own husband!
I am going after her . . .'

'No. I shall. Believe me, I did not intend it to sound so . . . so . . .'

'Cruel? Didn't you? You seem to delight in it, these days, with her. Do you want her that much, Quentin?'

'Want—her! Ridiculous!' It was something he himself was unable to accept, so how could he admit it to his mistress, of all people?

Margaret watched him make his way through the crowd after Sapphira. She saw some friends coming towards her, and went to greet them. Now, more than ever, she knew that Sapphira would remain Countess of Ravenswood long after a year was past. She had seen something in Quentin's eyes. A strange look, one she had never seen before. Pain—naked pain! As if she had opened a wound. Or as if he had just found himself facing something too fearful to contemplate. The collapse of his world, perhaps? The knowledge that he was, after all, capable of genuine feelings—even love?

Once she had left Quentin's company, Sapphira found herself detained at every turn, and much as she wanted to be alone, she found it impossible.

'A perfectly splendid affair,' a heavily jewelled woman purred in her ear. 'I am Letitia Singleton. You must call on me soon, my dear, and tell me all about yourself.'

Sapphira smiled and said she would, and quickly moved on. Lady Singleton had not been as unsubtle as some who had directed pointed questions at her without a qualm. She had lost count of how many invitations she had received. She would begin to go out—if she was still in London—and, looking around her, she could see no reason why she should not be. Everyone seemed most content. Her first priority was to find Molly and Lottie with Quentin's help. After that she would satisfy the curiosity of the bored wives and gossiping matrons. It was not the ordeal she had feared, she thought, as she made her way towards the french windows and a breath of fresh air. She had been worrying for nothing

A young man detached himself from his female companion and attempted to detain her with the offer of more wine, but she refused, and eased her way past him on to the patio. Laughter came from the shadows behind her, and she quickly picked up her skirts and hurried down the steps towards the tiny rose arbour, now gaunt and flowerless in winter, envying the unseen couple their moment of romance. In her life there was no room for such things. How empty it promised to be.

She shivered in the keen night air, and leaned her head against one of the timbered supports, suddenly drained of all strength. The sound of music floated out to her. People would be crowding on to the floor, flirting, smiling, passing careless remarks—and beneath the air of gaiety, of well-being, the undercurrent of intrigue remained like a dark shadow on the sun. How could people live double lives and be happy? With husband one moment, lover the next. Marriage vows meant nothing. She shivered and wished she had brought a shawl.

'You will catch your death out here,' Quentin said quietly from the shadows. 'Are you hiding from your guests—or from me?'

Despite his soft tone, Sapphira started violently and took a step backwards into the arbour. As though she were afraid of him, he thought, shocked. He had done nothing to make her fear him. He had given her everything she wanted. After tonight, she would have more if she so desired. The idea of having a wife clinging to him, to interrupt his staid way of life, had never appealed to him, and he knew that until it had been forced on him, he might never have married. For weeks he had fought against Sapphira's presence. Tonight he had accepted it for the first time—and her, as a person. Not so much a surrender but a truce, he told himself, unwilling to acknowledge that he was in any way mistaken as to her morals and character.

'I came out for some air,' Sapphira said, recovering

her composure. 'Please do not inconvenience yourself by remaining here with me, sir. You will be missed inside.' *By Margaret,* she almost added, but bit back the words in time. He had been Margaret's property long before he had rescued her from the tavern, and would remain so, even though he had taken a wife. She had no right to be jealous!

'Do not remain so aloof from me,' Quentin snapped, and she flinched at the sharpness of tone, 'or people will begin to believe we are not the happy couple we pretend.'

'What does that matter,' she flung back. 'Nothing matters to you except your precious name and the fact you won your battle against Corinna. How, doesn't matter. The means you used to justify it do not matter. Only that you are the winner. Well, my lord, you have what you want. Go away and leave me alone. Have you no friends to make new bets with? I am sure there is plenty to be wagered on here tonight.'

'So now we have it.' Quentin stepped towards her, but she stayed in the shadows, away from the moonlight which might have illuminated her face. 'You are angry with me for what I said to Margaret, and you have every right to be. The bet, that was nothing, but to speak of it to you was wrong. I have been wrong about many things, I think.'

Sapphira was speechless. What was he saying? That he no longer believed her to be a wanton? That he believed in her innocence? Or was he prepared, now that he had seen for himself how capable she was, to allow her to take her rightful place as his wife at his side? To accompany him to theatres, the Park, ride with him in the stead of his mistress and accumulate her own circle of friends? Which would, of course, make not a scrap of difference to his way of life. He still had the best of both worlds, as men always did!

'I accept your apology, sir.' Her haughty manner stung him, but he kept a rein on his quick temper. 'Now that you have delivered it, I shall detain you no longer.'

'Damn you, wench! Why do you always rub me the wrong way?' he exclaimed. He was so close to her that he could smell the light French perfume she wore. Not heavy and sultry, which would have been the choice of many of the women present, he thought, but a light fragrance which wafted in the air about her, reminding him of apple-blossom. 'You have pleased me tonight. Nay, more than that. I have been—proud—of you.' The words did not come easily, and he heard her give a soft exclamation of surprise. 'I am not given to casual compliments, as you have gathered by now, neither do I give praise when it is not due. I see no reason for Ravenswood to have such grace and beauty all to itself, do you? If you remain here, understand one thing. As my wife, you will be permitted no games such as are played by those we are entertaining. We entered into a bargain. Keep your side of it and I shall keep mine, and you will not find me ungenerous. Go your own way, but remember the proud name you bear. I will not have it sullied. Is that clear?'

'You say you are proud of me, yet you still think of me as a woman of—of loose ways, giving my favours to any man who looks at me.' Sapphira's lips trembled. She was shivering again, but not from the cold. 'Had I wished, sir, I could have cuckolded you a dozen times already this evening.'

'If you even think of it, I shall kill you. You have only to contain your desires for a year, after all, and then you will be free to do as you please.'

It was not what he meant to say. Again he had spoken before considering how his words would wound her, but she did infuriate him! Why would she not accept the peace he was offering? She would not lose by it!

A sob rose in Sapphira's throat. The evening was spoiled, her triumph ground down beneath his contemptuous words. Anger and humiliation rose up inside her, mingled with the bitterness of defeat and the loneliness she had known, would go on knowing until the day he gave her her freedom. Without Molly and Lottie, she did not have a single friend in the world. She was not given to tears, yet they came unbidden into her eyes and she could not prevent them, for the force with which they spilled down her cheeks was overwhelming. Years of poverty and hardship had been annihilated by her marriage to Quentin, but she had achieved nothing. She was still nothing—a nobody in the eyes of this man she had come to care for as no other before. She should have hated him for his cruelty and indifference, but what burned in her breast was far removed from hate. If what she felt was love, she would reject it as he rejected her. He would never know of it and use it to degrade her further. She wanted to be strong, but the tears continued to flow, and she leaned back against the arbour, sobbing into her hands.

How long Quentin watched her, he did not know. His first suspicion was that she sought to sway him from his strict control of her ways. Tears were a very effective weapon when used by a beautiful woman, and Sapphira was that. Beautiful and desirable and his! But her sobs reached him, and touched the heart he had protected for so long.

'For the love of heaven, child. Don't weep so. Do you want your guests to think I have been beating you? They will, if they see you with swollen eyes and cheeks.'

'I don't care. Go away,' Sapphira cried, not looking at him. He sounded kind, but he did not mean it. She struck out at the hands placed on her shoulders, and as she raised her face to his, he saw the misery mirrored in the depths of her lovely eyes—and he was lost.

The man who caught her to him in a fierce embrace, seeking her soft mouth, finding it despite her protests and feeble struggles, crushing it beneath his, dominating it and her within minutes with the expertise of many years, was not the Quentin Tyrell he knew. This man was a stranger, driven by desire and passions he would never have allowed to run riot over reason. This man sought to fulfil the dreams of a lifetime in a single moment, with no thought as to the consequences. He was bewitched by this child-woman who had haunted his thoughts since the first day he saw her, and nothing mattered except that she belonged to him!

'Sapphira . . .' Her name broke from his lips in a harsh whisper, and they caressed her wet cheeks, the hollow of her throat, the satin smoothness of her shoulders.

Dazed, taken completely unawares by his advances, Sapphira found her struggles diminishing, her mumbled protestations dying away. Despite the chill in the air, his fingers burned on her skin like fire. Fire to match the one he had unwittingly ignited in her heart—and in her body. This was how the Court ladies behaved, slipping away to meet lovers in the darkness. But she was Quentin's wife! She had a right to love him and be loved in return. But he did not love her . . . How could he, when Margaret remained in his life? Older, more worldly, more experienced. She knew nothing! A growing tide of passion swept away all doubts, all reservations. She closed her eyes in ecstasy as Quentin's lips travelled over her face, brushing away the last of her tears and returned to find her mouth again, devouring it with a hunger which was both frightening and exciting, for she had never known the like of it before.

Customers at the tavern who had stolen kisses had been rewarded with a slap or a curt rebuke. She had never given her kisses willingly to any man. Now she revelled in the sheer enjoyment of giving without restraint to the man she loved. She was hardly aware that Quentin had guided her back against the wooden seat at the back of the arbour. She made no protest as he lowered her on to it, still holding her tightly against him. He could feel the rapid beating of her heart against his chest. It matched his own. There was a strange madness in him as he laid his lips against the firm swell of her breast above the blue lace.

'You will never belong to any man but me,' he whispered savagely. This time he would ensure that there were no other men, even if he kept her under lock and key.

A long high-pitched laugh sounded behind him, followed by the unmistakable, chilling, sound of people clapping. Sapphira's eyes flew open, registering horror and disbelief at what she saw. More than a dozen men and women were gathered outside the arbour entrance. Her face bearing a wicked smile, Corinna stood to the forefront, hanging on the arm of a young man in his late twenties. As Quentin started to his feet, cursing vehemently, his sister burst into another peal of shrill laughter.

'Is your wife so accustomed to being tumbled in strange places that you forgo the comforts of bed, Quentin? You lose, Giles.' She addressed her companion. 'I told you that ten minutes was too short. Pay up everyone, and then let's get back to the house for some more wine. I think the entertainment is over for the moment.'

'How could you!' Ignoring the grinning faces, though it took all her will-power not to strike out at them, Sapphira rose to her feet, brushing aside the hand Quentin put out to help her. 'I'm sorry to have upset another of your wagers, sir. Perhaps if you had told me there was a time-limit, I might have been more obliging. Of course there would have been an extra charge.'

Quentin's hand caught her a stinging blow across the face, knocking her back on the seat. Violently pushing aside the onlookers, he strode out and stopped in front of his sister. For a moment Sapphira thought that he would strike her, too, so murderous was his expression, but he continued on without a word towards the house.

Aware of the curious guests drifting in her direction, Sapphira followed, her cheeks flaming at the suggestions that followed her. He had used her for the amusement of his friends! Animal! Monster! Did he have no regard for anyone? His sweet words had lulled her into a sense of false security. She would not weaken again, nor would she ever trust anything he said. She stumbled on the grass, moist with evening mist coming in from the woods. An arm went beneath hers, helping her to recover her balance. She swung around, angry words springing to her lips, and found herself looking up at Blaise.

'Come into the library,' he said gently. 'You are frozen. What happened there? Everyone suddenly disappeared from the card-game I was in, and came out here. What did Corinna do?'

'I can't tell you. It's too—too humiliating.' Sapphira shook her head, unable to continue. In silence he led her into the deserted library, closed the windows behind them, and poured her a glass of wine.

'Shall I ring for your maid?' He was looking at her pale cheeks and the smudges of dirt on the skirts of her gown.

'No. Please, I want no one to see me like this. Enough already have. She is evil. As evil as he is!'

'Who? Corinna? I agree there. Who are you comparing her to?'

'Quentin.'

'My dear Sapphira! He is a saint, compared to her. Sit down and compose yourself and tell me what happened.'

Sapphira swallowed a little of her wine and then put it to one side. Perhaps too much of the unaccustomed wine explained why she had been such an easy conquest for her husband's deceit. She laid her head back against a cushion and was silent for a long moment. Blaise sat in a chair near by, not daring to disturb her until she was more herself. When she raised her head and looked at him again, there was utter desolation in her eyes.

'Quentin followed me into the garden a few minutes ago and—began to make love to me.'

He looked surprised, though not unduly, by the revelation.

'Is that so wrong? In his place, I wouldn't leave you alone for a moment, and I would be wildly jealous of your seeking the company of anyone else.'

'You don't understand. Our marriage—it is not like that. He has not touched me. He said he never would. Tonight, I thought . . . I mean . . . It was another of those hateful wagers. He must have made it with Corinna. There were people watching us . . . listening . . . Oh, Blaise, how could he do such a thing to me?'

'Are you sure Quentin made a wager? It doesn't sound like him,' Blaise returned with a frown, and she nodded, the curls on each side of her cheeks bouncing furiously. 'Poor Sapphira! It is a strange world you find yourself in.'

'I wish I were back at the Black Horse.'

'I think not.' He sat beside her and took her hand in his, holding it fast when she attempted to pull away. 'You have nothing to fear from me. I am not for you, and I would not amuse myself with you or harm you in any way. I shall be your friend—I think you need one. Will you accept my offer? It has no conditions.'

'How can I believe that—after tonight?' Sapphira breathed. She liked Blaise and felt somehow comfortable in his presence. She did not begrudge his suggestion to Quentin that he would marry her. He could not have known the torment she would endure. He had kind eyes, like a stray puppy seeking affection and companionship. She suddenly came to realise that what she saw there was loneliness. 'I am indeed in need of a friend. Thank you. However, I must warn you, my husband also delivered a lecture to me on how I should behave tonight. Under the circumstances, it would serve him right if I ran off with the first man who took my fancy.'

'I doubt if you will do that—you are too sensible.'

'Too conscious of the money I would lose, don't you mean?'

'I didn't say that, nor did I imply it. You are a prickly little thing, aren't you? Rather like Quentin. Be very careful if such a thought should enter your head, for he would follow you wherever you went. If he did not kill you, he would most certainly kill the man with you.'

'I could never be like—them.' Sapphira looked towards the closed door. Beyond, the sound of laughter and music which had given her so much pleasure earlier now served only to increase her despondency.

'And I shall never betray your trust. Let's set the tongues wagging. Come and dance with me,' he urged.

'I—I'm not very good.' But why not? She had worked hard for this night.

'I know an excellent dancing-master. I shall send him to you.'

'Thank you, Blaise, I accept.' Sapphira rose from the couch, brushed the dry specks of dirt from her gown with a handkerchief and looked at him steadily. 'I don't know why I should trust you, but I do. It is almost as though we have known each other for years. How silly.'

Blaise did not consider it silly, for he had been thinking the same thing for some considerable time. He did not regard her in the same light as other women. Not as a conquest, or an amusing companion for the evening, but as a friend. It was the first time he had felt about a woman in this way. It was the way he would have felt with a sister, had he had one, he thought, as he escorted her back into the other room. Quentin was a fool to set her against him.

It was clear that the incident in the garden was common knowledge. Sapphira saw that as soon as she reached the dance-floor. Soft laughter had followed her as she walked at Blaise's side, and now speculative looks were cast at them by other couples and the fans fluttered furiously again. Her eyes searched the room for Quentin, and found him watching her from the far side, with narrowed, distrustful gaze. What right had he to look at her so, after what he had done? She hoped he would come to her so that she might apologise for the angry words which had passed between them, but he kept his distance and further provoked the wagging tongues.

Later, Blaise introduced her to his father. His mother had died when he was born, and Thomas Courtney had remained a widower, never seeking another wife. How he must have loved her, Sapphira thought, as she extended a slim white hand towards the distinguished grey-haired man who barely touched it to his lips.

'I see now why Blaise was so anxious for me to attend tonight. So you are Quentin's wife. I have always admired his taste in women.'

'You are too kind, sir. I am sure you are aware that I was not selected for my looks,' Sapphira replied.

'Scandal has never interested me, Lady Ravenswood.' Sapphira wondered if it was her imagination, after all she had been through that evening, or was he staring at her a little too intently? He was still unconsciously holding her hand. His gaze focused for a long moment on the sapphires at her throat, before returning to her face. 'I hope my son will bring you to dine with us some evening.'

'I should like that,' Sapphira answered politely, and she and Blaise moved on.

A woman came to Lord Courtney's side. Tall, very slender and red-haired, but pale, despite the heavy rouge and powder meant to disguise the signs of the illness which had plagued her for many years. Blue eyes, so much like those of Sapphira, stared after the girl. When she spoke, her voice shook with emotion, and Lord Courtney caught her hand, squeezing it reassuringly.

'You saw? The pendant she wears! Tell me I was not mistaken. Tell me it is the same one you gave me eighteen years ago?'

'There could never be another like it. I would know it anywhere. She must have come by it by accident,

Susanne. Don't build your hopes too high again. We have been through this so many times before,' he soothed. In her present agitated condition, he was afraid that she would pursue Sapphira before everyone, and cause another scandal for the gossip-mongers to enjoy. 'You should not have come. You are not well, my dear. Let me take you home.'

'No, I want to see her. When Blaise described her, I knew I had found her. I must speak to her . . .'

'No. I forbid it. Not here.' He was quite adamant, and held fast to her hand. 'Think of the girl, if not yourself. This is not something for the ears of those wretches. It must be done discreetly . . . if at all.'

'I must see her. I will see her. I shall send her an invitation to visit me. Help me, Thomas! Help me to see my daughter?'

'Our daughter. Of course I shall help you.' Thomas smiled, and began to guide her slowly towards the doors. 'Tomorrow, Susanne. We shall discuss it tomorrow.'

'My lady, the King's carriage has arrived,' Wilcox whispered in Sapphira's ear, and she gasped so loudly that Blaise looked at her in surprise. They retired to a quiet corner.

'The King here? The Earl did not mention that he was coming! I—I did not invite him,' she said tremulously. The King! She was overwhelmed; terrified!

'Corinna,' Blaise said, tight-lipped. 'I suspect that not only that little scene in the garden, but the invitation to Charles, is all part of a scheme to get back at both you and Quentin. She should have been strangled at birth!'

'His Majesty often arrives unexpectedly at gatherings such as this,' Wilcox said, his equanimity not in the least disturbed because he would soon be serving the sovereign of England. How Sapphira wished she could steal a little of his composure! 'I believe he has brought Lady Castlemaine with him.'

'Oh!' She knew that she was his favourite mistress,

who had borne him two children. She was said to be a great beauty, although somewhat hot-tempered, and had complete control over her royal lover. 'How—how do I greet her?'

'With a smile and honeyed words. She is a close friend of Corinna, and she's excessively vain,' Blaise replied blandly. 'The two of them set this up between them. Quentin will be furious. I don't fancy Corinna's chances of getting any money out of him for a very long time.'

'Then perhaps he was not to blame for what happened.' Sapphira was horrified when she remembered what she had said to him. She had made herself sound exactly the kind of woman he suspected her to be. Grasping, mercenary, faithless! Yet if Corinna had not appeared, what would have happened, she wondered? A faint tinge of colour rose in her cheeks, and she found Blaise staring at her questioningly and quickly returned her attention to the matter in hand. Would Quentin introduce her? He must! But where was he?

'Do not alarm yourself, my lady.' Wilcox's tone was as confident as always. 'When you receive His Majesty and Lady Castlemaine, I shall be a few paces behind you with a tray of wine. I have discovered—no, I have made it my business over the years—to discover the likes and dislikes of the Earl's many friends. It makes it so much easier to accommodate them when they are here, you understand. On the tray will be a large glass of the fine claret, which happens to be a favourite of his. It happens to have a slight addition to it—a little cognac. Only the Earl ever serves him this particular drink, as far as I know. And for the lady,' a slight twist to the thin mouth indicated that he had other thoughts as to her station, but as a servant would never have dreamt of voicing them. 'She is very partial to a certain liquor the monks at Market Cross have produced for centuries. The recipe is a well-kept secret, but the potency is not, hence the small glass.'

'Again you saved my life,' Sapphira breathed, and a smile, or as much as the severe features could manage, came and went briefly.

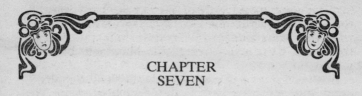

CHAPTER
SEVEN

THERE WAS no grand entrance. No announcement of
the King's arrival. Charles suddenly appeared in the
room with Lady Castlemaine on his arm, and the whole
room was agog. Men bowed, ladies curtsied, and whispered how elegant he looked and wondered at the
smugness of her expression. Some said she was again
enceinte. This would be her third royal bastard!

Sapphira had heard that the King was a handsome
man. Now she saw for herself the magnetism, the aura
about him, which had brought people flocking to his
side when he returned home from exile. For an English-
man, she considered him taller than average, and his
features were quite severe, she thought. His complexion
was dark, but bright eyes enhanced it. His long black
hair was curled naturally and fell about his shoulders.
His clothes were of cloth of gold, shot with silver thread.
Elegant—majestic. He moved easily and gracefully and
acknowledged the people on both sides of him with
warm smiles.

Clinging to his arm, Barbara, Lady Castlemaine, was
also a picture of elegance in a gown of pink and white
taffeta. Sapphira experienced a momentary twinge of
pity for poor Catherine of Braganza, the King's unfortunate wife. Not only did she have to suffer the indignity
of her husband being seen constantly in public with his
favourite, but the woman had also been given a position
as one of her ladies-of-the-bedchamber—on Charles's
insistence! Yet even Sapphira could not deny they made
a handsome couple.

As she started towards them, forcing herself over the

panic which urged her to turn and disappear into the crowd, she caught sight of Quentin coming out of a side room, and behind him—Margaret! People moved back to allow the couple free passage, and it was then that the small puppy the King was holding in his arms gave an excited bark and leaped free of them. It thudded to the floor and rolled over, dazed, and Sapphira bent and lifted it carefully into her arms, soothing it as it whimpered pathetically.

'Oh, you poor thing. Are you hurt?' It nuzzled at her hand, and a pink tongue darted over her cheek as she bent her head to fondle its ears, completely forgetful of the tall figure who had come to a halt before her.

'My dogs have always had excellent good sense in their choice of companions.' Her voice jerked up at the amused voice, and at the sight of the dark laughing eyes surveying her she went down into a deep curtsy. It was not the elaborate, graceful gesture she had practised over and over again in front of her mirror, not with a puppy clutched tightly to her breast. 'My lady, do not remain down there with those lovely eyes hidden from me. I would know who I am to thank for such timely intervention.'

A hand fastened over her arm. Even before she looked up into Quentin's face, she knew it was he, by the way the fingers held her so purposefully.

'Sire, may I introduce my wife, Sapphira.'

'So this is the beauty I have been hearing such rumours about. Shame on you for hiding her away for so long! I shall expect you to present her to us at Court before much longer.'

'As Your Majesty commands.' Quentin heard the ripple of surprise which ran through the onlookers. He did not know if he was pleased or angry that the issue had been forced on him. He would not be ashamed to present her, not after the way she had conducted herself tonight, but the incident in the garden was still too clearly in his mind. Her taunting comments that she expected payment for her services—like a whore! Had they been spoken in anger or truth?

A middle-aged man leaned forward and whispered something to Lady Castlemaine, who began to smile broadly. Instantly he felt uneasy. She, in turn, touched the King gently on the shoulder, and he inclined his head to hear what she said in a voice too low to carry beyond the two of them. Sapphira saw the laughter disappear from his eyes and the full, somewhat sensuous, mouth tightened. He had been told who—or rather what—she was, she thought, as his gaze fastened on her once again. One caustic comment from the King on Quentin's ill-fated choice, and no one would accept her into his house.

'My dog, if you please, Lady Ravenswood.'

Colour beginning to stain her cheeks, Sapphira handed the animal back to him. And then he smiled again, and chuckled.

'I don't know what she sees in you, Quentin, with your black moods. Lady Castlemaine has just reminded me that we have much in common, my lady. Once, not so long ago, I was forced to do my own cooking, too. Yet today I am King of England. Remain with us a while. I am interested to hear more of this unusual love-match.'

The King was favouring her! She could not believe it. Behind Lady Castlemaine, Sapphira saw Corinna scowl in vexation and she knew that it had been a deliberate attempt to shame her and humiliate Quentin before all his friends, exactly as she had done in the garden. It had failed. Lady Castlemaine, if she disliked the thought of being in the company of a low tavern girl, certainly had no intention of allowing it to show to her royal lover, or anyone watching.

'You are most gracious, Sire. All that I have heard about the King's benevolence is indeed true,' Sapphira replied, her courage returning. 'May I ask that you partake of a little refreshment?' Wilcox was at her side without a word being said. She selected the glass of fine claret, and held it out to Charles. 'As you like it, I believe, Your Majesty. And for Lady Castlemaine, her favourite from Market Cross.'

'Here—the animal looked more at home in your arms than in mine.' Charles gave her the tiny spaniel, and savoured his drink. 'Excellent. It is indeed how I like it. And yours, my dear?'

'The Earl never forgets me when he is at Ravenswood.' The woman smiled at Quentin and then looked surprised as he shook his head.

'My wife must take full credit for tonight, including this. As a hostess, she is second to none. I hope Your Majesty and you, my lady, will sample some of the other appetising refreshments we have to offer.' He knew that Sapphira was looking at him, but he kept his eyes averted from her face. He had gone some way to atoning for the slap he had given her, even if it had been deserved. He had never struck a woman before, and now that some of the anger had abated, he did not like the way it made him feel.

'It is the duty of a good hostess to know the—shall we say—idiosyncrasies of her guests so that she can provide only the best of everything for them,' Sapphira said. The puppy in her arms continued to lick her hand, and her eyes shone as she stared down at it. At the tavern, Silas had not allowed animals, except a cat to catch the rats, which it never managed to do as there were too many. She had often fed it scraps from the kitchen, for it was so thin that the bones could be seen through its scabby coat. Silas never gave it food. If it did not catch mice to eat, it was of no use to him. Like people, she had thought, discarded when their usefulness was over.

'Keep it,' Charles said, and she looked at him in amazement, as did the men and women gathered about them. Keep it! The King—whose love of his dogs was known the length and breadth of the kingdom! They slept at the foot of his bed and went with him whenever he went out, even to the Council meetings he considered so tedious. 'My Bess gave birth to a litter of six. I can see it will be well cared for.' His gaze fastened on Quentin, silent, disbelieving the impression Sapphira had made on the King of England. Charles had taken a fancy to her. Next, there would be invitations to dine with him privately. Why should she not accept what he had to offer; it was so much more than she would receive from the bargain they had made! The dark eyes of the monarch held a hint of reproach as they continued to look at him. They had been friends for over ten years. Had fought together, hungered together, reminisced of home together and of the new England awaiting them when they returned. 'You have always made me welcome in your home, Quentin. I hope you will not be too busy to do so in the future?'

'My house is always open to Your Majesty, as you well know,' Quentin answered, a trifle shamefaced at the trend of his thoughts. If he had not been so confident as to the utter impossibility of any woman successfully penetrating his thick shield of cynicism and sarcastic rhetoric, thus leading her to the weakness he knew dwelled deep inside him, he might have begun to think that he was not invulnerable to Sapphira. Why should he care where she went, or what she did? Or with whom? The bargain was that they would discreetly go their own ways. Yet, as he watched her walk away, laughing at something Charles had said, the spaniel clutched tightly in her arms like a little girl with her first toy, he knew that was the last thing he wanted.

The gown Sapphira had worn that evening lay across a chair. Beside it stockings and petticoats and shoes, left where she had dropped them. It had been very late before the last of the guests had gone. Many had remained to be near the King and his mistress, who had surprised everyone by remaining until the early hours of the morning and, to all accounts, had enjoyed himself immensely. He had danced with most of the pretty women in the room, and three times with Sapphira. He had made it quite plain that she met with his approval, and therefore, before the last toast was drunk, she found herself in great demand.

Wives, who had previously ignored or avoided her, now sought her company, as did their husbands, with more on their minds than a simple invitation to supper. How Sapphira climbed the stairs to her room, she did not know. It was ecstasy to pull off her shoes and be undressed by her maid. She had given orders to Mrs Grayson that only the food was to be cleared away, what little there was left, and then the servants were to go to bed. They deserved their rest as much as she did, and had worked as hard to make the party a success. It had been, she knew it! Even Lady Castlemaine had congratulated her on one of the finest evenings she had had for a long time. Charles had smiled warmly at her words, and Sapphira knew they had been solely for his benefit. She would probably never know if it was true.

Corinna and her escort had left early, much to her relief. She knew their paths must cross again at some future date, but the next time she would not be so naïve as to expect anything but treachery from Quentin's sister. She had left Quentin still drinking with two friends. He had said good night to her cordially, but giving the impression that he did not wish her to linger. Blaise kissed her hand, his brown eyes sympathetic as Quentin turned away to resume his conversation.

'Ride with me tomorrow?' he whispered. 'In the afternoon, when you have recovered from tonight's festivities.'

'Very well. Come for me at three.'

She wondered at the wisdom of her decision as she lay in bed, but decided there was no harm in accepting Blaise's friendship. It was all he offered, and she trusted him.

The sound of the door opening, as she began to doze, roused her into wakefulness again. Brushing the loose hair from her eyes, she sat up, her eyes searching the darkness beyond the foot of the bed where the spaniel puppy slept snug and warm curled up on the coverlet. Quentin moved into her vision. By the faint light that shone into the room and across her bed—for some mad reason she had opened the curtains to look down at the arbour where she had acted so impulsively, so foolishly, and had almost surrendered her innocence in a moment of unbridled passion to a man who had no conception as to the meaning of the word love—she saw he was still fully dressed.

'I did not mean to disturb you.' His tone she thought strange. As though he found himself suddenly ill at ease in her presence. Why did he seek it, then?

'I was not asleep,' she said, and he moved closer. The dark features were unreadable, yet in the depths of his eyes she glimpsed something which alarmed her. She had seen it hours before as she lay in his arms in the arbour. Had he come intending to finish what had been started there? She was his wife: she could not refuse his demands, but her whole being cried out against being used simply for his pleasure. Would he gain pleasure from such a relationship, or did he merely want to remind her of her place? The King of England might have shown her his favour, but she belonged to her husband in all things, if he chose to assert the authority he had hitherto declined.

'I was proud of you tonight. Everyone liked you, I am sure.' The words fell from his lips haltingly. He tried not to look at the figure, half-dazed with sleep, who regarded him from the bed. She wore something loose and diaphanous, reminding him of the warm, willing body he had held in his arms and which had been snatched from him by Corinna's inopportune arrival. How he wanted her! He ached with the longing to possess her.

'I am glad to have met with the approval of your friends.' How uninterested she sounded. Did she think, because she had had the King's smiles, she could do no wrong now? She had yet to learn how fickle the human race was. 'What of you, my lord? Are you satisfied with your acquisition? I find it hard to believe you are, for you spent more time with your mistress than with me, and everyone knew it.' Was she rebuking him? 'But then, I am not truly your wife, am I? I have no claims on you.'

'No, you do not! You have my name and all that goes with it. Be satisfied with things the way they are. I offered no more. Allow me to keep the illusion I have as to the innocence you protest so vigorously that you still retain. If I touched you and found otherwise, I would destroy you!'

His words chilled Sapphira. What ghost haunted him? Why would he not allow himself to love and be loved in return?

'Am I to understand I am free to lead a life of my own? As your sister does?'

'You are my wife, and you will behave as such. You shall never sully my name, as she has.'

'And if I take a lover? Discreetly, of course,' Sapphira challenged. He had come to tell her how proud he was of her, yet he did not want to remain with her or spend more time with her than was absolutely necessary. He was annoyed that the evening had been such a success, she thought, growing angry. The King had befriended her, and so society would accept her. He had been hoping to send her back to Ravenswood, out of his sight, out of his mind, leaving him free to be with Margaret.

Quentin came close to the bed, his eyes glittering dangerously. 'Then you need look no further, my wife.'

She cried out as he seized hold of her, bruising her bare arms with the fierceness of his grip. His mouth on hers was not at all gentle; the kisses he forced on her soft lips were meant to be dominate, to subdue her to his will. Sapphira had no strength left in her to fight him, but it was several minutes before he realised she was offering no resistance.

'Aren't you afraid?' he demanded tersely. 'What of your precious innocence?'

'If you wish it, it is yours to take.' Her lips quivered as she spoke. He could feel her whole body trembling beneath his. She was afraid, but of what? That he might discover her lies? Or, as he made the final assault, would he discover that he was the one who had been wrong? He raised his head and stared down into the pale face and quivering lips. Into the eyes which had an almost unearthly glow.

'I want you,' he groaned, putting her from him. 'God knows how I want you. But I prefer the illusion. I have had too many shattered in the past. I shall not take you, Sapphira. No more will you take a lover. One day I shall cross this threshold which separates us, and then there will be truth between us. Until that day, you will know no other man if you value your worthless life.'

He spun away from her. The door slammed after his departing figure, and Sapphira fell back on the pillows, her cheeks wet with tears. Tears for the love she knew she must deny herself. Tears for the man who did not trust her enough to reach out and take the love she offered. Tears and more tears, until exhaustion claimed her and she fell into an uneasy sleep.

With her breakfast tray, which arrived next morning at eleven, were at least two dozen invitations. Parties, soirées, balls, hunting trips, visits to the theatre . . . Who had instigated this, she wondered, pushing them to one side and reaching for her hot coffee. The King, or her proved ability as a hostess? She had no interest in them, this morning. Her mind was still full of Quentin. He would never accept her. One day, when his need grew too great, or she angered him beyond reason, he would take what he considered his, but there would be no love, no gentleness, in it and neither of them would gain anything.

If she told him of her love, perhaps he might respond, she reasoned, but she knew that such action would only drive a deeper wedge between them. He could not trust —could not love.

Her maid, still excited about the unexpected visit of the King, chattered on while she ate breakfast, but Sapphira hardly noticed. So she was to lead her own life, was she? Then she would begin by accepting as many of the invitations scattered on the bed as possible. She would not remain in the house or in Quentin's presence a moment longer than was necessary. She needed the help of both Mrs Grayson and Wilcox to put some order into them. She would reply in person to them all, starting that evening, she decided.

'This one from Lady Winterbourne asks that you dine with her today.' Wilcox held out the last of the invitations.

'Today? That's impossible. It's almost noon now. Let me see it.'

The card had been written in a fancy scrawl, so unlike her own careful efforts. There were many things she need to improve, she thought, as she continued to read. 'Sapphira, Countess of Ravenswood, is requested to dine with Susanne, Lady Winterbourne, at one p.m. Together with Lord Courtney and his son, Blaise.'

'Perhaps I could,' she murmured, casting an eye at the clock. If Blaise and his father were present, she would not feel so awkward. She could not remember being introduced to anyone by the name of Winterbourne. Why not? She had to begin her new life without reservations. 'Yes, I shall go. Have a carriage ready for me in half an hour. I shall be back about three. I have a riding engagement.'

The carriage drew up before a fashionable house in a

quiet cul-de-sac near Whitehall. It had a high wall
surrounding it, making it completely private. Sapphira
was admitted by a liveried footman through a large front
door into a glass-panelled hall, which reflected not only
the light, but her image from every angle. Her face had
lost its thinness, she saw, momentarily allowing herself
a little self-indulgent vanity and it became her. Where,
oh, where, were Mollie and Lottie? She wanted so
much to share all this with them! Despite all her new
acquaintances, she felt very much alone.

From a high-backed chair before a fire rose a woman
whose face was vaguely familiar. It was several minutes
before she recognised her from the party, but they had
never been formally introduced. How blue her eyes
were, Sapphira thought. So like her own. Above the
woman's head, her gaze was drawn to a portrait. She
felt her senses quicken as she discovered that she was
looking at a picture of herself. Yet how could it be?
And yet how not! For, in the picture, the girl was young,
with hair of burnished gold which hung low about her
waist. And . . . round her neck! She caught her breath
in disbelief. Round her neck was the very same sapphire
pendant she herself had worn only a few hours before.

'Come, my child. Sit down. We must talk.' Sapphira
ignored the friendly invitation, stepping backwards
towards the door. 'Don't go. I did not mean it to happen
this way—so quickly, I mean. I thought we could talk
first . . .'

'What have we to say?' Sapphira's voice was harsh
with emotion. 'You abandoned me eighteen years ago,
and now you expect me to fall into your arms?'

'No. Listen to me. Forgive me, if you can. Do you
not think I have suffered.' No denial! What more proof
did she need that this woman was her mother? The
woman swayed unsteadily, and reached for the back of
the chair to steady herself. She looked so fragile that it
was all Sapphira could do not to step forward and help
her. 'I had no choice in what happened, believe me.

You were taken from me by my mother, when I was ill. I wanted to keep you. You were such a beautiful little thing. All red curls and dimples.'

'Your words are wasted on me.' Sapphira fought to remain adamant in her decision to shun her true mother who had done nothing for her in eighteen years; whereas Molly had kept her, clothed her, loved her. 'You brought me here under false pretences. I shall hear no more from you.'

'Will you listen to *me*, then?' Thomas Courtney stepped from another room, Blaise at his side. Lady Winterbourne gave a cry and sank back into the chair at her fingertips, near to fainting.

'Water, Blaise, quickly.' Thomas all but snatched the glass his son handed to him, and held it beneath her lips with a tenderness in his actions that made Sapphira's eyes darken with suspicion. Had she found her father, too! Her suspicions were confirmed as he turned to face her, and said quietly, 'If you choose to walk out of this room without hearing what I have to say, you are at liberty to do so, and I shall not reproach you. But I beseech you to listen to me—to us. We have sought you for many years, Sapphira, never believing we would find the daughter who was taken from us.'

'Stay.' Blaise came to her side. She saw that he looked somewhat strained, and wondered if this was as much a shock to him as it was to her. He nodded, indicating his own ignorance. 'I knew nothing of this until a few minutes ago. When he thought you might leave without hearing the truth, he blurted out everything. Now I know why I was so comfortable in your company . . . the company of my sister. Sit down, please, and listen. Then judge, if you still feel inclined to do so.'

Feeling as though she were experiencing some kind of dream, Sapphira allowed him to seat her on a chair. She was very pale, but determined to remain composed. Nothing anyone said could wipe away those years she had been in Molly's care, and that was all that mattered.

'What Lady Winterbourne—Susanne—has said, is the truth. You were taken from her without her consent. She was very ill. Dying, her mother thought, and so she took you from her side and gave you into the care of the Sisters of Mercy. Until that moment, Susanne had insisted on keeping you, despite all the objections foisted on her. I knew nothing of this.' For a moment, as he met his son's gaze, Thomas looked uneasy. Blaise stood behind Sapphira's chair in silence, waiting, as she was. 'Your mother was not herself, Blaise. Some called it madness. I don't know. After your birth, she changed completely. She had never wanted a child. She saw herself as a society hostess, glamorous, always in demand. A child required too much of her time.'

'She spent little enough with me,' Blaise's tone was bitter. 'I remember that much, even though I was only seven when she died. She never laughed. Never joined us whenever we were together. Never loved me. Did she, father?'

As Thomas shook his head, Sapphira found herself thinking how ironic it was that Lady Courtney and Quentin had not been born in the same time. How they would have suited each other!

'I met Susanne two years before your mother died. She was but twenty then. A shy thing, dominated by her mother, who was a widow. We met always in secret. We loved each other, but we were not lovers. She would not have it, while my wife—your mother, Blaise—still lived. Afterwards. We made plans, but her mother had already selected a husband. Susanne opposed her, and there was talk of her being sent abroad. We became lovers, and she bore my child.'

Susanne Winterbourne, huddled in the velvet chair, silent until now, reached out a thin white hand and clasped that of the man beside her. Sapphira saw his eyes warm to her gesture and felt envy. They loved each other still, after all those years! Two pairs of blue eyes locked, and Susanne patted the fingers closed over hers.

'I wanted you, Sapphira. He wanted you. We planned to be married as soon as I was well, but . . . I developed a fever . . . my mother took you from me. When my strength returned, she insisted I went to Europe with her, hoping I would soon agree to the husband of her choice, but I refused until the day she died. I tried so hard to find you. I went to the Sisters of Mercy the moment I discovered what she had done, but you had been given away. To a good couple, they told me, who would care for you.'

'And the pendant. Your thirty pieces of silver . . .'

Susanne gasped, and Thomas started forward towards Sapphira's chair, his face red with anger as he retorted, 'I gave your mother those sapphires. A token of my love. She put them round your neck on the one occasion she held you, before fever almost took her to her grave. It was her way of being close to me while she held you. Of me being with her. Are you so heartless, girl? Have you never known love?'

'Father,' Blaise intervened quietly. 'Sapphira has every right to reject you both. Has she not suffered in her life? Shall I tell you what the Black Horse is like? The men who frequent it?'

'No.' Sapphira wheeled on him, cheeks flaming. 'I owe them no explanation.'

'Nor they you.' Blaise interrupted in the same composed tone. She stared at him, and understood. Neither Thomas nor Susanne Winterbourne need have exposed their secret to her. Neither knew how she would receive the news. If she wished to expose it to eager ears, she knew she could destroy the frail woman facing her. She had dreamed of this moment. Of finding her true mother, and rejecting her with the same callousness as she believed she had been rejected so many years ago. But that was not the way of it. How could she not believe this trembling creature who clung so tightly to Thomas's hand? The desire for revenge, compensation for those years of hardship and poverty, melted away as she gazed into her mother's ashen face. She had a name. Sapphira, daughter of Lady Winterbourne and Lord Courtney. Her blood was pure. She was as high born as any of the ladies she had mixed with the night before. Blaise touched her arm. 'Can you not find it in your heart to forgive, Sapphira? For myself, I am pleased to have such a delightful sister.'

'You are not shocked?' she whispered.

'All men sow a few wild oats. Why should my father have been any different? Come, make your peace with them. Is it not time we were a family?'

She had a family—Molly and Lottie! When would she find them? She fought and lost against the tumult of emotion which overwhelmed her. With tears in her eyes, she jumped from her chair and ran to her mother. As the painfully thin arms enfolded her and Thomas looked on, smiling, she felt as if she had betrayed them. Her tears were as much for their loss as for the parents she had found. Bitter tears which made Blaise frown as he watched her.

'I question the pain and misery you have both resurrected for yourselves,' he said, and Susanne looked across at him, tears swimming.

'Not pain. Joy at finding our daughter.' She touched the loose hair hanging past Sapphira's shoulders. She had come out in such a hurry that there had been no time to have it dressed. 'Do you hate me, Sapphira? Can you forgive this tired old woman who loves you? Has always loved you?'

Old? Yes, she looked old, but she could not be more than forty, Sapphira calculated. The years had treated both of them harshly. She lowered her gaze and found herself staring at the diamond ring on her finger, the emerald bracelet on her wrist. Her nails were clean and well manicured, her hands unblemished by cuts or burns, as they had often been before. She wore clothes in the latest fashion, rode in a carriage bearing her husband's coat-of-arms and drawn by two fine black horses. She had found favour in the eyes of the King of England and was shortly to be presented at Court. She no longer slept in a draughty attic, her stomach growling with hunger in the night, but in a comfortable bed, on a feather mattress, her stomach full of food. And when she awoke, there was a maid to attend to her every need. She had neither fears nor worries.

And now, in one short hour, she had found a mother and a father—and a brother!

'Blaise!' She looked round at him, seeking help—guidance—and he came to her and placed his arms about her shoulders, drawing her back to her chair. It was easy to understand now why it was so natural for them to come together as friends.

'You have a very distinguished heritage, you know.' His face broke into a boyish grin. 'The Courtneys can trace their ancestors back to the Knights of Saint John. Courtney men have always been fighters.'

He had taken the shock better than she had, she thought in admiration. She was more shaken than she would admit, and in a far different way from what she had expected. There was no hate in her, no malice or words of retribution to pour down on her mother's head. A scandal would kill her!

'Alas, I can offer you nothing more exciting than my great-grandmother, who was one of Queen Elizabeth's ladies-in-waiting,' Susanne said. She sat forward in her chair, her body as taut as a bow-string. 'I want to acknowledge you as my daughter, Sapphira. Make you my legal heir.'

'No! I forbid it,' Thomas intervened. 'Do you want to kill yourself, woman? By all means acknowledge her on paper, but not in public. You would be ostracised! Sapphira, I demand your word that what you have discovered will go no further?'

'Are you so ashamed of her, my dear? Last night you told me how proud you were of her.'

'Please, there is no need for any of this,' Sapphira

said. 'I have everything I want. I am content for things to remain as they are. You have my word, Lord Courtney, if it is so important to you.'

Was she? Could she continue with her life as if this day had never happened?

'But I want you to come and live here with me,' Susanne replied. 'There is no need for you to continue with that hateful bargain you made with Quentin Tyrell. You could be free of him.'

'How did you know about that?' Sapphira gasped, growing pale. 'Is it common knowledge?'

'Corinna has made no secret of it,' Blaise answered. 'Last night she intended Lady Castlemaine to persuade the King to snub you on some pretext or other, but he took a fancy to you instead. Don't look so alarmed! I do not think he will pursue you. He and Quentin have fought side by side in the field, and there is a bond between them that many envy. Sometimes I think Charles knows more about him, from those days in France, than anyone.'

Remembering the strangeness of the King's words to her husband the night before, Sapphira suspected he was right. Somewhere in the dark, distant past lay the secret of his bitterness. Would she ever discover what it was?

'Lady Winterbourne is right, you know,' Blaise continued. 'Why live with Quentin when you could live here? You have told me that things are not right between you. Surely this is a way out?'

'You are his friend, Blaise. The only close friend I think he has. You know why.' Sapphira was surprised by his words. 'To leave him now would mean that everything reverts to Corinna. Why, I do not know. I am not in his confidence.'

'During his absence, when he left to fight at the King's side, Ravenswood was taken over by one of Cromwell's officers. His men were billeted in the near by village. They raised hell, apparently. When Lady Ravenswood,

Quentin's mother, tried to reason with the man, he had her confined to the house and then took Corinna as his mistress.'

'Quentin cannot hold her responsible for that!' Sapphira gasped.

'Perhaps I should have said that Corinna took the Major as her lover. She gave no thought to anyone. Her mother was a virtual prisoner until she fell ill and died. The villagers were abused, starved, the women molested, crops stolen from the fields. Yet she lived in comfort at Ravenswood with her protector. I know very few of the details—this all came from Quentin one night when he was very drunk. He came home to find his mother dead, the village barely surviving, and his sister's name hated by everyone who drew breath. He is only now, after all these years, succeeding in his attempts to put the place back on its feet. He has had the schoolhouse rebuilt and made additions to the church. He has given the villagers money from his own purse to remake their lives, and they love him for it. But Corinna—I fear that if she ever returned to Ravenswood, some harm would befall her, such is their hatred and contempt for her. The war had broken Quentin's father. He lived on for a year after their return to England. During that time Corinna nursed him like an angel, he told me, until the old man really began to believe that the things he had heard about her were not true. He had threatened to shut her away in a convent after his death. She was terrified of that. I don't know what prompted his father to make such an odd will—Quentin never told me. Something must have happened between them while they were away. Whatever it is, he never speaks of it. Anyway, everything was left to him, but on condition he was married by his thirty-second birthday and remained that way for at least one year afterwards. If not, Corinna inherits everything. And, believe me, she would do anything to turn the tide in her favour.'

'Poor Quentin! Every hand turned against him.'

'Except yours,' Blaise murmured, and a smile lit up her pale features. 'You love him, don't you?'

'Yes.'

'He is a very lucky man. I hope that, in time, he learns to appreciate what is being offered to him.'

It was late in the afternoon before Blaise escorted Sapphira home. After dinner they had sat and talked, and the time had flown quickly. Their riding engagement was postponed until the following day. She had promised to visit Susanne again, too, and go to the shops with her.

Blaise helped her to alight. Holding tightly to her hand, he smiled at her. 'You look tired, little sister.'

'How nice that sounds. Oh, Blaise, I thought I would hate her. I wanted to, but I couldn't. She is so frail. I liked her—pitied her. Oh dear, I am so confused. I don't know what to do any more.'

'Allow things to happen in their own good time.' Blaise bent and kissed her on the cheek. 'Until tomorrow.'

No sooner had Sapphira entered the house than Quentin came out of his study, his face dark with suspicion.

'Where have you been?' he demanded, and she paused at the bottom of the staircase and looked at him in surprise. She had been wondering how best to tell him her news, but now all thought of doing so vanished from her mind. Why did he look so angry?

'Visiting friends. Lady Winterbourne. Do you know her?'

'We have met. And Blaise just happened to be there too?'

'No. Both Blaise and his father were also invited to dine with her. Have you any objections?'

'Your maid has laid out your riding-habit. Who are you going out with now?' Quentin snapped, his eyes narrowing. He had been watching the two of them from the window, and the sight of Blaise kissing her had made his blood boil. The one person he thought he could trust. She had ensnared him easily! How many assignations had she made last night? It was happening a second time! He would kill her if she took a lover!

He had planned to take her to the theatre with him that evening as a surprise. Her face was flushed with excitement and her eyes were brighter than he had ever seen them. What had happened to make her look so content? The successful conquest of his best friend?

'I was going to ride with Blaise. We made the arrangement last night, but I am too tired,' Sapphira replied, remaining calm before the fury she could see rising in him. 'I do not know what has angered you so. Am I not doing what you want—leading my own life, with friends of my own making?'

'Leave Blaise alone,' Quentin thundered, and her eyes widened as she suddenly understood. Jealousy? Impossible! Resentment, perhaps that she had found someone sympathetic and understanding, who did not treat her like an adventuress.

'He is a friend. I like his company.' How easily she could have dispelled his suspicions. The urge to do so was very great indeed, but the sight of his glittering eyes deterred her from blurting out the truth. Was there nothing she could do to please him? After last night, she had begun to think that their relationship might take a turn for the better, but his attitude made that impossible. She left him without another word and went to her room. That night she ate her supper alone.

Quentin took Margaret to the theatre in her stead, and did not return to the house until the following morning. He never told her he had found Molly and Lottie.

CHAPTER
EIGHT

THE FOLLOWING week Quentin formally presented Sapphira to the King and Queen at Court. By then, she had grown accustomed to the stares and whispers and ignored them. Despite Margaret's presence, for the whole evening, which included a firework display after dark and a trip in barges down the River Thames, Quentin remained constantly by her side, seemingly the most devoted and attentive of husbands. She enjoyed the moment for what it was—a proud, defiant gesture on his part to still the tongues of those who still continued to gossip about them, knowing that on the morrow he would go his own way again—to Margaret.

As she would go hers, to her mother and Blaise, who accompanied her everywhere when Quentin declined to join her. She knew her husband disapproved of the relationship, suspecting the worst about her. Had he spoken one kind word to her in the weeks which followed, or broached the subject in a friendly manner, she might have regretted the promise made that afternoon and confessed the truth to him, but, if anything, he sought to avoid her company, or so it seemed. They rarely ate together, and as spring came and went and sunny days heralded the approach of a welcoming hot summer after the bitter cold of winter, they were as strangers. She was seen by his side at all Court functions, often with him at the theatre, but their outward show of a contented couple was for the benefit of those who watched. In the house, there was little or no conversation between them. Without Susanne's company and that of Blaise, it would have been an unhappy, lonely existence.

Her friendship with Margaret remained steadfast, and often they went to the shops together further to confound the sceptics and it was a pleasure to have her to the house for the occasional dinner, for it meant that Quentin would remain at home. He was polite, but painfully distant, letting her know by the narrowed gaze of those glittering eyes of his, how much he disapproved of her new interests and companions. Her circle of acquaintances was not his. Most of Susanne's friends were intellectuals: writers, judges, lawyers. At first she had thought them uninteresting, then, as she grew to appreciate their worldliness and wisdom, her young mind, eager to learn, acknowledged that there was more to be discovered from such people than from bewigged Cavaliers and their fancy women. Never once did she suspect how memories from the past rose up to haunt him whenever he was with her, and returned as nightmares to plague his sleep. Black moods overshadowed him.

He and Blaise frequented the same taverns together, for the fact he had taken a wife in no way changed his mode of living. Which was how he had intended it should be. But there were times when he found himself staring at the younger man, and the dark thoughts which crept into his mind were not pleasant. The image of Sapphira lying in his arms had begun to haunt him, yet, when questioned, Blaise made their relationship sound purely one of friendship. But it would not go away. He could not forget the effect she had had on him that night he had held her in the arbour. She had been willing then —with him. Why not with Blaise, younger, handsome, a more fit companion for an eighteen-year-old girl than a man nearly twice her age? It would not be the first time a wife had been stolen from him. No—she had given herself before—and revelled in her affairs. She had been young, too—the same age as Sapphira, when he had married her in France . . .

* * *

It was inevitable that gossip should reach him, but he, too, chose to ignore it. He had made a bargain with Sapphira, yet it was no longer to his liking. He had developed a possessiveness towards her that greatly alarmed him. Jealousy was no stranger to him, but he had thought that the earlier time had made him immune to pain. A careless word spoken within his hearing sent him reaching for his sword. The following morning, an hour after dawn, he severely wounded the blustering offender, and knew he could still be hurt. There was only one way to prevent more, and his course of action was decided on that very same morning.

Sapphira was appalled when she heard of the incident from Blaise. They were riding, as they always did, in the countryside round the Royal Hunting Grounds.

'He had said nothing to me,' she gasped, turning pale. 'He could have been killed!'

'Quentin is an excellent swordsman. I was his pupil once. That's how we became friends. We were enemies when we first met, thanks to Corinna. She had told me some dreadful stories about him and, having seen some of his black moods, I believed her. Besides, I had fallen in love with the girl. I was blind then to what she was.' Blaise smiled at her, but there was a new bitterness in his voice.

'I didn't know,' she said softly, and reached across from her horse to lay her hand over his. 'Are you still in love with her?'

'Unfortunately, yes. She throws me a few favours sometimes—her company or her bed—but I can no longer believe that I am the only man in her life. There must have been dozens, the poor ignorant fools. She used them all as she did me.'

'Don't,' Sapphira entreated. 'You sound like Quentin. Somewhere there is a woman who will love you, Blaise. The right woman.'

'Perhaps. How is Quentin treating you now? I saw

you together at Lady Hampton's little soirée last week, and he seemed quite attentive.'

'That is an act, nothing more. I hardly see him unless we have to go out together. He spends more time with Margaret than with me. Once, I thought . . . It's silly, I know, but on one occasion he was even annoyed because I had been out with you! I could stand his jealousy, Blaise, even thought he has no cause for it, but not his coldness. There is a high wall between us. There is no door through which I might gain entry to him, and no ladder tall enough to scale it. Yet, sometimes, I feel him watching me. He wants me, I know he does . . .' She blushed and looked away, from him. 'I delude myself. Lust is not love, and he will never give me that. It is not in him.'

'Perhaps we should not see each other so often,' Blaise suggested. 'He is my friend, and I do not want him to think ill of me, although when we are drinking together he has said nothing, nor shown he disapproves of our friendship.'

'I want so much to tell him, but it would make little difference to his attitude, I am sure. I think some woman must have hurt him very much. At first I thought it was Corinna, but not now. Buried deep inside him is terrible, terrible, pain. I can sense it.'

'The pain of rejection? Or of the loss of the only woman he has ever loved?' Blaise asked.

Sapphira had not considered that alternative, nor did she want to. To accept that Quentin had once been in love, and then suffered the loss of the most precious thing in the world to him, spelled doom for her own love and the hope that one day he might turn to her and accept her as his wife. For a man of his complex character, there could never be a replacement!

'Isn't that Sapphira over there?' Corinna had a small pair of ivory-handled opera glasses trained on one of the opposite boxes. 'Lady Winterbourne, too, and Lord

Courtney. Those two are spending a lot of time together. Susanne looks positively radiant these days. Cupid does shoot his little arrows at some strange targets.'

The group around her sniggered. One or two of the more daring ones turned to cast amused looks in the direction of the next box, where Quentin sat with Margaret markedly ignoring the presence of his sister. Corinna's voice had deliberately been loud enough to reach him—and much further. Quentin's mouth tightened visibly as heads turned upwards to gaze at his wife and her companions. Beside him, Margaret lifted her hand and waved to the glittering figure in cloth of silver, her hair swept high on to the crown of her head.

'Dammit,' he said in a harsh whisper. 'Must you acknowledge them?'

'Do you want everyone to think you did not know she was coming here tonight?' Margaret did not even look at him as she answered. 'You said Sapphira had a headache, when you asked me to accompany you. She does look remarkably well!'

Another man joined the party in the box. Sapphira turned and smiled as he seated himself beside her, and Quentin's eyes glittered with a dangerous light. He had not even spoken to his wife all that day. She had been in bed when he went riding that morning and in her bath when he returned home to change for the theatre. The thought of taking her had crossed his mind. The sight of them together as soon after the duel might still wagging tongues, but when he had entered her bedroom and seen the evening clothes all ready laid out for her to wear, he knew she had another engagement. It would certainly be her last, he thought, as he turned away unseen. He had allowed her too much freedom, repeating the same mistake as before. Tomorrow the axe would descend on her pretty neck.

It should have been different with Sapphira. He did not love her. It should not have mattered what she was or how she occupied her time, but it did. There was only one way to exorcise the ghost which haunted him. This time, what was his he would keep.

He shut his ears to the laughter and innuendos being uttered a few feet away, and concentrated on the play about to begin. It was a drama by William Shakespeare, badly acted by a group of motley individuals who forgot their lines, evoked roars of laughter from the audience when none should have been forthcoming, and were booed off the stage on more than one occasion by rough-shod customers in the galleries. He was relieved when it ended.

He had not looked in Sapphira's direction all through the last act. The sight of her sitting so close to Blaise that their bodies were almost touching heightened the malice in him, the desire to teach her a lesson which would serve as a reminder of how she should act in the future. She was a constant visitor to the Winterbourne house. How many times had she met Blaise there? Remained with him unchaperoned? Were they lovers? He would kill them both if he discovered that they were.

He straightened in his chair as people rose to leave, often jostling in the aisles in bunches, chatting before they went off to eat somewhere, and his stare intensified. Neither Sapphira nor Blaise was in the box, only Susanne and Thomas.

'They left half an hour before the play ended,' Margaret told him quietly. 'Didn't you notice? Where are you going?'

She started up as he sprang to his feet and turned away from her.

'Where do you think?'

'Don't be a fool, Quentin. They could be anywhere. For heaven's sake, you don't think . . .'

'Yes, I do,' he snapped. His manner alarmed her, and she stepped back, a hand against her throat. 'Don't ever call me a fool again, Margaret.' He looked at her as he spoke as though she were a stranger, and then turned and left her. Corinna made some remark about her brother being so infatuated with his wife that he had to have both her and his mistress with him whenever he went out. Margaret did not follow him. He was past listening to reason. If he returned to the house and found Sapphira and Blaise together, she knew he would kill one or both of them. He was indeed a fool, she mused. He was in love with his wife, and he did not even know it!

Sapphira did not hear the door of her bedroom open. Silently Quentin entered the room, came to the foot of the bed and stood looking down at her. Alone! The house had been in darkness. She had sent the servants to bed. He had climbed the stairs, his hand on his sword, preparing himself for the return of his nightmare—the sight of his young wife naked in the arms of another man, whispering the same words of love as she had poured into his ear. Lies! Deceit! Treachery! Death! The terrible pattern was about to be repeated. But Sapphira was alone, except for the spaniel curled at her feet.

A single candle, which she had forgotten to extinguish, burned on a table beside the bed, throwing a soft glow across her body. It was a warm night, and she had unknowingly pushed away the covers. As she moved in her sleep, he saw the outline of thigh and firm swelling breasts beneath the thin silk of her nightgown, tempting him to reach out and take what was his by right. Not since France had he desired a woman so intensely, and never less in control of his emotions!

Her loose hair was spread across the pillow, a few reddish curls against a damp cheek. How peaceful she looked—how innocent! And then he remembered how she had smiled at Blaise, the air of intimacy always between them as though they shared some secret. Memories of Lucy obliterated Sapphira's features. The hair became raven black, the childish, often petulant, features mocking his hesitance to join her on the bed as she stretched languidly, arching her body invitingly towards him.

With a groan he stumbled out of the room and went down to his study to shut out memories old and new somewhere in the depths of a bottle.

Sapphira had left the theatre early, plagued by a throbbing headache that had begun not long after she saw Quentin and Margaret in the opposite box. Corinna's shrill laughter told her she was being discussed. She had wanted to leave immediately, but Susanne had reminded her how odd it would look if the did so. An admission that the rumours linking her to Blaise were not to be lightly dismissed. Quentin had already condemned her, by not acknowledging her presence, she thought miserably. She cared nothing for what anyone else thought of her, only he.

She would tell him the truth in the morning. She had no other choice, she decided. The situation was unbearable. Her relationship with Blaise was driving a wedge between two men who had been good friends for years. Quentin had to be made to accept how misguided he was in his suspicions. His moods were growing worse. The atmosphere in the house was as intolerable for the servants as for her. Most of them were afraid to approach him when he had been drinking—and this he seemed to be doing much more over the past weeks— lest he snap their heads off for simply asking if he would be in for dinner. They turned to Sapphira in all matters, and that, too, served to increase his bad temper. He rarely spoke a civil word to anyone. She wondered if he was different with Margaret.

Her rest was erratic, troubled by dreams. Molly and Lottie haunted her constantly. On the one occasion when she had dared ask Quentin if there was any news, he had curtly told her that there was not. She went repeatedly to the Black Horse, without his knowledge, to question Silas time and time again, with no success, and she had come to accept the painful fact that he did not know where they were. They were lost to her. A pouch of guineas was no payment for the love she had been given by them both. Did they believe she had abandoned them? Or, as she had previously suspected, had they taken themselves out of her life because of her new status?

She dreamed of Quentin. There was rarely a night when she did not. Always they were together beneath the arbour. One day he might take her in his arms, with warmth in his eyes, gentleness in his embrace, and she would tell him that her only desire was to be his wife and make him happy.

Below, in his study, Quentin drank continuously, unable to dispel the image of her from his mind. Yet sometimes it was not Sapphira, but the ghost of his dead wife, which rose before his eyes to torment him. In time the two became as one. Two hours later, when he returned to her room, although not drunk, he was in a dangerous mood. Drink had blinded him to everything but his desire for Sapphira. The need to satisfy the hunger that had burned in his breast since that night at the inn when he had clumsily, drunkenly, attempted to make love to her. Tonight he was able to acknowledge it for the first time, because tonight he was going to prove to himself, once and for all, that she was as tarnished as any whore selling herself in the streets. Tonight there would be no interruptions.

Sapphira awoke with a start as the dog at her feet growled a warning to the shadowy figure who had reappeared to disturb its sleep a second time. She was surprised, but not unduly worried, to see Quentin in the doorway, although she had not expected a reprimand until the morning, when he would curse at her for being so thoughtless as to appear in public in the same place as he was with his mistress. It would be her fault, of course. He could do no wrong! How she wished he had not disturbed her, she thought, sleepily sitting up. Her head still ached maddeningly. Without a word,

Quentin scooped the dog up into his arms, carried it to the door and dropped it in the passage. Sapphira came bolt upright, an uneasy feeling stealing through her as he closed and locked the door after it.

'What do you want?' she demanded. What had brought him back to the house so early? He rarely left Margaret until the next morning. On one occasion she could remember him not coming home for the best part of a week.

He advanced to the bed and in the candlelight as she saw the glitter in his eyes, she knew the answer to her question and it instilled a new quality of fear in her. His gaze devoured her. Never had he looked at her this way. His gait was unsteady and she drew back, alarm registering on her face, now pale and set.

'You are drunk!'

'I have been drinking, but I am in full control of my faculties,' Quentin said, and her eyes widened in horror as he began to undress. 'I want to remember having you.'

Sapphira gasped at the insult. It was the way he might have spoken to a whore! This could not happen. She had to tell him the truth now. She grabbed up the bedcovers and covered herself, but he snatched them away from her again with a low chuckle that made her shiver. She drew herself back against the pillows, her heart beginning to beat so loudly that she was sure he must hear it. If he sensed the fear in her, she would be lost.

What had been said to him to turn him into this crazed madman, determined to destroy her? What had Corinna whispered to him tonight—or in the days past? It had to be his sister who had made this sore in him fester until he could stand it no longer. She had turned a friendship between brother and sister into a sordid affair. He believed she was Blaise's mistress. She saw the accusation written on his face as he stripped of the last of his clothes.

'Our bargain . . .' she whispered. It was not what she had meant to say. She found herself staring at several thin white scars which ran from one shoulder to disappear into the labyrinth of dark hair covering the muscled chest.

'I have decided to end it!'

'Quentin, you don't know what you are saying! You have been drinking. Please, let me speak.' She stretched out a hand towards him, pleading. She was not to know that someone else had acted in such a fashion many years before. The sight of her doing so sickened him, and once again two women merged into one and, in doing so, committed Quentin to his chosen act of destruction.

'I want no lies, wench.' She knew that when he addressed her in this fashion she was once again the object of his contempt and derision. 'I have done with lies and weakness, and you shall not cuckold me again.'

'I have not . . .' She tried to scramble out of bed in a mad panic, but he grabbed her roughly and threw himself down beside her, one firm leg thrust across her body, effectively pinning her

'Not this time, my beauty. This time you will not run away. There is no audience to applaud our performance, but you will have to grow used to that. You and I shall be spending a great deal of time together—alone! Blaise is a boy— I am a man, and you belong to me! You will not betray me as you did before!'

What did he mean? It was as though he thought she were another woman! As if he were somewhere else!

Quentin caught her loose hair, roughly dragging back her head, seeking her mouth with lips of fire. Sapphira cried out in anger and outrage, to think that he was using her to satiate some desire for some unknown female from the past. She pummelled at his face until he, with an oath, coupled her wrists with his free hand and held them fast above her head.

'You are drunk! Mad!' she gasped, wincing as he

released her hair and his hand searched her body with almost feverish caresses. She tried to turn her face away, but he forced it back, devouring her lips like a man possessed. 'If you take me like this, I shall never forgive you. Quentin, you have been listening to lies! Blaise and I . . .'

'I am of the opinion you have too much time on your hands,' he growled, and she felt her nightgown rip as she continued to struggle against his efforts to subdue her. The agonising hold on her wrists brought tears to her eyes and she felt her strength begin to ebb. She could not—would not—submit to this indignity! 'What you need is a child to occupy your days.'

The thin thread of Sapphira's self-control snapped at his brutal words. The weeks of trying to please him, of conducting herself as a lady, not a tavern girl. The insults of his friends, the gossip at Court, Corinna and her contempt. And now this: her own husband, driven by motives she could not comprehend, was bent on mastering her with no more consideration than he would break a wild horse.

Turning her head, she fastened her teeth in his arm and bit with all her might. Quentin swore and momentarily rolled away from her. She seized the opportunity to spring from the bed. Sobbing, she stumbled blindly in the direction of the door, but her toe caught on the bedclothes tumbled in a heap on the floor, and she fell to her knees.

He was upon her before she could rise, flinging her down upon them, the weight of his body crushing her beneath him. She struck out at him weakly as the nightgown was ripped away. His searching hands made her moan in terror.

'Is that how you treated your amorous customers at the tavern, wench?' Quentin's lips whispered against her ear. Slowly they continued down, bruising the soft, unprotected skin. 'You will be well paid for your time if I am satisfied with you. Come, now, don't lie there as stiff as a corpse. Did your other lovers teach you nothing?' He flung the insults at her like a man demented, incensed beyond reason by her attempts to throw him off. He was asking no more than she had been willing to give others before him.

'You are wrong. There was no one—there is no one.' Sapphira tried again to reason with him, but her words were choked back by the ruthless pressure of his mouth.

She felt suffocated by the hard, lean body pressing down on her. Her senses began to fade. Pain suddenly seared through her, bringing her back to reality. She screamed, but had no strength left to push him from her. She thought she heard him swear—just once—with great vehemence, but in her horror and confusion she was sure of nothing except the assault on her body.

'You damned witch!' Quentin's voice was unsteady. 'You will haunt me no more.'

The pain returned, and a smothered moan broke from beneath his lips. He was suddenly still, and she lay dazed, listening to the sound of his rapid breathing.

'Sapphira.' She heard him whisper her name as though from a long way off. 'I am king of fools this night.'

The hands which began to move over her again were no longer rough, determined to subject her to his will, but gentle, at times teasing, rousing in her a sensation she had never before experienced. How could she lie here and enjoy his touch, she wondered in bewilderment? But she had no strength to do otherwise, and the fire which consumed her did so quickly and without warning.

She awoke to the touch of his hands on her body again and was ashamed at how swiftly he succeeded in rousing passion in her. She had never known such an ecstasy, and in the arms of the man she loved she could not control it. Surely she must have given herself away? When he drew away from her and began to dress, she lay drowsily watching him, content, and with new hope in her for the days ahead. He had taken her in anger, yet afterwards he had been kind, and she had glimpsed another side of her mood-ridden husband. How she loved him, despite the way he had abused her!

'Quentin, will you listen to me now,' she murmured.

He turned and stared down at her, curled beneath the sheets like a sleepy kitten, and she recoiled at the coldness in his eyes. Was this the same man who had cradled her in his arms, soothed her fears, caressed her bruised skin with velvet fingers? He knew now that no other man had touched her before him. Why did he not acknowledge the fact, and apologise for the attack on her which had amounted to nothing less than rape! A cold fear settled over her, and the brief moment of happiness that she had known suddenly vanished and might not have been. He had been making love to her, or to the woman whose name he had called out in his sleep after he drew away from her? She used the only weapon at her disposal with which to fight him—hostility.

'You do not seem over satisfied with your conquest, sir. Were you disappointed not to find the whore you sought? Or were you seeking to lose yourself still in the arms of a ghost?'

Quentin stared at her, but she saw by the tightness of his mouth that she had touched a nerve. 'I do not understand you, wench.'

'Did you make love to me? Or to her?' She drew herself up in the bed, her expression scornful. The eyes blazed blue fire at him. She had every reason to feel outraged, he thought, and he had no excuses with which to defend himself. He had come to her seeking to destroy the image of innocence she presented, to confront her with the lie, and thus bring her to heel—and, in the midst of achieving his aim, Lucy had taken her place in his arms, only to vanish again as his mastery of Sapphira was complete. He had exorcised his demon and in doing so had been forced to acknowledge that his wife had not lied. Until he had laid claim to her by force, she had been a virgin!

'Her name was Lucy, was it not?'

He flinched as though she had struck him. He had no recollection of anything after he had carried her back to bed, and climbed in beside her, until he awoke to find that he was still holding her in his arms and her nearness roused him to take her again.

'You reproach me for a harmless friendship, while you degrade me by flaunting your mistress in my face and are still obsessed with this other woman. It was you who broke our bargain, sir. You, who changed the rules of the game.'

'You and I play no games any longer,' Quentin said heavily. He was angry that he had allowed his feelings to get out of hand. Angry too, that she had misunderstood what had happened between them, yet he knew she could not be blamed for that. The stricken look on her lovely face told him that he had hurt her deeply, and with more than just the roughness of his caresses, the domination of his body. She expected an apology, he realised, and rightly, but the words he wanted so much to say would not pass his tight lips. For the first time since Lucy had died, and his world had died with her, and truth and love had become despised words to him, he despised himself, knowing he was in the wrong. He had deliberately, cruelly, asserted his rights on an innocent child, not deserving of his contempt.

'How you must have loved her,' Sapphira said, misinterpreting his silence.

'Love! Perhaps—once. Before I discovered what a treacherous bitch she was. I was young then—young enough to have dreams—to trust!' His voice grew harsh with bitterness. 'She destroyed every spark of decency in me, as I proved to you last night. Before her there was no one, but—by God—there have been many since!'

'Yet you love her still!' Sapphira fell back on the pillows, drained, defeated. She could not fight a ghost. All this time, when she had seen him looking at her and believed that he wanted her, he had been seeing another woman. He had fought and lost the battle within him to contain the desires which still raged inside him.

'She killed my love long before she died.' His tone became flat, without emotion. 'Last night I finally laid her to rest.'

'You talk in riddles.' She passed a trembling hand across her eyes. As she did so, she noticed for the first time the dark bruises beginning to show on her wrists and arms. The urge to wound him as deeply as he had her seized control of her.

'Your friends will be amused when you tell them it was necessary to take me by force. From the many invitations I received from them, they thought me an easy conquest.'

'You should not have fought me.' Quentin, too, saw the marks he had inflicted, and a flush of deep colour stole into his cheeks, although she saw not one flicker of regret in his eyes. Was there no remorse in him? How could any man be so totally without pity?

'Perhaps I would not, had you not lunged at me like a wild animal. Now your curiosity is satisfied . . .'

'You don't understand,' he interrupted in a harsh whisper. 'I had reason for the way I acted . . .'

'My friendship with Blaise? No, that was an excuse,' Sapphira flung back scornfully. 'You were drunk . . .'

'No. Driven by forces I did not understand . . . could not control . . .' He broke off with an oath. 'Dammit, wench. I don't have to explain myself to you. You are mine to take whenever it suits me. Remember that.'

'Go away and leave me in peace. I have nothing more to offer you.' He could not mean that he intended this new relationship to continue? She could not bear that thought. To lie in his arms, subjected to kisses and caresses which must eventually wrench from her the secret she had held back from him for so long.

Quentin turned to the door, but then he paused and looked back to the lonely little figure in the enormous bed, clutching the bedcovers about her as if afraid he might return and rip them from her grasp as he had done last night. She would never forgive him. He would never forgive himself—but she was in his blood now, and he had known the wonder of her body. She would remain his. Whatever he had to do to keep her, he would not let her go.

'Last night has made that impossible.'

With a tiny cry Sapphira buried her face in her hands. When she looked up again, she was alone.

'What is the matter, Betty? You are all fingers and thumbs this morning,' Sapphira asked, as her maid spilled most of the coffee she was pouring into the saucer instead of the cup. She had quickly slipped out of bed the moment Quentin left her, and put on a fresh nightdress and a loose wrap which covered the tell-tale marks. The torn nightgown had been pushed away at the bottom of a closet. 'Are you in love?'

'No, my lady, I wish I were. I'd have my man take me away from here tomorrow if I were.'

'Then you are not in any trouble? You can safely tell me if you are,' Sapphira assured her. Her manner was strange. Usually she was a happy, friendly, girl, but this morning she appeared nervous and clumsy.

'Oh, no, it's nothing like that. It's worse! There's plague in the city, my lady. Maisie came back from the market full of the news. Half the houses in Bethnel Street are marked with red crosses, and someone said that three houses in Drury Lane were marked last week. Now there's more!'

Sapphira felt her heart grow cold. Drury Lane, where the most fashionable theatres were. She and Quentin had been there the week before. Yet more terrible than

that thought was the realisation that Bethnel Street ran
alongside the waterfront where the Black Horse was
situated. If Molly and Lottie were in that area still . . .
Plague! She had never seen it at first hand, only heard
stories of the death and destruction it cast across whole
countries. No one was safe from the disease that could
cause death within five or six days. If the patient lingered
on for ten or eleven days, recovery was probable, but
not many did.

'The master mentioned to Wilcox that, if it spreads,
the house will be shut up and we shall all go to
Ravenswood.'

He would have to tie her hand and foot to get her
there, Sapphira thought, scrambling out of bed. Plague
or no, she was going to spend the day searching that
area. She would find out something, even if she had to
bribe every man and woman she spoke to.

'My lady, you haven't finished your toast.'

'Take it away, Betty, I have to go out. I have friends
who might be living quite near to Bethnel Street. I must
find them. Come back quickly to help me dress. And
tell Stevens I shall require the carriage.'

Half an hour later as she descended the stairs, Quentin came out of the sitting-room and deliberately
blocked her path to the door.

'Are you going out? May I ask where?'

She flushed beneath his searching gaze. Surely he did
not still believe she was having an affair with Blaise?
This was the first time he had demanded to know her
comings and goings.

'To see friends.'

'Susanne Winterbourne? You spend more time in her
house than you do here, and she has made no secret of
the fact she considers me a most unsuitable husband for
you. Are you going to tell her what a brute you have
for a husband? Perhaps she will send for Blaise to come
and comfort you, as he no doubt has done in the past.
Do you think me a fool, girl? You may not yet have

slept with him, but, with Susanne's help, you will.'

'Are you jealous that I prefer his company to yours?' Sapphira flung back her head and stared defiantly into the burning eyes. 'He is gentle and kind and I enjoy his company. He—he is like a brother to me.'

'Brotherly love is not something Blaise could feel for someone as lovely as you. I forbid you to go out. Besides, have you not heard that there is plague in the city? Until we know to what extent, it is wiser to remain indoors.'

'I had forgotten. I must remain healthy for one full year of our marriage, must I not?'

'Do not anger me further, wench,' Quentin growled. 'You will do as I say, or . . .'

'Or what? Will you use force on me as you did last night? Why should you care? Force is all you know.'

'That is not true, dammit!'

'I think it is.' She was very calm. She knew what she had to do, and she was going to do it, 'I am not going to see Susanne. Nor Blaise, although had I asked for his help, I know I should not have to search for them myself. He would have cared enough to help me.'

'What do you mean? Who?'

'Molly and Lottie. You never intended to find them, did you? I am sufficient complication in your life—you did not want two poor relatives to care for. People might have begun to believe that Quentin Tyrell had a heart, and that would never do, would it? You do not have one. You use people, and then discard them with a few guineas' compensation if they are lucky.'

'Enough,' Quentin thundered. He grabbed her by the shoulders and shook her savagely. 'You know nothing about me, do you hear? Nothing! By God, it's time I forced those pretty adjectives back down your throat.'

She stood rubbing her arms in a startled silence as he wheeled about and tugged at the bell-rope beside the fireplace. Wilcox appeared immediately.

'The carriage is ready?' Quentin demanded.

'Yes, my lord.'

'I shall be accompanying her ladyship. I don't know when we shall return.' Purposefully he took Sapphira by the arm, ignoring her questioning look.

'Where are we going?' she protested, as she was ushered none too gently out of the room. A wild hope was rising inside her. She looked up into the satanic features, seeking confirmation. Was it possible? He knew where they were! He had known all the time, and had said nothing!

As they reached the carriage, he waved away the hovering servant, helping her inside himself, and said grimly, 'Where do you think?'

She sank back into her seat, beginning to tremble. Why had he said nothing? He knew how unhappy she had been, unable to reassure herself that they were safe and well.

'I think I hate you,' she whispered. 'You are an inhuman devil.'

A smile deepened the sardonic twist to his mouth as he looked across at her. 'You do not know the meaning of the word, child.' His voice was almost gentle and yet still mocking. 'I pray you never may. I would not care to look into your face one day and see an image of myself.'

'One day?' Sapphira echoed, and in the bright sunshine he saw the sudden pallor which crept into her cheeks. 'You will have to bear the sight of me only a short while longer, sir. Then you will be free of me.'

'No.' The single word sealed her fate. She knew exactly what he meant, even before he added quietly, 'I have decided that you will remain my wife. There will be no further discussion on the subject, so please do not provoke me by mentioning it again.'

'You can't mean that,' she gasped. 'Why? As revenge against her! She is dead, you cannot hurt her, and so I am to be a replacement, the subject of your scorn and ridicule. I won't stay with you. I'll run away. To some place where you will never find me.'

'I should find you and bring you back,' he told her. 'Perhaps you would like to reconsider those words, or shall I have the carriage turned round and return us to the house?'

'You—you would do that?' She looked into the merciless features, and nodded bitterly. 'I had forgotten the lengths you will go to in order to have your own way. I shall stay.' What other choice had she but to agree? It reminded her of the day he had asked her to marry him and then, in the same breath, threatened her with prison if she refused. She had committed herself to prison with her answer. A life sentence with a man incapable of feelings.

CHAPTER
NINE

As THEY neared the poorer part of the city, Sapphira became aware of an air of tension among the people in the streets. Faces were pale, expressions worried. She even saw several carts being loaded with belongings and furniture. Panic had already set in, the frantic desire for people to distance themselves from the city.

The heat was unbearable. She was constantly using her fan throughout the journey, but she was never cool. The sun beat down on her unprotected head in the open carriage and she became conscious, more than ever before—probably because she had been away from it all—of the odours that lingered in the narrow cobbled streets. The stink of rotting vegetables thrown out on to the baking stones, the nauseating stench of open sewers. Flies swarmed around them.

She felt Quentin's narrowed gaze on her as she pressed a perfumed handkerchief to her nose, and looked away as they passed a public whipping.

'Is it much further?' she ventured to ask.

'We can go back, if you are afraid.' Neither the sickening smells nor the flies seemed to annoy him, she thought, and wondered if he had become hardened to such things beneath the blazing sun of France.

'I am hot and uncomfortable. There are so many houses marked with the plague sign here. Can it not be contained before it spreads further?' She averted her gaze from a man splashing a scarlet cross on the walls of a house. In the doorway a small child clung to the skirts of a weeping woman. 'Poor things.'

'The plague has no compassion on man, woman or

child.' No more had the God above him who had
brought it to the city, and sights like these to make him
relive those last nightmare days of his marriage. 'Do
not worry. If it shows signs of intensifying, you will go
to Ravenswood.'

'You have seen it before, haven't you?'

'Yes.' The carriage came to a halt and he rose to
alight. Sapphira sensed that, otherwise, he might have
said more.

They stood before a newly-painted house with small
latticed windows. A large board was wedged in one of
them with the single word 'Rooms' written on it in large
black letters. It was by far the most pleasant-looking
building in the whole street, Sapphira thought, looking round her. In the last street, she had counted six
houses in all with the dreaded red cross, but so far no
houses here were marked. She breathed a sigh of
relief.

Dear God, don't let them be stricken with it, she
prayed, as Quentin opened the door and she went down
three steps into a cool, low-beamed room, sparsely
furnished, but comfortable none the less. The woman
who came from the room beyond, smoothing down a
crisp white apron over the front of her plain gown,
stared at the two people before her for a moment
without recognising either of them, and then her hands
flew to her mouth.

'Sapphira! Can it be you?' Her wide eyes flew to
Quentin's face. 'Why have you brought her here? I told
you I did not want to see her again. How could you do
this to her?'

'The girl has been fretting for you since the day I took
her away, woman. She has a right to know you are
well,' Quentin returned sharply.

'Oh, Molly, are you angry because I did not come
back to see you?' Sapphira cried, mouth quivering as
she fought back her tears. 'I came as soon as I could,
but you had left the tavern. No one would tell me where

you were. Why don't you want to see me? Have I changed so much?'

'Look at you—a fine lady! What am I? A woman who runs a rooming-house. This is no place for you, especially at a time like this. Take her away, my lord, I beg you.'

'No, I will not go.' Sapphira ran to the woman and put her arms around her and kissed her thin cheek. 'I am no different. I have clothes and money, and I live in a fine house, but my heart is the same. I love you and Lottie as dearly as I ever did. Please believe me.'

Without warning, Molly burst into tears and returned her embrace, and Sapphira realised that she had been terrified of rejection. Quentin found himself strangely moved as the two women kissed and hugged, oblivious of his presence in the emotion of the moment. There was nothing false about his wife's joy at the reunion. There was great love in her for this woman who had raised her from infancy and showered on her the affection and care her own mother had denied her. He envied Molly the touch of Sapphira's arms, her kisses given so freely, and with laughter, between the tears which streaked her cheeks. None of these things were given willingly to him, and he had only himself to blame.

'Where is Lottie?' Sapphira asked, when they eventually drew apart and she began to compose herself. 'She is not ill?'

'Good heavens, no. A picture of health she is these days. Since we left the tavern and she isn't kept on her feet working half the night, she's greatly improved. And we have money to buy food, decent food, and all my rooms are full. At least they were until this morning. News of the plague sent three of my boarders heading for the door. The last one leaves tomorrow.' Molly shrugged, wiping the last of her tears on her apron. 'What a mess I'm in, and forgetting my manners! I've not offered you a seat, or something to drink.'

'If you have some wine,' Quentin came forward. 'Did I not do right to bring her?'

'Yes, my lord. Forgive my sharp tongue. Come into the parlour and sit down while I open a fresh bottle. I'll make some tea, too. Lottie will be back from Widow Scott's in a little while. She goes there twice a week for sewing lessons. That girl's needlepoint is the finest to be seen anywhere.'

'And you have enough money to support yourselves?' Sapphira asked, lowering herself into one of the wooden chairs beside a small table with a bowl of fresh fruit in the centre of it. Once, such a thing would have been unknown to them, she thought. Life had changed for them all.

'More than enough, thanks to Lord Ravenswood. Every Friday his man brings it to me.' Molly looked at the silent man reclining in the one and only armchair. Her opinion of him had greatly altered since the day he had carried Sapphira out of the Black Horse and out of her life. 'He came back the very day after you left to make sure old Silas hadn't taken the money from me. He had, of course, never expecting anyone to know. You should have heard him beg for mercy as your husband thrashed him within an inch of his life. Then he brought us here, and told us it was ours to do with as we pleased. But then you know all this . . .'

She turned away to open the bottle of wine she had taken from a cupboard. Sapphira looked at Quentin, but he was staring thoughtfully into the tiny kitchen beyond the parlour, a frown creasing his brows.

'Remember to boil every drop of water you use, woman, and if either you or your daughter feel the slightest hint of sickness or sudden chills, call a doctor at once. It would be better if you left here.'

'Leave? No, my lord. I lost my livelihood before, after the death of my husband. I will not lose it again. Nothing shall drive me away from here. If we left, the place would be broken into and looted by waterfront scum before an hour had passed.'

'Molly, you cannot stay here if the plague worsens. It is in the next street already,' Sapphira protested. 'What about Lottie? Come to us. We have room for you.' Her mind was reeling with questions. Quentin was their benefactor!

Realising what she had said, she looked hesitantly at her husband, expecting swift opposition. *I shall do anything you ask of me*, her eyes pleaded silently, *only do not part me from them again*. A tiny flicker of acknowledgment passed across his face as he contemplated her. Molly, busying herself with bringing clean glasses and pouring out wine, noticed nothing.

'Sapphira is quite right. I should have thought of it myself. When the last of your boarders leaves tomorrow, come to us. I shall send the carriage. Shall we say about five in the afternoon? There will be men to help you close the place up and board the windows and doors. I assure you the place will still be intact when you return. It will be cared for.'

'Live—with you?' Molly echoed shocked, and almost spilled the glass of wine she was holding out to him. 'I —we couldn't! My lord, we are simple folk . . . What would your friends say? Oh, no. It is not possible.'

'Until this threat is past. I will hear no refusal. It is settled.' Quentin's tone belied further argument, and the woman stood in a stunned silence.

'But we shall work for our food and lodgings,' she insisted. 'I want no charity. I can cook and sew, and my Lottie can turn her hand to almost anything now.'

'Molly, dearest Molly, you will do no such thing,' Sapphira said firmly. 'I am going to repay you for all the years you took care of me. Now it is your turn and Lottie's. Maybe I can find her a good-looking husband. One for you, too, to care for you as you have always cared for others. Please, Molly—let me show you how much I love you both. I can offer you so much more than words now.'

Sometimes words were all that were necessary, Quentin thought, as he drank his wine and listened to the two of them making plans. How he wished he could find words to make Sapphira as happy as she was now. To make those blue eyes sparkle as they did gazing tenderly at Molly. He knew that by his actions the night before he had forfeited the right to ask anything from her, but he would continue to do so by any means necessary. The last vestige of pride remaining in him would still not let him admit he had been wrong.

His attitude puzzled Sapphira, who had been expecting a rebuke for the things she had said to him, but her stammered attempt at an apology had been brushed aside as if it was of no consequence. She would never understand him. She had said she hated him, believing, as she did then, that he had been instrumental in keeping her from Molly and Lottie to save himself further embarrassment, but that was not true. On the way back to the house he had not spoken to her at all, except to ask if she was content with the arrangements. No reproaches, no caustic comments to spoil the wonder of what he had done. The joy at what was to happen.

She climbed into bed that night still unable to comprehend the strange moods of the man she had married. He was, after all, capable of kindness and thoughtfulness. Was it something in her which brought out the worst in him? Would he come expecting gratitude for what he had done? She fell asleep, still alone . . .

The next day her spirits lifted even more as the time drew near for her guests to arrive. She personally supervised the preparation of their rooms, close to hers, and placed vases of fresh flowers in each one. She went out early, and returned having bought for Lottie some fine fabrics, shoes, and pretty ribbons for her hair. For Molly there was a rope of pearls. She called the servants together and instructed them to meet the every wish of the newcomers who were close and dear friends. Later, when they were alone, Mrs Grayson smilingly told her that Quentin had given similar orders before he had left the house.

As the carriage pulled up outside the door, Sapphira ran downstairs, her cheeks flushed with excitement. To her great surprise Quentin alighted first, and then helped the two women down. He had said nothing about going to fetch them. Why was he showing such an interest in their welfare? It was obvious by the way Lottie was gazing up into his face that she thought him to be a perfect gentleman, the kind she had always dreamed about. Molly was looking up at the house, and the open front door where Sapphira stood, Mrs Grayson and Wilcox beside her, with more than a little apprehension in her expression. As Quentin took Lottie's arm and started up the steps, he sensed her reticence and slipped a firm hand beneath her arm. The warm smile he gave her dispelled her fears, and as Sapphira watched them, she was ashamed to feel a pang of envy. Such charm and impeccable manners, but always for someone else. It was becoming increasingly painful to hide her feelings and continue with the role he demanded that she play. Unwanted, except when memories and stifled passions drove him to her bed. Unloved, yet denied the attentions of other men—even the most innocent of friendships. Expected to remain at home and bear his child while he went to his mistress.

A child? Would she become pregnant from that wild night? Did she want to? She knew she did, with all her heart. A boy with his looks, or a girl inheriting his hair as black as night and her blue eyes with which to bewitch him as hers never could.

Lottie's wet cheeks against hers luckily broke the spell of her thoughts. How the girl had grown! They were almost as tall as each other, and much of the unhealthy pallor had gone from her cheeks, but Sapphira thought that, nevertheless, she would have a doctor to see her. Perhaps Quentin's suggestion that they retire to Ravenswood was not such a bad idea, after all. The country air would do them all good. There would be long walks in the woods; she might even teach her little sister to ride; perhaps find a nice young man from the village to court her.

It was not until later, as she escorted them to their rooms to retire, wondering whether she had looked in such awe of her new surroundings when Quentin first brought her to the house as they did now, that she became aware that, no longer, was Lottie either her sister, or little. She was a young woman, fast growing pretty. Should they be told of Susanne? Molly had always wanted her to find her real mother, and would be pleased, but would they change towards her? Would they feel they did not have a place in her life and try to leave it once again? Yet, out of fairness to the woman who had brought her up, she knew she must speak. If they loved her as she did them, then nothing could part them again.

'Sit down, both of you. On the bed, Lottie, there's no one to tell you off here,' she laughed as the girl looked hesitantly around her. 'I must talk to you—I have so much news.'

'Sapphira, my dear, would you mind keeping it until tomorrow?' Molly asked, sinking down on to the bed beside her daughter. 'What a day this has been! I am exhausted and I swear I would be asleep before you utter two words. Tired and full to bursting. Your cook did us proud. Those meat pies were the recipe from the Black Horse; I'd know them anywhere. You have a fine man, do you know that? Not at all as I expected him to be.'

No, Sapphira thought to herself, Quentin had surprised more than one person tonight. He had not gone out, as was his usual practice these days. She never knew where he was, and it was not her place to question him. Sometimes, most times, she suspected that he was with Margaret, but he also spent a great deal of time in the King's company of late, playing cards or hunting. He had sat at the head of the dining-table, Sapphira opposite and Molly and Lottie between them. His constant, easy flow of conversation wiped away all awkwardness between them. A far different man from the one she had shared a meal with the first night beneath his roof. He had made no attempt to make her feel welcome.

'Do we . . . I mean . . . must I sleep alone in this enormous bed?' Lottie asked in a small voice, hiding a yawn as she did so. 'I don't think I would like it very much.'

'We've slept side by side for so long it's become a habit.' Molly slipped an arm around her daughter's shoulder. 'You stay with your old mother, if you like. Sapphira won't mind, will you?'

'Of course not. Habits of a lifetime don't change overnight, although, I have to admit, most of mine were altered in a very short time. Quentin saw to that.'

'But that was necessary. You are a lady now. It's different for you.

'Then you think I have changed, Molly?' Sapphira said slowly.

'No, child, not you. Circumstances. Our lives are different now. You are happy in yours, and Lottie and I—well, we have the house, and money to keep us, thanks to the generosity of your husband. I told him tonight that one day I would repay him, but he only laughed and said I was stubborn, like you, and he doesn't want anything from us.'

'Do you mean that, when it is possible, you will return to the lodging-house? You will not stay here with me so that we can be a family again?'

'We were never meant to be part of your life, Sapphira. Did I not always say that good fortune would be sure to find you?' At the firmness of Molly's tone, Sapphira saw all the plans she had been making dissolving before her eyes. She would have them for a short while only.

'Then you must let me make the most of the time we have together, and deny me nothing,' she declared, a brave smile masking her disappointment. 'Tomorrow we shall go to the shops, and I have some very special friends you must meet. Oh, look! Poor Lottie is almost asleep. Do you have everything you want? You have only to pull on the bell-rope beside the bed and someone will come immediately. I am going to pamper you every second you are here, so expect to have breakfast in bed.'

Molly's face was a picture. She had never been afforded that luxury before, and Sapphira was delighted that she did not refuse it.

'Good night, dearest Molly . . . Lottie. Sleep well.' She kissed them both, and then for a moment laid her head against the woman's shoulder as she had done so many times in the past.

'What is it you have not told me?' Molly held her for a moment and then gently put her away, tired eyes searching her face. 'You do that only when you are afraid— or lonely.'

'I miss you,' Sapphira whispered, bright tears starting to her eyes. Lottie murmured something quite unintelligible and curled up on the coverlet, oblivious to the two of them beside her. 'I have so much, yet I have nothing.'

'What are you asking from me that your husband cannot give you?'

'Love.'

'You silly girl, do you still have those foolish notions in your head?' Molly reproved, and Sapphira drew back, hurt by her lack of understanding. She had never misunderstood before. 'Has he not given you his name? Do you not live in this beautiful house, surrounded by many fine things, and servants at your beck and call? All this—and still you want more?'

Sapphira smiled at her through a mist of tears. Molly's husband had been a kind, uncomplicated, little man and their life together until he had died had been uneventful. If they had ever loved each other, and she liked to think they had, then the fires of youth had long since mellowed into nothing more than comfortable companionship. An uncomplicated, uneventful way of life. The months she had spent thus far with Quentin had been the exact opposite. The demands placed on her now far exceeded any she had thought possible when she had stood at his side at Ravenswood in her lace gown, and they frightened her. In all her married years, she suspected, Molly had never felt the way she did.

'Perhaps, like my mother, I love foolishly, unwisely, with my heart and not my head.' Quentin had once loved that way, too, but that other woman had killed it for ever.

'You have found her?' Molly gasped, suddenly alert.

'Yes. You shall meet her soon, I promise. I want her to meet you too. She has much to thank you for.'

Outside in the corridor, tears came without warning. Sapphira leaned against the wall, her face in her hands. She could understand Molly's decision to remain at arm's length. She was right, their worlds were far different, but she balked at accepting it, losing them both again. How long would she have them with her? God knows, she did not want the plague to continue, but, while it did, they could not safely return to their home. The longer they remained, the harder it would be for her to accept that they must part again.

'What is it, Sapphira? Are you ill?'

In her moment of distress, she had not noticed the door of Quentin's room opening. As she raised her head and he saw her wet cheeks, he caught her by the arm and ushered her inside.

'Please, I don't want to trouble you,' she began, as he guided her to a chair, left her side for a moment and then returned to press a glass of brandy into her hands. 'Are you not going—out?'

An eyebrow quirked as he caught the hesitation, and knew that she had almost said 'to Margaret'. At first he had been pleased at her acceptance of his mistress, for it meant no change in his pattern of life, but of late he had noticed how she always hovered between them, and Sapphira's outburst the previous night had finally enlightened him as to the extent of her displeasure. She could not reconcile herself to accepting Margaret as her friend and his mistress any longer. Sapphira was his wife, and although Margaret's company had been far more satisfying, he had spent too much time with her. A long sojourn at Ravenswood was what they both needed. She would have no cause to complain of neglect there.

'You can go, Robert. I shall not need you tonight,' Quentin said to the manservant across the room. The man bowed and left them. The sound of the door closing made Sapphira look up, and when she saw that they were totally alone, he saw a shadow cross her face. 'Why were you crying? You are not often taken with tears. I am not going out, so you have plenty of time to tell me. Is it Molly? Are you not pleased to see her?'

She sat in an awkward silence as Quentin removed his coat and the cravat at his throat and tossed them down before relaxing into a chair. A gleam of mockery crept into his eyes as she continued to sit stiff and silent. Colour flamed into her cheeks as he declared amusedly, 'Confound it, girl! Tell me what troubles you before I think of a better way to occupy my time.'

His meaning was only too clear, and she gulped at the drink in her hand, exploding into a spasm of coughing as the first flames reached her throat.

'I forgot, you don't like spirits, do you,' he said, as she hurriedly put it aside. 'Well, are you going to speak, or am I . . .'

She told him. He listened attentively and without

interruption until she had finished, his expression one of concern.

'Surely you realised she would not stay? She would not be comfortable here.'

'Why not? I had no choice, but for her there is one,' Sapphira replied. 'I could give her so much.'

'And make her feel she is living on your charity. I've never taken you for a fool, girl. Like you and me, she has her pride. The lodging-house gives her a certain status. Nothing elaborate, I admit, but as its owner she can hold her head high and be proud of what she is—what she does. They shall want for nothing; I shall see to that, if you are still concerned. But you must allow her to do what she thinks is best for herself and Lottie.'

'Why should you go on helping them—they are nothing to you? Why did you go back to the tavern that day?'

'To prevent the money I had given them falling into the hands of that odious uncle of yours.'

'Did—did you really beat him?'

'It was a pleasure.' Especially as he recalled the marks on her back, Quentin thought, and wondered why he did not tell her so. It was not often that they were completely alone like this. Usually there were servants hovering in the background, listening, watching. He saw at once how uncomfortable she was with him. Did she feel the same vulnerability as he did looking at her? Was she remembering what had happened between them the night before? Abruptly he rose and poured himself a drink. 'I think you had better go to bed. You look tired.'

'Yes. I shall need to be fresh for tomorrow. I have so many plans.' She was frightened to be alone with him, yet his dismissal hurt her. Margaret would not have acted like a tongue-tied dolt, she thought, as she turned towards the door. Quentin's voice halted her.

'What plans? Do you not understand they must remain here for several days under medical care? This disease strikes without warning, and not even the most brilliant doctor in the land really comprehends how it spreads so rapidly and to so many places. Both Molly and Lottie will stay in their rooms for at least three days, and in the house for the remainder of a week. Then, I think it should be safe to allow them outside again. I made enquiries, and no house in their street was infected when we left.'

'A week,' Sapphira whispered. 'And then they will be safe? You are sure?'

'No one is ever sure about plague,' Quentin told her, unsmiling. 'You will allow the doctor to examine you also. If we leave here for Ravenswood, I must be sure that none of us carries it.'

Was he concerned about her health, Sapphira wondered, as she returned to her room, or was the safety of the villagers at Market Cross, and his servants, his prime concern? Could he have not made his words a little more personal?

For seven long days Sapphira did not venture out of the house, choosing to remain close to Molly and Lottie who, thankfully, developed no ominous signs. The week passed quickly. Sometimes in the afternoons she read to them or she told them of the plays she had seen in Drury Lane, the night of the ball when she had met the King of England and the famous beauty, Barbara Castlemaine. Lottie became so attached to Sapphira's little dog during those days that she allowed it to sleep at the foot of her bed, and Sapphira never once said how much she herself missed its company.

She found several bolts of new cloth in a storage-chest, and they cut out a dress for Molly. As they all sat sewing in the candlelight, she remembered those days in the Black Horse when they had not had a moment to themselves. Those days had become to Sapphira no more than a bad dream. For the others, too, they were slipping away into the realms of unreality, she realised.

Molly was complaining she was beginning to put on weight when their confinement indoors drew to an end, blaming Mrs Grayson for caring for them so well. It was plain that she had settled into the life of a lady far more easily than she had imagined, and Sapphira laughed away her fears that she might become too used to it. She did not want Molly to think she was being deliberately manoeuvered into making a decision that she knew was not right.

For an hour Sapphira had lingered in a scented tub before she retired. The windows were thrown open wide to allow a breeze into the room, but waves of unhealthy heat wafted in on the night air despite the lateness of the hour. Was there no respite from the continuing heat?

News about the plague was worrying. The hotter the weather, the higher the mortality rose, until in that first week in June the City authorities enforced an Act, first introduced by James I, which divided it into districts in an effort to contain the spread of the deadly disease. Each one was to have examiners, searchers-out of those ill, volunteer nurses willing to risk their lives for the sick, and watchmen, so necessary to guard against plunderers and robbers, and all those so eager and still able to take advantage of the appalling situation.

Sapphira took the light silken wrap from her maid and drew it around her. It was still too hot to go to bed. Even the touch of the sheets on her body was uncomfortable. She smiled at the girl, knowing she had a sweetheart below stairs, and gave her permission to withdraw.

She was engrossed in penning a belated letter to Blaise, explaining her absence the day before, when a soft tap on the door roused her.

'Come in! Have you forgotten something, Betty . . .?' Her voice trailed off as Quentin came into the room and shut the door behind him. He looked a trifle pale, she thought, the letter forgotten. He had been spending much time at Court over the past week. There was talk of moving to Salisbury, in the hope of avoiding the spreading plague. Had he come to tell her it was so and that they could now go to Ravenswood? She had begun to look forward to it.

'I thought you might like to hear some good news. The doctor has pronounced them both fit. You can visit the shops tomorrow, if you wish,' he said, and she leapt to her feet with a glad little cry.

'Oh, Quentin, that's wonderful.' Not until she saw the surprise which spread across his face did she realise she had never used his name before. 'I am so relieved,' she added, hoping he would not notice her embarrassment.

'So I gather.' He gave her a searching look, and Sapphira drew the wrap more firmly about her as his gaze lingered on her bare shoulders. 'You did not have to confine yourself, too, you know. These past two days you could have gone out somewhere.'

'And leave them alone? No, that would have been unfair. It's of no importance now. I have not thanked you, have I? Will you let me, or will you refuse my thanks, given from my heart—laugh at my happiness.'

'Do you consider me such an ogre? Yes, perhaps I have given you cause. But just cause,' he corrected himself quickly. 'Your eyes are shining. I never thought to see the day I should succeed in such an impossible task.'

'I don't understand you. Never mind.' She leaned up and gently brushed his cheek with her lips. 'Thank you a thousand times for giving them back to me. Even if it is only for a little while.'

As she went to draw back, his hands caught and held her face, and a fierce light sprang to his eyes—a wicked, devilish, light that she recognised. For a moment he held her, not moving, not speaking, and then his hands began to caress her purposefully.

'No, Quentin. Please,' Sapphira cried in alarm. Did

he intend to force himself on her with the same violence as before?

Bending his head, he kissed her slowly, gently, and with the same expertise that had brought her so quickly to surrender the last time. Sliding the wrap away from her shoulders, his fingers began to explore her skin, damp still from the night warmth. The aroma of scented oils was in his nostrils as he lifted her and carried her naked to the bed.

Sapphira offered no resistance, no protest, made no sound as he pinned her beneath him. She was utterly helpless against him and, as if he was aware of it, she felt the tight hold on her relax slightly.

'Sapphira.' Her name was lost on his lips as he buried them in the cloud of loose hair, in the deep hollow of her throat.

She forgot the brutality of that other time, and her solemn vow that he would never touch her again, but, as before, she was aware of the unbridled passion he could rouse in her. It greatly frightened her, for she could not hide it from him. Desperately she fought to contain it, knowing that to surrender would give him the thing he desired most—total control over her. Not only as her husband, but her master, too, at will to dominate her whenever he chose, and always succeed. But as his lips moved across her body, to each of the fading bruises on her soft skin, her battle was lost.

Quentin had made love to many women without love in him, and none had ever complained. To rouse an innocent like Sapphira was no great challenge to his skills, but he took his time, enjoying the warmth of her and the smell, the wonder of this new pleasure which had always been his for the taking, had he not been such a fool. Not until a low moan broke from her lips and her body arched up to meet his, seeking fulfilment of her need, did he satisfy his own desire of her.

'You see, I am quite capable of giving you pleasure.' Some while later he rolled up on to one elbow and

looked down at the flushed face close to his. Sapphira
stared at him sleepily, wishing she had been allowed to
stay within the confines of his arms. She had felt so safe
and content. So happy. The shadowy face smiled, but
she saw that the eyes contained a wary expression. Was
he still unsure of her? How could he be, after this?
However, his next words confirmed it. 'You will not
take a lover now, will you?'

'How can you even ask such a thing?' she gasped, the
spell of the idyllic moments shattered. 'You know such
a thought was never in my mind.'

'Not yours, perhaps,' he returned meaningfully.

'Will you never trust me? She destroyed love in you,
but surely I deserve your trust. Have I not earned it?'
He gave no answer, and her lips quivered as she spoke
again. 'The man you almost killed in a duel. Did you
suspect I was his mistress too?'

'I wondered when your curiosity would get the better
of you,' Quentin drawled, toying with strands of her
hair that lay across his arm. 'Did you think that was for
you? My dear girl, the man insulted me by casting a slur
upon my name. Any man would have acted as I did.'

'Not any man, only one consumed with unreasonable
jealousy.'

The dark eyes glittered. He pulled away from her and
reached for his clothes. He wanted her. He had proved
that by not being able to stay away from her, yet he
could neither trust nor love her, only use her to quench
the fires raging inside him. He would never belong to
her. Suddenly it no longer mattered. She had sufficient
love for two.

'Quentin.' He turned slowly and looked into her
pleading eyes.

'Dammit, wench, what do you want from me? I have
nothing to give you!' he demanded roughly. Her hand
touched his. He caught and held it and allowed her to
draw him back down at her side. Her fingers touched
his face, the black brows drawn together into a fierce

frown, the firm line of his mouth, and she smiled. Such a strange smile, he thought, not understanding her thoughts or the sudden boldness of her actions. Yet he did not, could not, move away from her.

'Can you not spare me a little of your time, my husband?' she asked softly. It was she who kissed him. She, who willingly went into his embrace and, with her willingness, unknowingly tightened the web which entrapped him.

She awoke the next morning to find that he was still with her, but as she sat up, feeling a little shy in his company after the long night of love-making which she had boldly instigated, he turned from the window where he stood and she saw that he was fully dressed. Something in his expression made the smile fade from her face. She had been too bold! Surely he did not think the worst of her again! The coldness in his eyes held back a question. He came to where she sat, and held out his hand. She stared, puzzled, at the paper he held, then, as recognition dawned, a look of horror spread across her face.

'It is not what you think,' she began, only to have him interrupt her with a harsh laugh that struck terror into her heart.

'Liar! Even while I held you in my arms, you lied. With your lips, your body. God help me, I should kill you now. And him,' Quentin said bitterly, and flung down in front of her the letter she had been trying to write to Blaise. The words leapt up at her '*I could not meet you, but I shall soon. We have much to discuss . . . Give Susanne my love and bless her for me. Had I not met her, I would never have known you, dearest Blaise . . .*

'He is no more than a friend,' Sapphira cried, aghast. 'Did last night tell you nothing? Oh, how blind can you be . . .'

'Be careful, wench, my temper is at a dangerous

level,' Quentin warned, his face working furiously. There was murder in the eyes that gazed at her, devoured her nakedness and looked away almost with disgust. 'Cover yourself, and call your maid. At once, before I take a stick to you. Your uncle knew what he was about, after all. You will pack and leave for Ravenswood today. Take Molly and her daughter with you; I want no sight of them in this house to remind me of you. The servants will follow in a day or two when I have closed up the house. You shall never come back here. I never want to set eyes on you again. You will live in seclusion in the country until I can be free of you. Or I kill you!'

'Will you not hear what I have to say?' Sapphira drew herself upright, struggling into her wrap. She could tell him that Blaise was her brother, and bring him to his knees, begging her forgiveness. That was what she should have done, but she did not. She had committed no crime except to love this heartless man, and she was paying dearly for it. Why should she vindicate herself to salve his wounded pride?

'If you utter another word to me before you leave, I shall have you bound and gagged until you get to Ravenswood,' he threatened, hands clenching into tight fists. It could not be happening to him again, but it was! And he had only himself to blame. He had allowed her to penetrate his armoured shield and she had succeeded in plunging a sword into his heart. The heart he had sworn would never be vulnerable again! The blind rage which seized him when he discovered the half-finished letter brought him to the point of murder, and only with a great effort did he refrain from rushing out of the house and confronting Blaise that instant.

He had betrayed a long-standing friendship, but Sapphira had taken the one unguarded moment he allowed her, seized on it maliciously, and then flung it back in his face. How she must hate him! His wife, and the only man he had ever called friend, save for the

King! They would both pay, but his revenge would be exacted in the cold light of day when his temper had cooled and he was capable of rational thoughts again, and neither would know when it would descend on them.

'Give me no trouble, wench.' Sapphira shrank back from him as he seized her, his blazing eyes only inches from hers. 'Be ready to leave by this afternoon. Do not be here when I return, or I will kill you. By all means send a farewell note to Blaise. Perhaps he will come seeking me, and save me a journey.'

He crushed her lips beneath his, devouring them like a madman, bruising them with the wildness of his kisses until she sagged limp and near-fainting in his grasp. Then, with a contemptuous laugh, he flung her back on to the bed and strode from the room. By the time Sapphira had gathered her reeling senses and composed herself sufficiently to follow and seek him out, he had left the house.

Preparations were begun in a feverish haste to make ready for travel to Ravenswood. Trunks were dragged down from the attic and dusted, the carriage and horses and hampers of food and wine made ready. In the midst of all the hustle and bustle, Sapphira dressed to go out herself, like someone in a dream, untouched by what was going on around her. She had no interest in anything but finding Blaise before he encountered Quentin.

She would have to walk to the house Blaise shared with his father, just off the Strand. She left Lottie helping her maid to empty the closets and pack away the contents. Below, Mrs Grayson and Molly were continuing with getting everything ready for the long journey, which had not been expected until the end of the month at least.

She would take everything she possessed with her, Sapphira decided, and wait and pray daily that Quentin would come to her at Ravenswood. If he did not, she would never dare to return to London in search of him,

and incur his wrath. She would remain there alone
and somehow remake her life without him, yet at that
moment such a thought was impossible to contemplate.
Without him, her life would be meaningless. Nothing
could replace what he had unknowingly, perhaps unwill-
ingly, given her during their short turbulent nights
together. Yet she knew she would never be able to send
word to him, begging his forgiveness as if she were in
the wrong. She had her pride, too!

As she approached the front door, a servant there
ahead of her opened it to admit a visitor, and she found
herself face to face with her brother. So overwhelming
was her relief that she fell into his arms, oblivious of
who might be watching, and then, as sanity returned,
she caught his sleeve, tugging at it urgently.

'Come inside quickly. Before you are seen!' She was
terrified that Quentin would return unexpectedly and
find them together. And challenge him!

Blaise followed her into the morning-room. She
looked so agitated that an army could not have dragged
him from her side until he knew the reason why. He
had missed her so much in the last few days; her company had become so important to him.

'Sapphira, dearest, what is it?' As she turned in the
middle of the room, he took her in his arms and kissed
her pale cheeks. Over his shoulder she caught sight of
the maid who had let him in hovering outside. Something in the girl's face disturbed her. She broke free of
him and quickly shut the door.

'Quentin is looking for you! He means to challenge
you.'

'What? Why? I have given him no reason,' Blaise
gasped. 'Besides, he knows I would never lift a blade
against him. We are friends.'

'If you faced him and did not, he would surely kill
you. He believes we mean to become lovers. Oh, Blaise,
forgive me! I have brought you to this. I wanted to be
accepted for myself, not because you are his friend or

because of my relationship with Susanne. If I had told him the truth . . .' her voice faltered and broke, but she knew Blaise had to be told everything. He listened in a stony silence, his face hardening as she spared herself nothing. 'And then he found the letter—part of a letter I had been writing to you. He became like a wild man. Even after all that had passed between us, he would not let me explain. And because of the promise I made to your father, I could not!'

'He need not look for me. I will find him!' Blaise drew her into his arms and felt her trembling. Quentin was the cause of her distress, but he also blamed himself. Had he remained silent that night in the Black Horse, and not arranged for his friend to be entertained in the upstairs room, Sapphira would not now be so desperately unhappy. But then, also, he would never have known her.

'No, he would like that. You are no match for him.'

'All I know he taught me, but if there is no other way to bring him to account for the way he has treated you . . .'

'He is sending me to Ravenswood. I am to remain there. He said he never wants to see me again, but I shall wait for him, however long it is.' Sapphira smiled through a mist of tears. She did not feel brave, but for her brother's sake she had to make him think she had accepted her exile, or he would do something foolish and perhaps lose his life.

'In vain!' Blaise retorted. 'Quentin does not easily relent, once his mind is made up.'

'He will come to realise how mistaken he was about me—about us—given time.'

'I could make him accept the truth now. It is my duty as your brother.'

'I do not want him coming cap in hand, mouthing apologies. If he comes to me at all, it must be because he wants me, needs me as he did last night.'

'Can you survive, knowing that you are merely a replacement for another woman?' Blaise demanded. 'Come away with me now, Sapphira. Father is taking Susanne to our estates in Berkshire. We leave tomorrow. They marry there next month. Finding you has finally made them decide to wed after all these years. I came to tell you that Susanne naturally wishes you to be at the wedding.'

'I will, but my mind is made up. I am going to Ravenswood first. Promise me you will leave with them, Blaise, and not look for Quentin? Promise me you will hide yourself away until tomorrow?'

'What you ask from me is the act of a coward. What if I do, and he comes seeking you instead, to use you as an instrument of his revenge?'

'Then I shall tell him everything, and afterwards I shall leave him for ever, for he will have shown me how worthless he considers the love I offer him.'

Sensing the struggle raging inside her brother, she put her arms about his neck and drew his head down to hers, pressing his cheek to hers. 'I don't want to lose you. If you approached him now, he would not listen to you. He was beside himself with rage. He said he wanted to kill us both! I have never seen him like that before.'

'I have, and he is capable of killing us, believe me. Some devil drives him, but I know not what it is.'

'I do,' Sapphira replied softly, a shadow crossing her face. 'When we next meet, I shall tell you about Quentin. There is much you do not know. Go now, before he returns.'

'For your sake, then. After all he has done to you, would it grieve you so much if I called him out and killed him?' Blaise held her at arm's length, and stared down into her wet eyes.

'You would no more bring me happiness by depriving me of him, than he would by taking you from me. I am selfish. I want you both. I love you both. One day, God willing, I shall be able to repair the damage I have done to you both.'

'Because you ask it of me, so be it.' He nodded slowly, and she walked with him to the door, clinging tightly to his arm. She was aware of the same maid hovering there to open it for him. Why should the presence of a mere servant disturb her so?

'I shall explain everything to Susanne.' Blaise bent and kissed her again, reluctantly releasing the hands he held. 'I shall come to you at Ravenswood.'

'Yes.'

After he had gone, Sapphira was seized with a terrible sense of foreboding, which remained with her throughout the day, completely engulfing her, so that by the time she mounted the carriage conveying her to Ravenswood, she was in the depths of despair and no one could cheer her up.

How foolish she was to think that Quentin would follow her. He would go with the King and the Court to Salisbury, and take up residence there with Margaret. He was lost to her for ever. *'I never want to set eyes on you again.'* He had meant those terrible words. *'I should kill you now.'* He did not know it, but he had, as effectively as if he had taken a knife and plunged it into her body.

It was then, as she forced herself to accept the fact that he had abandoned her, that the first tears came . . .

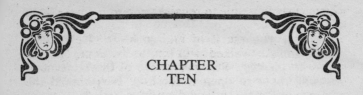

CHAPTER
TEN

IN THOSE first unspeakable months of the plague as it swept the City, more than thirty-five thousand people were left alone and frightened by the departure of their employers to havens of safety. The King was generous in his contribution of over eleven thousand pounds per week for their care, while the City, its reserves drained, gave a mere five hundred pounds. But he was not there in person to stem the growing tide of wild rumours that God had forsaken the people—and he was to blame for the riotousness and debauchery both of his Court and of his own life.

London became a place of the dead. The tolling of church bells brought those still able to walk into the streets with corpses of their loved ones—husbands, children, wives. Whole families perished, and were thrown into deep pits outside the City limits. Their departures passed unmourned, and their graves were unmarked. People avoided each other in the streets if it became necessary to venture into them, covering their faces with cloths and handkerchiefs, and stealing like thieves over the cobble-stones where already grass was beginning to spring forth from the deserted roads.

A strange madness seized some people. The thought that to follow the King's example, and revel in licentious behaviour, would keep the dreaded disease away sent many into the already full houses of pleasure and the taverns, where they associated with whores and drank themselves into oblivion in the hope of escaping the inevitable.

The numbers rose as the weeks passed. One thousand

became two, then three, then five—until, at the height of the epidemic, it was thought to have reached the staggering figure of eight thousand souls in the short space of one week.

Ghosts of the dead were said to haunt the evil-smelling streets. Judgments were delivered on the King and his mistresses by wild-eyed men who claimed visitations from heaven. Fervent clergymen still preached in half-empty churches to congregations more concerned with the preservation of their lives than the saving of their souls. Preservation was the order of the day, no matter how it was achieved. To live!

As some prayed, some starved, the plague continued to spread. Some, either crazed by hunger or mad, took their own lives by leaping to the streets below from high windows. If they did not die outright, they met a more horrible fate at the hands of their fellow men, for no one was allowed out of a house bearing the red cross for a full month after it had been painted on the door. To do so meant death. To remain meant death, a slow lingering death waiting for the disease to claim another victim. Hungry and afraid and waiting!

Corinna spent her days in an orgy of drinking and debauchery which, had anyone seen her, might have instantly placed her in the same category as one of the King's women. She kept a full house in those shameful weeks, uncaring in whose arms whe woke the next morning, so long as she woke.

Beyond the quiet little village of Market Cross, no such panic prevailed. With Quentin absent, Sapphira had taken it upon herself to assume control of the estates and also of the village. Every day she rode over the land and among the people, hoping to reassure them with her presence. She gave orders that no outsiders were to be allowed on Ravenswood land, or to stay in the village. Guards kept a constant vigil on the road leading to and from the village, turning away those seeking shelter. What food could be spared was given to the weary travellers, but they did not remain for even one hour. She was determined that the horror and death, the desolation and loss, that rampaged through London would not come to this peaceful haven that was Quentin's domain.

She would undertake his responsibilities. His village and his people, his home and servants would be safe until he chose to return to them. Unlike his faithless wife, she would not betray him, not even in her thoughts. Her love would remain steadfast and, one day, God willing, he would discover that she lived only for him.

If he came and found her mistress of Ravenswood, would he change? Could she melt his stony heart with her loyalty? Her love? The hope rose and died in her as she remembered the wildness in him when he had laid claim to her, the coldness, the indifference, in the weeks that followed before he despatched her from the City and left for Salisbury with Margaret. He had used her as he used all women. It meant nothing to him. She meant nothing to him.

Margaret, returning from an evening out, found Quentin more or less where she had left him four hours earlier. The decanter at his elbow was empty, and her mouth tightened in disapproval. He had done little else over the two months they had been in Salisbury. Soon after they left London he had told her what had happened, but had never spoken of it again. Neither had she, but as the weeks passed and his moods grew more difficult, though she ignored them, others did not; the previous night the King himself had remarked that Quentin's absence from the side of his lovely wife was turning him sour, and gave his permission to join her at Ravenswood.

It had been decided for him, Margaret thought, taking a fresh decanter of brandy from the sideboard. Yet it was what he wanted. He said nothing at all to her, but she knew Sapphira was never out of his thoughts. Whatever he believed her to be, he wanted her still.

'I am leaving in the morning.' He looked up as she took a chair opposite him, and she was surprised to see he was quite sober. 'Please retain the house for as long as you need it.'

'You are going to her, then.' It was framed as a statement rather than a question. He nodded, his mouth deepening into a humourless smile.

'I have damned little choice. It is a Royal command.'

'He thought it was what you wanted. And he was right, wasn't he? Your prolonged stay here has added to the gossip that you and Sapphira are no longer in love. Don't glare at me like that, Quentin. Of course you love the girl. Why else are you behaving like this? Go to her, and settle what is between you.'

'You are so sure it can be settled.' Quentin rose and poured brandy for them both, and then sat beside her.

'I am sure of one thing—Sapphira has not betrayed you. Call it a woman's instinct, if you like. I have never known you to be so blindly prejudiced against anyone —that's how I know you love her. You are wrong, but you cannot bring yourself to admit it. Do so, before you lose her.'

'Margaret, my dear, I am in no mood for your romantic fancies,' came the sarcastic retort. 'Here, I have a present for you. A parting gift to remember me by.'

'I shall not forget you, Quentin,' she laughed softly, as she allowed him to remove the necklace she wore and replace it with one of flawless rubies, fifteen in all, set in gold. 'This is beautiful. And what gift do you take for your wife?'

'Myself.' He glared at her challengingly, and she laughed again.

'I think she will be well satisfied with that.'

'She will have to accustom herself again to my presence.' Would she be alone at Ravenswood, or had she taken advantage of his absence, the thought that she would never see him again, to reveal her true colours? Would he find her with a man? No, she was not to blame for his suspicions. He was at fault and had always been so. Eight long weeks of hungering for her, dreaming of the softness of her body against him, the memory of the last time they were together. It would be that way again when he returned to Ravenswood. No more accusations or recriminations. If only the memory of that letter did not return so often to haunt him.

When Blaise had not appeared at Salisbury, Quentin had made enquiries immediately as to his whereabouts and discovered that he had accompanied his father to their family home near Windsor. So he had not followed Sapphira. The urge to challenge him still lingered, but the King had demanded his presence almost every other day, and an absence without good reason would have provoked unnecessary bad feeling between them. Once he had considered confiding in Charles, but as he watched him in ardent pursuit of another woman while Barbara Castlemaine looked on, green with jealousy, he came to the conclusion that neither of them was the same as he had been during those years of shared misfortune. He remained silent and withdrawn, brooding on what course of action to take. As the weeks passed, doubt began to creep into his mind. Blaise had always been a good friend, and he loved Corinna, for all the good it did him. Sapphira was all she had held out to be, an innocent whom he had used. Had she turned to him out of desperation, seeking the gentleness and kindness he could not give her? He knew that Blaise possessed both. Was it conceivable that they had merely shared a harmless friendship?

'I also have some news.' Margaret's head was resting against his shoulder. He slipped his arm round her and drew her close against him, but made no attempt to kiss her. His thoughts were miles away, she realised. She had lost him for good! 'Quentin, are you listening? I am to be married.'

'Married?' Amusement sprang to his face, then died as he saw that she was serious. 'Who is the lucky man? I mean that! You have wasted yourself on me for these past years.'

'There we are in complete agreement,' she replied, not unkindly. 'I am tired, Quentin. You know about the characters of my two husbands. The man I wed now is older than me, much older, and his health is not all it should be. When he dies, I shall be a very rich widow. I have been perfectly honest with him, mind! I told him that I want a home and that I expect to be kept in the custom to which I have become accustomed, and I want few demands made on me any more. That kind of life is his wish, too. We shall live quietly in the country for most of the year, in Cornwall. I shall entertain for him, care for him—and I shall, never fear—and I shall know the peace I seek.'

'I wish you well, Margaret.' The kiss Quentin bestowed on her mouth was without passion, and she smiled up at him. 'Why are you looking at me like that?'

'Once we could not have been in the same room together for more than two minutes before you made love to me. Now here we are like two ageing lovers, each bored with the other. No, my dear, that does not apply to us, I know, but in time it would have. You would always be thinking of her, as you are now.'

'We have been good for each other,' Quentin said quietly, ashamed that she could read him so accurately.

'And now we part and go our separate ways to a different kind of contentment. Happiness. You will be happy, Quentin. You will see.'

'As you will be. It seems that we both have what we want, do we not?'

Margaret rose to her feet, waving him back when he began to rise. 'No. Let us say goodbye here. You will be gone in the morning before I am about. Be happy, Quentin. Make her happy.'

'I shall name my first girl after you.' He gave her an

almost awkward smile, wishing he could impart more sincerity into his tone. She knew that Sapphira was the only woman who meant anything to him, despite all they had shared together, and it hurt her. Was he forever to hurt people he was fond of—loved? As he had once been hurt. Would the devil in him never cry enough?

Tears began to spring to Margaret's eyes as she turned at the door and looked at him.

'Devil take you, Quentin Tyrell. No man has made me cry in over ten years!'

'Corinna! What the devil are you doing here?' Quentin stared in disbelief at the person who awaited him in the small sitting-room of the house in Salisbury. When the maid had come to tell him that a woman wished to see him, his heart had leaped unexpectedly. Sapphira! It was not his wife, however, who rose from the couch to greet him, but his sister, and he was appalled at what he saw.

In two short months she seemed to have aged as many years. She was thin, her face heavily rouged, with no care having been taken over its application. For a woman whom he knew to consider her looks the best asset she possessed, and had used them ruthlessly to his knowledge to have her own way with every man who took her fancy, it signalled desperation—defeat! Where were her many lovers, the men she had gathered around her to share in her pleasures? She looked tired and very much alone. As he advanced into the room, she sank into a chair.

'I need a drink.' She sounded tired, and drained of life.

'I think you have had more than your fair share of that, and many other things, these past months,' he said heavily, but he poured her a large brandy and watched her drink it with the eagerness of one to whom strong liquor was a necessity. 'What do you want? How did you get out of London? I hear the roads are watched, these days.'

'The same old Quentin. Cold, hard and indifferent! God, how did Sapphira stand you, even for a short while? I bribed a most accommodating young man to let me through.' She smiled meaningly.

He ignored the jibe, the inference that his wife had sought solace elsewhere. Corinna had been the main instrument in arousing his suspicions in the first place with her sly remarks. He had put it down to jealousy at first, because Blaise had begun to show a preference for Sapphira's company, but later . . .

'I asked you what you wanted. I am about to leave for Ravenswood, and I do not plan to be delayed. If you want money, tell me, and you shall have it so that you can return to London or go wherever you wish. So long as you stay away from me, you know I don't give a damn what you do,' he snapped, and she looked at him and smiled. He did not like that smile, or the mockery in her eyes. What lies had she come expecting him to believe now?

'So you are going back to her? I wish you well of Blaise's leavings.'

'Your mind and your mouth must have developed in the open sewers,' Quentin stared at her coldly, forcing down the rising tide of anger. He must not allow himself to be provoked. 'Explain yourself before I throw you out into the street where you belong.'

'Blaise is at Ravenswood with your wife.' She purred the words at him like a sleek cat enjoying a saucer of cream. In two short strides he had crossed the space between them and slapped her across both cheeks. The sounds hung in the air for several minutes, and then she laughed, and the sound chilled him to the bone. She was mad! Or else she was in possession of knowledge with which to destroy him finally!

Blaise at Ravenswood? That was not possible; he was at Windsor with his father and Lady Winterbourne, whom, it was rumoured, he was shortly to marry. Or was he? Rumour also had it that Susanne Winterbourne had collapsed shortly after her arrival at the Courtney home and it was said that Thomas himself kept a constant vigil at her bedside. But his son would not share his devotion—what reason did he have? Had Blaise left for Ravenswood? Was he there now with Sapphira?

'Why, dear brother, I think you are in love,' Corinna said, and laughed again. She thrust out her empty glass for him to replenish. He ignored the gesture and she rose and did so herself, placing the decanter close to her. How many times had he done the same thing, he thought. Desperation had driven him. Hate drove her, the hope of destroying him and the wife who had ousted her from her position of importance. If he believed her . . . No, he did not. He would not!

'Go back to whatever lover you are keeping at the moment, Corinna. Leave me alone. I want no more of your wild tales '

'You are still going to her, then. Good, I shall accompany you. I want to be there when you find them together. I want to watch your precious world disintegrate, Quentin. When you do, I shall expect payment for the information I have brought you. Enough to get me out of this accursed country. Well, brother? Do we have a bargain?'

'Do you think I go blindly to Ravenswood? Accuse an innocent woman on adultery on your word?' her brother scoffed. 'You would do anything to harm her and me. Why are you really here, Corinna? Have your men deserted you?'

Her face went pale beneath its powder, and he knew he was right. She had been abandoned. He felt no pity for the situation in which she found herself.

'Giles left me when my money ran out. You are to blame for that.' She spat the words at him. He felt she would like to sink her long nails into his face.

'No, for that, you have only yourself to blame. Money

was all he wanted. I gave you a chance to leave London, if you remember?'

'To live under your thumb? Never! Do you want proof of her unfaithfulness? Is that what you are waiting for? I can give it to you, you know.'

'Then do so, before I lose my temper. You have seen me in a rage once before. I warn you, this time it would be more terrible. You would not survive it. Speak, woman. Spit out your poison.'

'One of your own maids overheard Sapphira and Blaise together when he came to your house before she left for Ravenswood. You didn't know that, did you? He saw her beneath your own roof. They were overheard to make plans to meet again at Ravenswood. He said so himself, and she agreed to meet him there. At Ravenswood, Quentin! She is planning to go away with him. Perhaps at this very moment they are lying in the bed the two of you shared together, making love as they make their future plans.'

One look at her brother's furious features told Corinna that neither of them would have a future if he found them together. She did not flinch from his anger as she would have done once before. Her confidence was unnerving.

Throwing open the door, he shouted for Wilcox to begin loading the carriage. He did not want to waste one precious moment in proving her wrong. If Corinna was right . . . if he found Blaise together with his wife . . . He shut his mind to what could happen. His dreams had been so full of those nightmares from the past . . . This time, it had to be different.

Dear God in heaven, let her be different, he prayed. He could not remember the last time he had asked a favour of God or his fellow man!

Blazing summer sun had hastened the crops in the field, and it seemed to Sapphira as if she had only just begun to settle at Ravenswood and now harvest time was fast approaching. As Ravenswood had never had a steward, Quentin always managing quite ably to oversee everything that was taking place, she selected a man from the village, the blacksmith, to advise her. He and his family lived in a small cottage not far from the main house, so that he was always on hand to attend to Quentin's many fine horses. His forefathers went back as many generations as the Earls of Ravenswood. She suspected that there was nothing he did not know about the estate or the village people, although he was a most mild-mannered man and always seemed reticent to give an opinion.

The first crops were harvested and the corn began to be gathered, and still the skies were blue and cloudless and the heat oppressive. Often Sapphira's thoughts returned to London and the poor people trapped there in the nightmare of the epidemic. The evil-smelling vegetation rotting in those sweltering streets, the closed-in houses with their red crosses. The fear and insecurity which prevailed. How lucky she was to be at Ravenswood, and safe, even if she was alone.

She tried not to let herself think of Quentin and Margaret together in Salisbury. She had long since given up hope of him coming to her, and for weeks she suffered in an agony of silence. Then estate affairs demanded more and more of her time, and it became easier to think of other things. Easier—until she lay in bed at night, alone and tearful, aching for him to be at her side. She would suffer any indignity he chose to inflict on her, so long as he was at her side.

Lottie, at her own request, had taken on the job of chief sewing-maid at the house and was already being courted by one of the young village boys, the eldest son of the tailor. The new independence brought with it fresh confidence and she was blossoming under the careful eyes of both Molly and Sapphira.

Between the latter had developed a deeper relationship than they had shared before. Sapphira had grown up quickly—too quickly, perhaps, with her marriage to Quentin, and she no longer needed a mother, but a friend, and in Molly she knew she had found the staunchest of allies, the dearest of friends.

There was a horse being led away towards the stables as she returned to the house one mid-morning. Her windswept hair lay about her shoulders, freed from the confines of a ribbon by her dashing ride from the village. She had become quite an accomplished horsewoman since the day Margaret first sat her on a saddle. The freedom she felt on horseback sometimes eased the feeling of being a prisoner. She was mistress of Ravenswood, and she knew the villagers had come to respect, even love, her for her efforts since she arrived, but the house was still a prison and Quentin would always be her gaoler. She was a prisoner of her own love!

Jumping to the ground, she flung the reins to a waiting groom, her heart pounding with rising excitement. Had he come after all? Could she have been so wrong about him? It was not Quentin who awaited her, but Blaise. With a soft cry, she went into his outstretched arms and buried her face against a firm shoulder so that he would not see the disappointment in her eyes.

'Blaise, you came after all! I had almost given you up. I thought perhaps you might have gone to Salisbury to look for a little excitement? Windsor must be very dull after London.'

She drew him to a chair, ordered coffee to be brought, and turned to him expectantly, awaiting all his news. Then, as she looked into his face, she saw all was not well. 'What is it? Do you bring bad news? Oh, no! Not Quentin!'

'No, little one. Susanne, your mother.' Blaise took both her hands in his and held them tight. Neither of them was aware of the servant who came and went, leaving a tray of hot coffee and brandy, or of the impression they unwittingly gave of a pair of star-struck young lovers holding hands. It took no more than ten minutes before the whole household was aware that the mistress had a rather special visitor. 'She died last week —quite suddenly.'

'Dead?' Sapphira said through trembling lips. 'Why did no one send me word? I would have come at once.'

'My father would not hear of it. In his own way he is a very cold man, although had you seen him with her those last few minutes before she died, you would not have agreed with me. I listened to them talking. All those years ago, she did not tell him she was with child because she knew that a scandal was the one thing he feared. His name was so important to him in those days. It still is. If it were not, he would not have extracted that damned promise from you, and you and Quentin would be together now,' Blaise said fiercely. His bitterness distressed her. 'The first he knew of it was before Susanne's mother took her abroad. She told him he had a daughter, who had been taken from her. She asked him to find and care for her until she returned to England. He never did, of course. Over the years it became an obsession with Susanne to find you. When he realised the pain and grief his indifference had caused her, he did everything in his power to help her. And then, when he comes face to face with you, he still refuses to acknowledge you publicly or allow her that right. He wanted no gossip to touch the name of his future wife. Susanne made him wait a long time. Not until you were returned to her, she told him, would she marry him.'

'He loved her very much to have remained faithful all these years. Whatever you think, Blaise, you cannot deny that.' His words explained so much. They exonerated her mother from the guilt of abandonment—of not caring—and they intensified Sapphira's sorrow. 'Did— did she suffer?'

'No. She collapsed soon after arriving at Windsor, but seemed to recover. She spoke of coming here to Ravenswood and persuading you to live with them after they were married. Then, a week ago, quite suddenly she developed a chill and then a fever, and began to ramble on about the past. She lasted only two days. I hated Father when I left the house, but, on the way here, I have had time to think a little more. Who am I to pass judgment? I could not hold even Corinna!'

'Don't talk like that!' Sapphira folded her arms about him and sat quite still for a long while. She knew the emptiness she felt now would never totally go away, nor could anything replace what she had felt for Susanne during the brief time she had known her.

'You realise what this means,' Blaise murmured, and she raised her head and looked at him, tears swimming in the deep blue pools of her eyes. 'At last you can tell Quentin the truth. Go to him, little one.'

'Would—would you take me to Salisbury?' Sapphira asked tremulously. She would go. She would find Quentin and make him listen to her. She would give him the chance he had denied her in his arrogant pride!

'We shall leave first thing in the morning.' Blaise smiled and kissed her. 'I'm too tired to stir from here before then. I've had little sleep since leaving Windsor.'

'Forgive me. I am not thinking clearly. Of course you must rest.'

She rang for Wilcox. Arm in arm she and Blaise walked out into the Great Hall, not speaking until he appeared. It was not a time for mindless chatter.

'Lord Blaise will be staying overnight. Please see that a room is made ready for him and that he has everything he requires.'

'The Blue Room is always at his disposal, my lady. A standing order of the Earl,' she was informed, and she looked at her brother in surprise.

'I've often stayed here. Before you and Quentin were married, that is. Many a night we have spent in here before a blazing fire, getting well and truly drunk. Reminiscing.'

'You will again. It will be just as it was,' she promised.

'Nothing will ever be the same again. No one should want it so. It will be better for all of us. I think it advisable for you, too, to rest. My news has been a shock. I am going to help myself to another glass of Quentin's excellent brandy, and then Wilcox can show me upstairs.'

He watched Sapphira slowly climb the stairs to her rooms. She had taken the news of her mother's death too well, he surmised. No tears! It was a bad sign. Quentin had taken precedence over everything, damn him! When she came at last to accept what had happened, he hoped that her husband would be at her side to give her comfort. If he was not . . .

'My sister and I leave in the morning for Salisbury, Wilcox,' he told the stony-faced servant who was waiting patiently to escort him to his room. 'We shall require the carriage to be ready by eight, and please see that there is food for the journey.'

Wilcox, who had shared the Earl's confidence for many years, and thought himself beyond being surprised at anything the aristocracy did, echoed in a startled tone, 'Sister, sir?'

'You heard me quite correctly, man. The lady is my sister, and I shall deal harshly with anyone I hear maligning her good name.'

'All in this house think highly of the Countess,' Wilcox returned stiffly. 'These past months, with the master absent, her presence has brought comfort to the villagers, and hope. She has great strength of mind, and we have much to be grateful for.'

'If only Quentin saw her through your eyes,' Blaise murmured softly.

Sapphira and Blaise dined together in the Great Hall. The last time it had been used, she remembered, was for her wedding feast. As she picked at her food, her thoughts returned to that evening when she had been entertained by jugglers and clowns, and the villagers had come to pay her their respects, and she had first understood the importance of the role Quentin had thrust upon her. She had not wanted it then. Now, it was almost the most important thing in her life. He came before everything, of course. Soon, he would know how wrong he had been.

'What is it?' Blaise asked. She saw that he was staring at her intently. 'You look . . . apprehensive.'

Her thoughts had been dwelling on the moment they had met. What if, when he learned the truth, the full extent of his mistakes, he still did not want her!

'It's nothing,' she answered, forcing a smile to her lips.

'Do not doubt your own capabilities, little sister. Quentin is not made of stone, nor is he an unfair man.'

'He has a heart of stone, and an arrogant pride that blinds him to his own faults,' she flashed, and Blaise chuckled at the outburst.

'How well you know him. Did I not tell you that you have nothing to worry about?'

They sat together under the trees after their meal, each dwelling on what the morrow would bring. Blaise's thoughts were of the woman he loved, whom he believed to be still residing in plague-infested London. Sapphira's were of her confrontation with Quentin. She would use no womanly wiles to hold him if he did not want her, she told herself. That would only remind him of his faithless wife, the ghost who separated them. She did not want that. His love, that was what she desired.

'Sapphira.' Blaise looked down at the head pressed against his shoulder. She looked up at him in the sunlight that shone on the fading rose-bushes and flower garden all around them. 'I thought you were asleep.'

'Dreaming a little, that's all.' How content she was in his company.

'Of an idyllic life with Quentin?' he teased.

'It will never be that. I must never own him, Blaise, never lay claim to him at all. Just love him, and show him by my love that I am the most faithful of wives. I shall never deceive or betray him, even in my thoughts,' she declared fervantly.

'How you love him.' There was envy in his tone.

'I shall go to him and tell him about us.' Neither of them was aware of the two shadows also in the garden. The man and the woman drew closer, unnoticed, to hear the conversation. 'He will have to listen. He must accept the love I have for you, Blaise, and understand it. We must never be separated again. I shall tell him everything. It cannot hurt Susanne now, and your father must forgive me this chance I take to find my own happiness. Quentin must accept it.'

'I accept only that you are a lying, scheming female, like any other!' came a harsh voice from the bushes behind them. As Sapphira and Blaise came to their feet simultaneously, Quentin stepped out on to the grass and, behind him, Corinna! Sapphira shrank from the evil look of satisfaction blazing from her features. 'And to think I came here wanting you. My God! Has he no mercy left in him?'

'Quentin! listen!' Blaise stepped forward, his hand on his sword. Sapphira pushed him aside and ran to the man she loved, arms outstretched. He had come to Ravenswood! No matter what his reasons were, he had come. He had given her the chance she desired.

'Quentin! Oh, my love, listen to me! I don't know what lies she has told you, but listen to me.' She stretched out her arms imploringly towards the rigid figure before her. He stared at her in silence, then, with an oath, lifted his hand and struck her aside with such violence that she toppled on to the flower bed and lay dazed.

A red mist rose before Blaise's eyes. He knew he was no match for Quentin, yet fear and anger gave strength to his sword-arm as he pulled his weapon free and lunged at his one-time friend. Taken unawares, his eyes still focused on Sapphira where she lay on the ground,

Quentin found himself at a disadvantage. Even as he reached for his sword, Blaise's weapon slashed down across his right arm, cutting deep to the bone. He reeled back on to Corinna, who instantly thrust him away, her eyes dilating at the sight of the bright red blood which stained his velvet jacket. He was struggling to draw his sword left-handed when Sapphira dragged herself to her feet, her senses reeling still, and thrust herself between the two opponents.

'No! No!' Her screams brought Wilcox and Molly, and a multitude of other servants from the house to gaze upon the ghastly scene. 'Stop! Blaise! For pity's sake, hold!'

'Why?' Quentin glared at her. The pain in his arm numbed his senses, yet still he fought to draw his sword, and at last succeeded, only to have Sapphira clamp her hands firmly over the hilt. 'Let him finish me, if he can,' he snarled. 'I warned you once that you would belong to no man but me.'

'I never have, I never shall,' Sapphira cried, her eyes blazing with blue fire as she stared at him—challenged him! 'Blaise is my brother. He brought me word this morning that my mother is dead. Susanne Winterbourne, Quentin. I am her daughter! I made a promise, a stupid promise, to tell no one . . . For the love of God, would you kill my brother, your friend, because of Corinna's madness to destroy us both? Have you not had enough of fear and hatred and bitterness? Did my body tell you nothing when you held me . . .' She broke off, colour flooding into her face as she realised what she had said before such an audience. Yet what did it matter? She cared not who heard her declaration of love!

Quentin shrugged himself free, but made no attempt to use the weapon in his grasp. He stood as if transfixed by the words she had spoken; then into his eyes came a look of terrible pain.

'Look at me, my husband.' Sapphira placed herself

squarely before him and Blaise, so that neither could make a move towards the other without first touching her with his weapon. 'I have never lied to you, nor shall I begin now. I care not who hears what I have to say, although my words are for you alone. Hear me. I love you! I know I can never take her place—that of the woman you will always love in your thoughts and dreams, but I love you still. I shall be whatever you wish me to be. I have no shame where you are concerned.'

Quentin said nothing. Slowly, very slowly, he reached out, and his fingers touched her cheek, her mouth. She could feel them trembling, and sudden hope rose inside her. The sword dropped from his grasp on to the path. He did not even notice it.

'Woman—don't you understand I love you?' he said harshly.

And then she was in his arms, her tears soaking through the velvet of his jacket, mixed with the blood from his wound. Fingers, suddenly strong and decisive, gripped her chin and forced back her head. For a moment she glimpsed his black glittering eyes, full of passion, before he lowered his head to hers and his mouth took possession of her lips to blot out everything but the splendour of his kiss which told her she had won her battle.

She did not want to move. She wanted to stay for ever within this magic circle which held her spellbound, gave her everything she had ever wanted. She clung to him sobbing, tears mingling with the kisses she gave so freely. Blaise, watching them, turned his gaze enviously towards Corinna, and was horrified by what he saw mirrored in the pale, tired face. Hatred and triumph, but not defeat. Even as he came to realise what she had done, she came unsteadily towards the couple locked in each other's arms. Her eyes were dilated, her face red with the exertion which had sapped the last of her strength.

'You poor, stupid fool!' she spat the words at her

brother. Quentin released Sapphira, but kept his arm tightly round her so that she was still close to and a little behind him, away from the advancing menace which, he now accepted, had always been there, intent on destroying them both. 'Kill her! She has lied to you, deceived you. Brother! Do you really believe he is her brother? He is mine? He would have told me if he had a sister. I know everything about you, don't I, dear Blaise?'

'Not quite all, Corinna.' Blaise looked at her and felt disgust for what she had become. For what he had allowed her to make him become. 'It is no lie. Sapphira is my sister. I love her as I have never loved any woman. I loved you as I shall never love any woman again, but that is now over. My sister is more important than you to me.'

Corinna gave a wild scream and launched herself at him, nails flexed to scratch at his eyes. She took two steps, swayed, and then stood, the blood draining from her face, a terrible smile on the waxen features.

'May you all rot in hell alongside me,' she whispered, and then slid to the ground at Blaise's feet.

'Don't touch her!' Quentin barked, as he bent to touch the inert form. 'She has brought the plague to us, unless I am very much mistaken. Stand away, Sapphira! Let me see her.'

'No! Quentin, don't touch her,' Sapphira begged, suddenly afraid.

Blaise caught and held her firmly, while Quentin knelt at his sister's side. He gently eased her over on to her back and stared for a long while at the distorted features. When he rose, his words were like the tolling of the London bells bringing a forecast of doom to all who heard them.

'I suspected she had it, even in Salisbury, but I was not sure. I took a risk, and I have lost. And, in doing so, I have brought death upon my house and those who dwell within it,' he said gravely.

'I would have done the same to be with the one I love,' Blaise said quietly. 'What must we do? Sapphira tells me you have seen it before. You survived then, so why not now? I have no intention of dying just to please Corinna.'

Quentin was still staring down at his sister. He seemed lost, Sapphira thought, and quickly went to his side, entwining her fingers through his.

'Let me see to that wound—you are losing too much blood,' she said matter-of-factly. 'And while I do, you can tell us what must be done to keep this horror from our door.'

'Don't you understand,' he turned on her fiercely. 'It is here. I—you—Blaise . . . perhaps we are all contaminated. Yet maybe there is a way . . . a slim chance.'

'Then we must take it. Wilcox, bring towels and warm water quickly,' she cried.

'No! No one must come near,' Quentin warned. 'We three must isolate ourselves from the rest of the household, and pray to God that he has not marked us for Corinna's end.' He looked at the silent servants hovering white-faced and trembling on the steps beyond. 'Wilcox, I want a coffin made for my sister. Bring it to the bottom of the staircase in the Great Hall and leave it there. No one—no one, do you hear, is to venture upstairs to us until you have leave from me. The Lady Corinna will be placed in the vault. No one is to go there either. We shall take care of her burial. News of what has happened here must not spread to the village, do you understand? It would cause a riot.'

'My lord, you will need help,' the man began. In all his years of service, he found himself suddenly lost for words.

'We shall manage. We shall live on the first floor. You will leave food each day at the bottom of the stairs, and fresh water, but you will not come further. You do so at peril of your life. Perhaps this accursed disease

will not claim us; only time will tell. Four weeks, that
is the time-limit in London. Four weeks! If, at the end
of that time, we are all dead . . . you will burn the
corpses where they lie. Is that clear? Fire is the only
cleanser I know of. It is how we disposed of the dead
in France. It must be done.'

'It shall be done, my lord. If it is necessary,' Wilcox
answered quietly. Sapphira was sure she glimpsed tears
in the old man's eyes as he turned and ushered all those
hovering about him out of the way. He had to drag
Molly forcibly inside. For a moment, Sapphira had
thought she meant to remain.

'Let me,' Blaise began, as Quentin stopped and lifted
Corinna, wincing with the pain of his injured arm. But
he shook his head and strode into the house, leaving
them to follow.

It was a nightmare of a different kind, Sapphira
thought, as she followed him, hanging tightly to Blaise's
arm. For four whole weeks they were to isolate themselves from the rest of the household and pray for
survival. Yet what else could they do? To stray from
the house meant possible infection for the rest of the
village. Quentin had seen it all before, she assured
herself, as he laid his sister on a bed in one of the spare
rooms. She must trust in him and the knowledge he
possessed. Knowledge he had gained in France, along
with so many other things. Trust and love!

A hastily prepared coffin made of oak was left early
the next morning at the foot of the staircase. Blaise and
Quentin brought it back to the room where Corinna
lay, and placed her in it. They said a prayer before the
lid was sealed, each hoping that she had not died in
triumphant victory over those she had hated.

'You must rest.' Sapphira looked into Quentin's
drawn features when he came back from the vault,
having transferred the coffin there to await burial, which
they had planned to do at first light. 'Quentin, please,
lie down. You can do no more for the moment.'

He shrugged and turned away towards his own room without a word. She stared after him, huge tears gathering in her eyes. Blaise squeezed her hand reassuringly. 'Go with him. Does he have to ask?'

'I don't think he knows how,' she whispered. 'It does not matter. If he wants me . . . Blaise, I'm so sorry . . . about Corinna. You loved her.'

'Feel no sorrow for her, little one. I no longer feel anything. In her way she has won, hasn't she? Even dead, she is capable of destroying us. Even if we bury her in the ground, she will infect it. Fire is the only answer. Quentin was right.'

'Blaise, don't dwell on such morbid thoughts! I am frightened enough,' Sapphira pleaded. 'Go and rest. In the morning we shall give her a Christian burial.'

Quentin's room was in darkness when she entered, but for a single candle burning beside the bed. It barely illuminated the still figure on the bed, and she hurried quickly forward, her heart in her mouth. He was so still . . .

'Who is it? Sapphira, is that you?' His voice was slurred with tiredness. Or was it something more? With a sob, she flung herself down beside him, pressing her head against his chest. 'You little fool, stay away from me. You don't know what you are doing. I have been with Corinna for the past three days . . .'

'It is you who are the fool! Don't you understand that if anything happens to you, I have nothing to live for? I love you more than life itself! You are my life—I won't leave you. I won't! I won't!'

'Hush. Hush, my love.' A strong arm enfolded her. She felt his lips against her hair. 'Lie close to me. God knows I need comfort and reassurance as much as you do. I know not if these measures I have taken will work. If they do not . . .'

'Don't.' Sapphira laid her fingers against his mouth, and felt him press a kiss upon them. 'We are together. It is all I ask.'

'I have more. Forgiveness. No, let me speak while I am still able. I feel a fever is almost upon me. Tomorrow I shall be of little use to anyone. My pupil listened well to his master's words. I always taught him that surprise was the best weapon of all, and by God, he did me proud tonight, even if I am suffering for it! But then I deserve to suffer for the grief I have caused you—the way I misjudged him.' He broke off, pain creeping into his tone. She dared not move, lest she caused him more. 'I was married in France. You have no doubt guessed that by now. She was young, no more than eighteen when I first met her, abandoned, I thought, by the father she had followed and whom she adored. Or so she told me then. She had no one to care for her, and she was such a child! God, how could I have been so ignorant of the truth! Yet perhaps I did not want to see it. Perhaps I knew what she was from the start, but I loved her, and I married her to give her the protection and security she needed. Within a month I discovered that she was unfaithful to me. The man she truly loved was in my regiment. Her father had been dead a full year. She had come in search of her lover and, having found him, gave him what she could not give me. When he was killed she turned to others, always with the protection of my name keeping her from where she belonged—a whore-house.'

Sapphira shuddered at his words and felt his arm tighten round her as if he were afraid that she might try to leave his side. She had no intention of doing that. She lay quite still, and waited for him to continue.

'The plague struck the village where we were. She went down with it, and died. I nursed her for seven long days and nights. With her last breath she laughed in my face, do you know that? She mocked my devotion, my love. In that moment she killed the love I felt for her . . . killed every decent emotion I possessed. I watched her body burn on the funeral pyre of corpses, and felt nothing. I thought myself incapable of feeling again, until . . .' His fingers touched her cheek, the loose hair spread over her bare shoulders '. . . until you came into my life, to turn it topsy-turvy with your total innocence. I found that I was capable of real love after all. A wiser, more adult feeling than that I shared—thought I shared —with her. This love consumes me like a fire. It demands that you remain faithful to me as I shall remain faithful to you. It demands that I give all, and I do so willingly. If it is not too late. Is it, Sapphira? Have I made you hate me too much?'

She turned within the confines of his arm and he drew in his breath as he discovered she had loosened the ribbons of her bodice and that his fingers had free access to the softness, the warmth, of her body. No word passed between then. None was necessary as she brought his mouth down to hers and gave him her answer.

The fire which began in the vault far below the main house, where generations of Tyrells were laid to rest, began suddenly and without warning. The coffin bearing Corinna's body was alight immediately, apparently from the upsetting of one of the huge candles set in wrought-iron frames which stood one at each side of it. Blaise brought word of it to Quentin and Sapphira early next morning, and also a reassurance that it had been completely extinguished and would give no further trouble.

'An accident. An act of God.' Blaise shrugged his shoulders. His clothes were covered with specks of charred wood and his face blackened with smoke. He had allowed no one else near the vault because of the risk, and had dealt with it alone. His hands were scorched and burned.

Quentin stared at him with a strange expression on his face, which was streaked with sweat as he strove to fight off the fever descending on his weakened body. He held Sapphira's hand tightly in his. His free hand reached out towards his friend.

'Thank you.' His voice was choked with emotion. The fire had been no accident. It had been Blaise's way of ensuring that Corinna did not spread her poison beyond the house. It was contained here with the three of them, and they would fight it and win. What must it have cost him to do what he did! 'Take my hand, dammit!'

Blaise took it and smiled. In that moment, Sapphira knew that their friendship would never again be in doubt.

Four weeks. Twenty-eight long days of watching the outside world through the windows of their bedroom after Quentin's fever had subsided and his strength returned. Long evenings of gambling between the two men for enormous sums of money that each knew would never be paid. Plans for the future. Reminiscenses of the past, pleasant ones, this time, in which they all shared.

Long nights of lying at Quentin's side and making love, of praying for a child. Of giving herself without restraint, and feeling from him the same response, and knowing that they were one for ever more. Of knowing the plague had ended at Ravenswood with Corinna's death, that they were unaffected . . . untainted . . . Life lay ahead of them . . . Love lay ahead of them . . .

And then, at last, their quarantine came to an end . . . Blaise and Quentin looked at each other's new growth of beard. The last days had begun to tell on them all. Sapphira, in contrast, had maintained a strict routine of bathing and making herself look presentable. The servants had been wonderful. Without them, they knew, survival would not have been possible.

She felt as nervous as a bride about to meet her husband as she dressed to go downstairs on that final day, the day of their release from the hell in which they had dwelled for so long. There was a noise outside the windows. Quentin came into the room as she went to look, full of curiosity, and as she turned and looked at him, the love and tenderness in his eyes made her legs grow weak.

'Wilcox,' he said simply. 'I should flay him alive, but I am too happy just to be drawing breath. He told the village what we were at. They have all been praying for us, every last man, woman and child. God, how proud I feel this day!'

She went to him and placed her hand in his and together they went out to the head of the staircase. Below them the Great Hall was crowded with people. Those she had sought to protect while he was away had returned in their way to express their gratitude and to welcome the return of their lord and master. To welcome the return of them all, she thought, smiling up at the man at her side. Blaise joined them, bearded, unkempt, looking a little bewildered by what he saw below.

'These are our people,' she said simply. 'They have come to welcome us back to life. Will you not take my hand, brother? Is it not seemly that we should meet them together after all we have shared?'

Blaise's fingers caught and held hers. In Quentin's eyes was such a look of love that she wanted to throw her arms about his neck and weep on his shoulder for their deliverance, but this was not the right time. They had all the time in the world, now, to be together and to be themselves.

Hand in hand, proudly, the three of them descended the stairs to the tumultuous applause from below. It was a moment never to be forgotten in the history of Ravenswood . . .

New from Violet Winspear, one of Mills and Boon's best-selling authors, a longer romance of mystery, intrigue, suspense and love. Almost twice the length of a standard romance for just £1.95. Published on the 14th of June.

The Rose of Romance

Mills & Boon

Your chance to step into the past Take 2 Books FREE

Discover a world long vanished. An age of chivalry and intrigue, powerful desires and exotic locations. Read about true love found by soldiers and statesmen, princesses and serving girls. All written as only Mills & Boon's top-selling authors know how. Become a regular reader of Mills & Boon Masquerade Historical Romances and enjoy 4 superb, new titles every two months, plus a whole range of special benefits: your very own personal membership card entitles you to a regular free newsletter packed with recipes, competitions, exclusive book offers plus other bargain offers and big cash savings.

AND an Introductory FREE GIFT for YOU. Turn over the page for details.

Fill in and send this coupon back today
and we will send you

2 Introductory
Historical Romances
FREE

At the same time we will reserve a subscription to
Mills & Boon Masquerade Historical Romances for
you. Every two months you will receive Four new,
superb titles delivered direct to your door. You
don't pay extra for delivery. Postage and packing is
always completely free. There is no obligation or
commitment – you only receive books for as long as
you want to.

**Just fill in and post the coupon today to MILLS & BOON
READER SERVICE, FREEPOST, P.O. BOX 236, CROYDON,
SURREY CR9 9EL.**

Please Note:- READERS IN SOUTH AFRICA write to
Mills & Boon, Postbag X3010,
Randburg 2125, S. Africa.

FREE BOOKS CERTIFICATE

**To: Mills & Boon Reader Service, FREEPOST, P.O. Box 236,
Croydon, Surrey CR9 9EL.**

Please send me, free and without obligation, two Masquerade Historical Romances, and
reserve a Reader Service Subscription for me. If I decide to subscribe I shall receive,
following my free parcel of books, four new Masquerade Historical Romances every two
months for £5.00, post and packing free. If I decide not to subscribe, I shall write to you
within 10 days. The free books are mine to keep in any case. I understand that I may cancel
my subscription at any time simply by writing to you. I am over 18 years of age.

Please write in BLOCK CAPITALS.

Signature _____

Name _____

Address _____

_____ Post code _____

SEND NO MONEY — TAKE NO RISKS.

Please don't forget to include your Postcode.

Remember, postcodes speed delivery. Offer applies in UK only and is not valid
to present subscribers. Mills & Boon reserve the right to exercise discretion in
granting membership. If price changes are necessary you will be notified.

4M   Offer expires June 30th 1985.

EP9M